A BORROW. PAST

A BORROWED PAST

JULIETTE LAWSON

SEATON CAREW PRESS

To Orna Ross

Who showed me how to unlock my creativity
and helped me to believe in myself as a writer

CONTENTS

PART I

CHAPTER 1

OCTOBER 1875: SEATON CAREW, NORTH EAST
ENGLAND

It was only a blank piece of paper, but it held so many possibilities. William Harper turned towards the brass telescope that stood at his bedroom window and peered through it, trying to imprint the scene on his mind before returning to his seat at the dressing table to start the sketch. He picked up a stick of charcoal and began an outline with the lightest of touches: a flurry of clouds, a straight horizon and a ship in full sail. Relaxing his hand, he let it sweep across the paper in soft strokes, creating waves around the ship. If only he could do this all day, every day, instead of his lessons.

Now for the shading, building up layers, blending the charcoal with his finger to change the mood, the clouds an ominous grey, the bleached sails billowing in the wind. He bit his lip as he worked, using small strokes to capture the movement of the sea as it grew to a swell and crashed into bubbling foam against the prow. Standing back, he assessed it. That wasn't quite the effect he was aiming for.

A brush would remove some of that heaviness. He reached for the wooden box, running his fingers along the exquisite carvings of oak leaves and acorns on the lid. The sense of awe hadn't left him since the day he'd found it, a treasure trove of art materials lying in wait for him, as if it knew about his secret desire. Mama still wouldn't explain why it was in the attic, but she had allowed him to use the contents. They both understood the terrible risk they were taking. If Papa found out…

The rustle of Mama's skirts announced her arrival.

'How are you getting on, my darling?'

'Fine, Mama.' She was wearing her cloak and bonnet. 'Is it time to leave already?'

'I'm afraid so. Make sure everything's packed away; you mustn't leave any trace.'

'I know.' He flicked away the spark of resentment at the implication that he was still a small child who couldn't be trusted to remember this vital instruction. He gathered together every piece of charcoal and returned them to the box, then wiped his hands on a damp cloth.

Mama studied the sketch. 'You're improving, I can tell. It's such a pity you can't show anyone your work. But I'm looking forward to seeing your flower stands in church. Mrs Wilson said your colour choices were just right.'

William smiled to himself as he put the sketch and the box on the top shelf of the wardrobe and covered them both with an old blanket. Compliments were hard to come by, but Mama would surely be proud of him when she saw the harvest display. It had been a rare opportunity to do some-thing artistic in plain sight. Far better than his weekly visit to Papa's office, stuck inside all day, his neck aching from bending over the desk. He could almost see the lines of figures in the shipment registers in his sleep, dreading the day when he had to start his proper job there.

It would soon come, now he was fourteen. Mama's attempts to make Papa delay it had only caused more arguments. With a shudder, William recalled the last one, when Papa's face had reddened with anger at the very suggestion that his decisions could be challenged. There was no way out; his destiny was to take the helm of the business one day. The thought was unbearable.

'Where are you both?' Papa's booming voice echoed from the hall up to the landing.

Mama jumped. 'Oh goodness, we should be downstairs by now. Be quick.'

William put his jacket on, fumbling with the buttons.

'Hurry up; you should have been ready long before now. Don't make him angry. Come here.' She fussed with his collar, making sure it was lying flat.

William studied her face. How hard would it be to draw her? Not like this, worried and rushing, but in her calm, loving moments. Her lemony scent filled the space between them, as she brushed a speck of dust from his jacket then stood back to inspect him.

'We'd better go,' she told him. She checked the fastenings on her cloak and adjusted her bonnet, then gestured towards the door for him to leave first.

William looked at his shoes. Were they shiny enough? Oh, the shame of it, if his appearance was found lacking. There was no time now to do anything but run the top of his feet up and down the back of his legs and hope the fabric of his trousers didn't pick up the dust.

'What are you doing?' Mama steered him out of the room with a hand at his back. 'Quickly now!'

He led the way down the stairs, hoping he would pass muster.

Papa was pacing along the hall, never a good sign. 'Come on, William, or we'll be late. How many times do I have to tell you that punctuality is important?'

At least once a day, thought William. Along with the lectures on eating cabbage, standing up straight and not talking to the lower classes.

Outside, the usual tedious walk to church had turned into a colourful procession of villagers making their way along the promenade. William's spirits lifted at the sight of all the ladies wearing their finest dresses and extravagant hats, and the gentlemen strutting in smart frock coats, some left open to display waistcoats in brocade or silk. The light caught the sheen of their silken top hats, like the glossy hard shells of the beetles that scurried out when he lifted a rock in the garden. What a wonderful array of colours and fabrics. Even the tradesmen of the village had made an effort, in their best woollen jackets and caps.

The shopkeepers' windows along the route boasted impressive harvest displays. A wheat sheaf made of dough had pride of place at the baker's shop, and at the grocer's, baskets spilled over with a rainbow of fruit and vegetables, framed by plaits of corn.

As they reached the bottom of Church Street, Grace Robinson arrived at the opposite corner, followed by her parents. Her three brothers were running around them, laughing and jostling each other. William sprang forward. 'Grace!' he called out.

She smiled and waved back, but William felt Papa's hand on his shoulder. 'Remember your place,' he said.

William sighed and fell back into step with his parents.

The vicar greeted them at the door of the church. 'Welcome, Mr and Mrs Harper, and William too. My dear wife told me how helpful you were with the displays, young man. God bless you. You must be very proud of him, Mr Harper.'

Thank goodness Lord Forbes from Chambers House was heading towards Papa. That would distract him.

Inside, William smiled at the transformation, proud that he'd had a hand in it. The colours brought the scene to life, with rosy apples, bright oranges and countless vegetables occupying every spare space. Huge vases of white lilies stood on the altar, behind which a banner in blue and gold proclaimed 'I am the living bread from Heaven'.

His choice of moss and foliage for the stands provided a perfect muted background for the bright spiky dahlias and colourful chrysanthemums. He glanced at Mama, hoping for a nod of approval, but she was lost in her own thoughts. It was better not to interrupt when she was in that sort of mood.

The church filled up, the gentle murmuring building to a crescendo as friends and neighbours greeted each other.

'Where have all these people come from? It's a good thing we pay pew rents,' said Papa, as they filed into the row that bore their family name card in a brass holder.

William copied Mama in positioning a kneeler on the floor and lowering himself onto it with hands together in prayer, glad to hide his embarrassment at Papa's snobbery.

The organ wheezed and coughed out the opening bars of 'Now Thank We All Our God', the signal for everyone to stand up. William scanned the congregation. The whole village must be here. So many families; how different it must be to have brothers and sisters to play with.

With so many things to look at, the service was soon over, even with one of Reverend Wilson's interminable sermons. While Papa spoke to one of the Local Board members about the state of the paths around the village green, William stayed in the pew, enjoying the sight of the sun's rays streaming through the windows, casting jewelled colours from the stained glass into the church.

He jumped as Papa's voice broke into his thoughts. 'Don't sit there daydreaming, William. It's time to go to the school-room for refreshments. I have business to discuss.'

~

THEY'D HARDLY WALKED through the door when Papa spotted the Mayor and led Mama over to have a word. William seized his chance to see Grace. She was wearing her best dress of dark green velvet, signs of wear around the cuffs and collar revealing its origin from the second-hand stall at the church sale.

She handed him a plate of cakes. 'Here you are. We're under strict instructions to fill ourselves up.'

He grinned. 'You might be. We're having Sunday lunch when we get back.' But when he saw the cakes, he couldn't resist.

In between mouthfuls, Grace told him what the boys at school had been getting up to, instead of going to lessons. Some had been caddying at the golf club and others had helped with the harvest on the farms. 'It's a shame you can't come to school,' she said. 'I miss your awful caterwauling at hymn practice.'

'I wish I was still there too,' William admitted. 'Miss Lawson's not bad for a governess, but there's nowhere to hide when she starts asking questions. And now I'm going to Papa's office on Fridays to learn the business. I can't bear the thought of doing it every day. I'll die of boredom.'

Grace grabbed a sandwich and put it on her plate. 'At least you're guaranteed a decent job. I'll be going into service.'

'That's so unfair. You deserve better than that. Can't you try to get an office job, or look after the money at one of the big lodging houses?' It was unbearable to imagine her stuck in a basement kitchen, peeling vegetables all morning, or even worse, cleaning.

'You know that's not how it works for girls like me. Don't you worry. I'll be glad to bring a bit of money home to help Mam and Dad, at least until I get married.' She pulled a face. 'But it's different for you. You'll have years of work ahead. You should do what makes you happy. Something creative.'

'And how do you reckon I'm going to manage that?'

She shrugged her shoulders. 'I have no idea. Run away?'

'Very funny. Come on, Grace, be serious.'

'Well, I don't see any other way of making your parents take notice.'

William shook his head. 'How can you even think that's a good idea? I'd have no money, and nowhere to live.'

'You never know what you can do until you try. I bet you'd find a way of surviving. Starving artists do it all the time, don't they? Anyway, I'd come with you.'

He turned away on the pretext of putting his plate on a table, to hide the flutter of pleasure at the idea of making his way in the world by doing what he most loved, with Grace at his side. It was an impossible dream, best forgotten.

All too soon, Mama and Papa came to find him. He wiped the crumbs from his mouth and tried to brush the rest off his jacket.

'Come along, William,' said Mama. 'We're going home now. I hope you haven't over-indulged. Cook will be upset if you can't eat your lunch.'

Grace followed him, telling a tale of a new teacher who was having a hard time controlling the class.

'William, come here,' commanded Papa. William changed direction and Grace followed.

Papa scowled at Grace. 'I didn't ask you to come with him. Get off home.'

'I heard that.' Mr Robinson looked furious as he strode

over to Papa. 'You have no right to talk to my daughter like that.'

William shrank back, dreading what would come next.

'I will talk to whoever I want, however I want,' said Papa.

Mr Robinson came much closer to Papa than was acceptable and looked straight into his face. 'Not to my family, you won't.'

'Dad, don't,' pleaded Grace. 'Let's get home.' She took her mother's hand, and they walked towards the gate.

William ran after her. 'Grace, I'm sorry.'

She turned round. 'It's fine, William. You'd better go back to your Papa. Don't worry; it's not your fault.'

He looked back towards Papa and Mr Robinson, dismayed to see they were still arguing. Mrs Robinson put her arm around Grace, and they all stood together, watching and waiting. Even at a distance, they could hear every word. Most of the villagers shuffled past in embarrassment. Only a huddle of elderly widows hung back, sensing trouble worthy of an audience. William's cheeks burned. His family would be the subject of gossip around the whole village. Papa didn't seem to care.

'William is destined to join the family business. I'll thank you to keep your daughter away from him.'

Tom Robinson stood his ground. 'I'll do no such thing. Our Grace is the only real friend he has. The poor lad doesn't have much of a life, kept at home.'

Mama shrank back, trying to fade into the background. William rushed to her side.

Papa's cheeks were flushed with temper. Didn't he realise everyone was staring? But he wouldn't give in.

'You need to mind your own business. I don't have to listen to this nonsense from someone like you.'

William edged closer to Mama.

'And you need to mind your manners.' Mr Robinson's face was inches away from Papa's.

'Stop it! Stop it now!' came a voice, tearful and angry. William was taken aback to realise it was his own. 'I'm sick of all the arguments, sick of being told what I can and can't do.' He turned and ran out of the gates, ignoring Grace's outstretched hand as he stumbled past her. At the end of the street, he sprinted in the opposite direction to home, towards the row of labourers' cottages where Grace lived.

He crossed the track and climbed over a stile, then paused to catch his breath. With a backwards glance to make sure no one was following him, he took the path to the beach. It was deserted, save for the seagulls whirling around overhead, shrieking as they mocked his misery.

Why didn't he fit in? Why was he always in trouble, never able to please Papa? A lump lodged in his throat and he fought against the sob that threatened to emerge.

It was all his fault, for wanting to be close to Grace, the only person who truly understood him. Why couldn't Papa accept his friendship with her? He'd seen Mr Robinson being gentle and loving with Grace and her brothers. He was a hero, too, a lifeboat crewman who saved lives. Papa was none of those things. It wasn't fair.

Pushing back the annoying tuft of hair that flopped over his forehead refusing to be tamed, William lifted his face to the wind, letting it cool his skin. If he stayed out, they might think he wasn't coming back, and Mama might make Papa understand how wrong it was to argue with Mr Robinson like that. Everyone expected him to act like a man now, so why couldn't he choose his own friends?

What if Grace's dad told her to stay away from him, to avoid another argument? He couldn't face not seeing her. She was his only door into a normal world. It seemed that whatever he did, he upset someone.

He spotted an overturned rowing boat on the sands and climbed on top of it, sitting deep in thought as the sea ebbed and flowed at the edge of the sand and the waves crashed against the pier in the distance.

It was only when a ship on the horizon caught his eye that he realised he'd been staring at a fixed point without seeing anything. How long had he been sitting there? He wasn't sure. But it was long enough to make his point.

As he made his way along the beach towards home, he cringed at the sight of Mama standing on the path, a forlorn figure scanning the shore. His determination dissolved in an instant. He'd made things worse by running off. Papa would have the belt ready for when he got back. His skin grew hot at the thought of it. Best get it over with. The longer he left it, the more lashes there'd be.

He hurried over the sands, stumbling and scattering stones with his boots, full of guilt for upsetting Mama.

'William, oh my darling, thank goodness. Are you all right?' She pushed back his hair with a gentle touch. 'Come, let's get home,' she said.

They set off, William barely able to take in her chattering about how worried she'd been. All he could think of was the atmosphere that would greet them on their return.

Once inside, he stood still while Mama removed her cloak, tracing the geometric patterns of the floor tiles with his foot. The ticking of the clock echoed in the stillness. Papa must have gone upstairs to his study.

Mama took off her bonnet and smoothed her hair. 'I realise that was difficult for you, but running off didn't help matters.'

William studied her; she looked even paler than usual. Had he made things worse? 'Did Mr Robinson hit Papa?' he asked.

'No, of course he didn't,' said Mama. 'But it wasn't pleasant, with everyone listening. It's best if you keep out of Papa's way for a while. I'll get Cook to put your lunch plate on a tray, and you can eat it in your bedroom.'

Just as William was about to ask her for more details, Papa's voice rang out from the landing. 'William, come here at once!'

He exchanged an anxious glance with Mama. 'You'd better do as he says,' she told him. He wasn't fooled by the matter-of-fact voice she put on; her eyes were wide with fear. William climbed the stairs towards trouble, and Mama gathered her skirts and followed him.

PAPA WAS WAITING for them on the landing. 'In your bedroom. Now!' he roared, his face contorted with fury, his fists clenched. William scuttled past him, dreading what he might find.

There on the bed lay the three paintings he'd completed, and the oaken box. Oh no. How had Papa found them? William dug his fingernails into his palms, ready for the explosion.

'I assume these are yours? You deceitful, wretched boy, after everything I've said about your future career. No gratitude for what we've done for you, no ambition. Well, I'm going to put an end to this.'

Papa reached for the schooner painting he'd finished last month. Oh, how proud William had been the day he'd sneaked Grace into the house, when she'd told him she loved that one best. Dread landed like a stone in his stomach as Papa lifted both arms and rammed the canvas over the metal bedpost. The ripping sound tore into William's heart.

Papa hesitated for an instant.

Please. Please stop there. Don't destroy them all. But it

13

was no good; William could only watch, helpless, as Papa threw the other two paintings on the floor, the seascape and the lifeboat, and stomped all over them, crumpling the canvas.

Mama was just standing there. Why didn't she say something, try to stop him? Papa was breathing so hard that when he lifted his head, William could see the hairs in his nostrils quivering.

He fought back the tears. 'Stop it!'

Papa's face reddened as his hand reached out and grasped the box.

'No!' William leapt forward, but it was too late. The carved casket with its tiny acorns slammed against the wall and fell apart. The lid shattered into pieces, and paintbrushes flew in all directions.

He knelt and gathered up a fragment of wood, running his fingers over the carving as he looked into Papa's furious face. He had to go, get out, out of that room with its ruined paintings, away from the house. Mama reached for him but he pushed past her, a mist of tears blurring his sight as he stumbled down the stairs and ran out of the front door.

There was only one place to go.

CHAPTER 2

William ran as fast as he could towards the row of cottages near the lifeboat station, struggling against the wind, his breath catching in his throat. He hammered on the door of Grace's cottage as if his life was in danger.

Mrs Robinson opened the door. 'William? What on earth are you doing here? Come on in.' She called for Grace as she ushered him in to the living room. 'Sit there,' she said, steering him to a tattered sofa. 'I'll get you a drink of water. You look dreadful.'

He sat down and tried to calm himself. Grace's three brothers broke away from their game of marbles, then returned to it as if deciding he wasn't very interesting, squabbling as the tiny glass balls clinked and rolled across the floorboards. There was a clatter of footsteps on the stairs, then Grace rushed in.

'What are you doing here? What's happened?' She sat next to him.

Struggling to keep his voice steady, he described how Papa had destroyed his paintings. The boys broke away from their game to listen, their eyes widening. Mrs Robinson shooed them upstairs and gathered the marbles into a cloth bag.

It was the first time he'd seen Grace stunned into silence; she hadn't interrupted him once. At last she spoke. 'How could he do that to your paintings? You spent hours on them, and they were so realistic. I can't believe it.'

William sighed. 'They were only my first attempt. But Papa will never allow me to paint again. That's what hurts the most.'

Mrs Robinson sat next to him. 'I'm sure things will calm down. From what Grace says, you have a real talent and they should be proud of you.'

If only it was that straightforward. 'That isn't the way Papa sees it.'

'Maybe not now, but in time he might think differently.'

Grace shook her head. 'William's Papa is a bully. Look how horrible he was to Dad after church.'

'And your dad stood up to him, I'm proud to say. But William can't fight back. It'll take time to win round his Papa.' She turned back to him. 'What does your Mama think?'

William sighed. 'She wants me to do whatever makes me happy, but she won't go against Papa's wishes.' He stopped. It wasn't right to criticise his parents in front of another family.

'He's a snob as well,' remarked Grace.

'Now then, that's enough,' her mother warned her. 'We have no right to judge others. We never know the full story.'

William shivered. The fire had dwindled away, leaving only a few dying embers in the grate. To think of all the fire-places at home, every one of them burning to keep Mama warm, and Ada always on hand to top them up with the best coal. It was past lunchtime now. Despite the cake he'd eaten, his stomach gave a growl. Grace's mother had better not have noticed it. He couldn't accept food from them.

The door creaked open and Tom Robinson came in, followed by two men clad in blankets, soaking wet and shivering.

Mrs Robinson rushed to her husband's side. 'Oh, thank God you saved them. Come in, shut the door. Hurry.' She steered the men towards the rug by the fireside. 'Tom, get two towels from the cupboard.'

She turned to the rescued sailors in a natural movement that told William this was a common event. 'Let's get you a set of dry clothes. Grace, open the chest.'

Grace turned to a grimy leather chest in the corner, opened the lid and began to sort through the contents.

William blushed as he realised Mrs Robinson had noticed him looking. 'All the neighbours give us their old clothes, and I clean and mend them, ready for rescued sailors like these two,' she explained.

He took the bundle Grace offered him and put them on the floor for the sailors to make their choices. They huddled together on the rug in front of the fire, shivering until Mr Robinson came in with the towels and sent them into the kitchen to dry and dress themselves.

'Get another log for the fire, Grace,' said Mr Robinson. William saw the worried look she gave her mother.

'Their need is greater than ours,' Mrs Robinson reminded her.

How little they had, yet they were willing to share it with strangers. He took the log from Grace and put it on the fire.

'So, William, what do you want to do?' asked Mrs Robinson. 'These things are often best sorted straight away.'

'I'm not sure,' he replied. 'But I can't go home yet. Papa will still be furious.' He couldn't tell her he'd much rather stay and find out about the rescue.

She gave him a sympathetic smile. 'But your Mama will

be frantic with worry. I'm surprised they haven't come knocking at our door.'

'Huh, I don't think so,' said Grace. 'They wouldn't want to be seen coming here.'

Mrs Robinson glared at her, forcing her into silence.

'I understand you're still upset, William. But I can see it from a mother's perspective. Your Mama loves you very much. Imagine how she'll be feeling at this moment.'

'Yes, I can see that,' admitted William.

'I can walk back home with you, if you like? Grace can look after her brothers while Tom sees to the sailors.'

He thought for a moment. 'But if Papa sees you, it might make things worse.'

'Well, I could take you to the corner of the village green. Will that help?'

'Yes, I think so.'

'Come on then. The sooner you get it over with, the better.'

Grace gave him a hug and put her hand into the pocket of her dress. 'Here, take this,' she said, pressing an object into his hand.

William studied it. It was an oval piece of jet, smooth, black and shiny.

'It's a good luck charm,' she explained. 'My uncle brought it from Whitby. I keep it in my pocket and whenever I'm worried about something, I turn it over in my fingers and make a wish. It always brings me comfort. I want you to have it.'

William put the jet in his trouser pocket. 'Thank you, that means a lot to me. Wish me luck.'

'You know I do.' She stood at the doorway and waved as they left.

William dragged his feet the whole way. All he could see was Papa's face, red with raw hatred, and his whole body trembling with rage as he slammed the painting against the end of the bedstead. What if he'd turned on Mama? He stopped and wiped his eyes on his sleeve.

Mrs Robinson returned to his side and laid a hand upon his shoulder. 'Be brave. Your Papa's had time to settle down, and your Mama will be relieved to have you back. Don't forget to apologise to your Papa for deceiving him. Bide your time, and everything will work out.'

She looked towards the village green. 'I'd better leave you here, in case they're watching at the window. Take care, William.'

He gave a brief nod and tried to say 'Thank you', but the words wouldn't come, so he turned away and edged forward. Inside lay the devastation of his paintings. He could never forgive Papa for this.

On the day he had found the box in the attic, he'd been lost in wonder at the skill of the person who had carved the intricate pattern of leaves and acorns. Now it lay in pieces on his bedroom floor, except for the fragment in his pocket. He ran his fingers over it, thankful that the piece he'd grabbed had the acorns attached, a comforting smoothness in contrast to the broken edges.

The last part of the walk was the hardest, his steps unwilling, until at last he stepped into the porch and took off his shoes. The only sound was Ada's humming as she tidied the drawing room. In he went, up the stairs to the landing. At the top, he stopped. His parents were in their bedroom, arguing by the sound of it.

William gripped the bannister to stop himself from turning and running back outside. Be brave, Grace's mother had said. But how? He wasn't ready to face them, but neither could he bear to go into his own room where his ruined paintings lay. Instead, he sat on the floor and leaned against the side wall of Mama and Papa's bedroom. What sort of mood was Papa in?

~

WILLIAM STRAINED to hear Mama's words as he sat with his ear pressed against the wall. She was pleading with Papa, her voice wavering.

'Won't you go out to look for him, Matthew? He's been missing for almost an hour now.'

'I'll do no such thing. He will have to come home eventually. You have fussed over him too much, Anna. He needs to grow up.'

'He needs to understand that we love him. After what you did to his pictures, he'll be upset, not to mention worried about what you'll say when he returns. If he returns.'

The familiar knot twisted in his stomach. The same old argument, Mama trying to make Papa see sense. Why did people marry, only to spend their days arguing? And he always seemed to be the cause of it, no matter how hard he tried to please them.

Mama was sobbing now. If only he could run in and hug her, to let her see he'd returned. But the heavy tread of Papa's boots reverberating along the floorboards told him his fury hadn't abated.

'I won't countenance his disobedience. He knows I have forbidden him to waste his time on this art nonsense. It's insupportable, after the risks we've taken for him.'

Risks? What did that mean? He could barely hear Mama's reply, except for a few fragmented words; something about wanting a baby. Then her voice rose more clearly. 'Is that what this is about? Are you jealous of your own son?'

The pacing stopped and Papa's voice boomed out again. 'Now you're being ridiculous. Me, jealous of a weak boy? I have quite enough to occupy my mind, with the way opportunities are opening up at work. If William is to take the company forward in the years to come, he has to conform to my expectations.'

It always came back to this, a destiny he wanted no part of. He tucked his knees in and held them tightly against his chest, retreating from the real world into his own tiny space. A noise filled his ears, buzzing and pounding, drowning out Mama's failure to persuade Papa to go out to find him. It faded again, and his attention returned to his surroundings.

The ticking of the grandfather clock rose from the hall, marking time while he waited.

Papa cleared his throat. 'I shouldn't have stopped. Not on such a foul night. I should have continued on to the doctor's to get some medicine to settle you. Our lives could have continued as normal, and we'd never have known another way existed.'

William sat up straight. He'd never heard Papa admit he'd made a wrong choice. But what did he mean?

There was the scraping of a chair, and Mama's voice became faint, as if she'd moved towards Papa. He pressed his ear closer to the wall to catch her words better.

'But medicine wasn't the answer. I wouldn't have settled. Being childless... it was a curse. When you returned that night with him, it was a sign from God, a reward for our patience.'

Returned? When was this? Where had Papa taken him? What did she mean? A pang of guilt overcame him. It wasn't right to eavesdrop; there'd be trouble if he was caught. But something kept him there: a need to know, a tiny hope that there was a time when Papa cared for him.

'You can hardly call his disobedience a reward. You know how hard it was for me to break away from all my Tynemouth contacts and begin again. Once he's started at the office full time, he will become accustomed to it and we'll have no more of this foolish wilfulness.'

Mama's pleading voice returned as she asked Papa to remember he was a child, and they were responsible for him. 'Think what a tiny, vulnerable baby he was when you found him that night. If he hadn't cried, you'd never have realised he was there. What was the point of saving him from the wreck, and making a new life here, if you're abandoning him now?'

CHAPTER 3

Saved from a wreck? William's breathing turned into urgent gasps as Mama's words buzzed in his head. The walls closed in, his vision blurring, every sound muffled, as if he was in a tunnel, everything narrowing down to one fact. He didn't belong.

A rattling noise from the doorknob made him jump. He'd be in trouble if they found him here, but shock held him fast to the floor.

The door creaked open. 'I've said everything I'm going to say on the matter, Anna. I will be in my study for the rest of the evening, preparing for my board meeting tomorrow.' The door slammed and Papa marched the other way along the corridor towards his study.

William curled up even more tightly, rocking his body back and forth. No, it couldn't be true. But there could be no other meaning. They weren't his Mama and Papa. He was nothing more than a shipwrecked orphan, picked up on a stormy night like flotsam washed ashore on the tide.

Was this why he had always felt different? Now he had the answer: he was a stranger, an interloper. What should he do? Mama was on her own now. He could run into her arms and tell her he was back. But one clear thought burned through his confusion: she had lied to him too. How could she? All the times they'd been alone together, and she had never once thought she owed it to him to explain the truth. Everything was a pretence. The realisation slammed into him like a pail of icy water thrown in his face.

Neither of them must find him here; they mustn't know he'd overheard. He scrambled to his feet and ran to his room, but as soon as the door swung open, he remembered.

Oh Lord, look. The ripped remnants of his paintings, the splintered fragments of his beloved box. The box that had held his brushes and the promise of a different future. He brought his hands to his face. Why hadn't they told him?

He had to get out; there was nothing here for him now. In a daze, he pulled out a battered soft leather bag from the wardrobe and stuffed a few clothes into it, then scooped all his pocket money from a drawer and put it in his pocket, suppressing a sob. The oaken shard snagged the fabric of his jacket, so he disentangled it and put it in the bag. Keep going, be quick, don't get caught, work it out later. What else? He added a notebook, a pencil and a few handkerchiefs.

Down the stairs he went, cringing at every creak, dashing across the hall, only pausing to put his shoes on before emerging into the cold air. At the corner of the village green, he paused. Which way? His fingers closed over the piece of jet in his trouser pocket.

What about Grace? She'd told him she was prepared to run away with him. But he couldn't expect her to leave her family, and they wouldn't let her go. It would break her heart and theirs. Her mother had been so kind to him after Papa had ruined his paintings; he had no doubt that she'd take him in. But sooner or later Mama and Papa would come for him and drag him back. How could he stay, knowing he didn't belong to them? How could he knowingly live a lie?

No, not back to Grace's, much as he longed to see her. He had to do this alone, leave as soon as possible, so that Papa couldn't find him.

Northwards was the best bet, where the land rose to form shallow cliffs, away from the main part of the village. Towards the town, where there'd be some form of transport to take him far away: a boat perhaps, or a train.

William strode away from the house he could no longer call home, not daring to look back, keeping his head down and praying that no one would recognise him. One thing was certain: he had to get away. Away from the terrible lies; speed up, run fast, before Mama missed him. Past the houses, on to the track near the edge of the shallow cliffs, his feet pounding the ground, covering the distance as fast as possible.

After a few moments, he dropped his bag and leaned forwards with his hands on his knees, gulping for air. The dark sea crashed against the rocks, arcing and splashing into white foam. He tasted the raw tang of the salty spray, storing the sensation away for another day.

William took one last lingering look along the beach he loved, before picking up his belongings and continuing on towards the town. He had spent hours looking at the sea, and now he knew the joy of painting it. If he settled somewhere else, he might be able to paint again. Something good had to come from this disaster.

The railway station was close by. He could catch the first train that arrived and put his fate in its hands.

The ticket office was quiet. A poster attracted his attention: an impressive cathedral, ancient walls, a blue-green river and bridges of intricate ironwork. 'York - cathedral city', he read. All he'd heard about it was that it was south of here, and inland. It sounded as good as anywhere; Papa only dealt with coastal ports and it would be easier to hide in a busy city.

He approached the counter. 'A single ticket to York please,' he said in a small voice.

CHAPTER 4

William sat on a bench, self-conscious and insignificant, and waited for the train. He'd never been out of the village alone before, never mind on a train. Papa had told Mama she fussed over him. Perhaps she had; it didn't matter now. There was no going back.

There was a rumbling, growing louder, then the sound of clanking and grinding as the locomotive pulled into the station like a magnificent mechanical beast emerging from a cloud. He'd never been this near to one until now. Billy Corner used to miss school to sit on the bank and watch the engines go by. He was slow at his lessons but could tell you everything about these machines: how much coal they used, their top speed, and how the steam turned the pistons. William concentrated on the sounds and the movement of the wheels, trying to push aside his anxiety that someone would spot him before he could climb inside.

Once in the compartment, he stored his bag and took a seat. The guard waved his paddle as if signalling his new start, then blew the whistle. They were off.

The station receded and the sea came into view. Oh no.

They were heading back to Seaton Carew. After an anxious few minutes, the train sped past the platform. In what seemed no time at all, it was slowing at the approach to Stockton station. The lady in the ticket office had told him to change trains here.

William climbed down on to the platform and headed for a poster that showed the timetable, afraid to show his ignorance by asking someone how to interpret it. It was better to occupy his thoughts by deciding what to do when he arrived in York. He would need to find a bed for the night first, then tomorrow he would look for a job. He must think of the practicalities and ignore the image of Mama alone in the bedroom at home, still unaware he was so far away.

What about Grace? She wouldn't forgive him for leaving without saying goodbye. It might be a long time before he saw her again, if ever. He reached for the piece of jet in his pocket, finding comfort in knowing her fingers had rubbed it when she'd been scared.

A noise made him turn towards the tracks. The York train was coming, clouds of steam billowing from its funnel. He climbed on board, his pulse racing, trying to calm himself with deep, slow breaths, and eased himself into a seat by the window. As the train chugged through the countryside, he stared out at the changing landscape. There were so many shades of green, like daubs of paint blended on a palette. In the distance he spotted villages clustered at the base of valleys, and flocks of sheep clinging to the hills. Why had Papa never taken him on a journey before now? He had spent his whole life in Seaton Carew.

Or had he? The thought landed like a punch to his stomach. He had no idea if he'd lived anywhere else before he formed any memories. Mama and Papa had never talked about the past. He'd often wondered why he didn't have brothers and sisters like the other children in his class, but

Mama always looked sad when he raised the subject, so he'd stopped asking. Now he knew why.

How had she managed to keep up the pretence? The gossips would have spread the word in no time; it was that sort of village. But how could they produce a baby as if by magic, without everyone asking questions?

Then he remembered: Papa had mentioned moving from Tynemouth. That must have been straight after the shipwreck, so people in Seaton wouldn't have been any the wiser. It was better not to dwell on it. He would never go back. If he clung to that decision, it might stop any regrets. It was better to plan for the future and make the most of the choices open to him, even if it took every ounce of the limited courage he had.

His thoughts occupied him all the way to York, where he dismounted and stood on the platform watching travellers being reunited with their loved ones. A pang of longing overcame him as he remembered he was alone in the world. He ran his fingers through his hair. Don't look back, don't think about Mama crying at the realisation that he'd gone, bewildered, not knowing the real reason for his disappearance.

Where now? He spotted a sign for the way out and walked towards it. It was best to keep his head up and look confident and purposeful, even though his heart was breaking inside. Now it was his turn to pretend, as a matter of survival.

As he emerged from the station, the city walls came into view, their grey stones looming above him, weather-beaten and watchful. He followed the flow of people across the road and under an archway, assuming they were heading for the city centre. Excitement fluttered in his stomach. Or was it hunger? He wasn't sure; he'd never had to wait for a meal before.

It was already getting dusky, and he needed to find a

place to stay first. Somewhere warm and clean, with a comfortable bed and a means of getting washed in the morning, so he could make himself presentable and ready to start searching for work.

There were so many streets, full of shops. Of course, they were closed on a Sunday; his first chance would be tomorrow. The curtains were drawn at the first and second-floor windows, where the owners must live. Gas lamps flickered, casting shadows on the pavements as people milled around, some heading to the inns for refreshment.

The poster at the station had depicted a river. There were bound to be boat trips for the tourists, and they might need workers. He liked the thought of helping visitors to enjoy their day.

A lady stood just ahead of him, another traveller, judging by the bag at her feet. She was well-dressed, her hat fashionably set to one side just like Mama's. She fingered a stray curl of hair as she studied a piece of paper and frowned.

William was about to approach her and offer help, but before he could make a move, an older man, with untidy whiskers and a scar on his cheek, strolled up and spoke to her. His cap and rough jacket suggested he was a workman. The lady shrank back from him. It was rude to stare, so William turned round and pretended to examine a shop window, observing them in the reflection.

'You're a lovely thing, aren't you?' the man said, stroking the lady's face. She pushed his arm away, but he persisted. 'On your own? If you're short of money, I can help out. 'Ow about threepence for a bit of a fumble?'

'Get away from me,' she said. 'How dare you?'

William turned round and saw the man make a rude gesture and walk away muttering to himself. What should he do? He didn't like to interfere, but the lady looked distressed.

She pulled a handkerchief from her bag and dabbed her eyes with it.

He decided he'd better walk on by. Mama had often said it wasn't wise to get involved in other people's troubles.

'Excuse me… young man?' Her voice was punctuated by sobs.

He turned around. 'Yes?'

'I'm sorry to trouble you, but I'm lost. Can you help me find somewhere to stay? I've got this map…' She faltered. 'But I can't…' A tear stained her cheek.

'If I could, I would,' he said, stepping closer. 'But I'm new to the city myself, and I need a room for the night too. I've just arrived by train and it's getting rather late.'

Her face brightened. 'That's fortunate. Should we pair up and try to work it out between us?'

William considered her question for a moment. It seemed like a good idea. He suggested walking to the end of the street to check for landmarks. After comparing the map with their surroundings, they worked out where they were. There were several possibilities, and he started to feel more hopeful.

'I can't thank you enough,' she said. 'Can I treat you to a drink and a bite to eat? It was scary back there, when that man approached me. You've restored my faith in men.'

She thought he was a man; how grown-up that made him sound. He nodded in agreement. After all, he was ravenously hungry, and thirsty too, and he wasn't sure how long his money would last. He followed her into the nearest inn and settled himself at a table while she beckoned someone over and placed an order. Thank goodness she was willing to take the lead.

It wasn't long before two mugs of ale appeared. It would be embarrassing to admit he'd never drunk it before, but if he refused, it would offend her. After a cautious sip, he decided it wasn't too bad. She must have forgotten to order food, or else they had run out. This would have to do for now. They shouldn't be dallying here anyway, not when they had lodgings to find. He gulped it down, glad of the refreshment.

'You must have been thirsty,' she said, a smile playing about her lips. Fingering the jet pebble in his pocket, he stored away the moment to share. What would Grace say about him drinking alcohol with a stranger? He dismissed the thought that he might never be able to tell her about it.

'I was parched,' he agreed. 'It's been a few hours since I last had anything.' How he regretted missing lunch.

She raised her hand, and the innkeeper appeared with another mug. 'I didn't...' He stopped, thinking it sounded ungrateful. 'Thank you. Oh, you didn't tell me your name.'

'Elizabeth,' she told him.

This time, he sipped his drink at a more leisurely pace while she suggested a few lodging houses from the map. Would being with her reduce his chances of finding one? They'd need two rooms. But he couldn't go off on his own now. Anyway, she had the map. It was much harder for him to find somewhere suitable without her help.

'Finish your drink; we'd better be on our way,' she told him.

He drained his ale and reached for his bag, then tried to stand. The room swam before his eyes, and the chatter of the customers buzzed around his head like a swarm of bees. He reached out with one hand to steady himself against the table. 'Oh... I got up too fast there,' he said.

'Not used to drinking? I'm sorry, I just assumed... Come on, follow me. I'll look after you.' She took her own bag and made towards the door.

William followed, unsteady on his feet, convinced the floorboards were rising up to meet him. It would be better once he got outside in the fresh air. At the door, she reached for his hand. As they stepped out into the street, the coldness hit him full in the face and he gasped, blinking in the half-light. The upper floors of the buildings seemed to lean in as if sharing a confidence, ready to spill their secrets.

The man with the scar was standing over the road. William glanced at Elizabeth, unsure whether he should point him out or lead her away. It was hard enough to walk straight, much less think coherently, so he stood beside her while she consulted the map again. Then she lifted her head and looked straight at the man.

He crossed the road in a flash and stood in front of William, eyes blazing. 'You pinchin' my girl? You need to be taught a lesson.'

William let go of Elizabeth's hand. 'No,' he said, 'I've only just met...' He reeled back as a fist hit him in the stomach. He dropped his bag and doubled over in pain. Then a push from behind made him topple forward.

'Get his wallet,' the man called out. William curled into a ball on the floor, dimly aware of Elizabeth rifling through his bag. It was futile to even try to stop her; things might get worse if he resisted.

'Stupid boy,' she whispered into his ear, before she rushed off with the man, her shoes clattering on the cobbles and her laugh echoing along the street.

William clutched his stomach as a dull ache spread through his body. Surely someone must stop to help? A procession of feet skirted round him and muttered voices signalled disgust.

Two red velvet shoes came into view, with a lace hem fluttering above them. A lady would take pity on him.

'Disgraceful. The drunks get younger every week.'

She tutted and walked on.

THE DAMPNESS SEEPED into William's body as he lay on the pavement. He couldn't stay like this; someone might trip over him, or worse, give him a good kicking. But if he moved, he might make his injury worse. Gingerly, he rolled on to all fours then sat back on his haunches, still light-headed and weak. After a few moments, he struggled to a half-bent position and stumbled a few steps. When he tried to straighten up, the pain stabbed at his insides. Where should he go now?

One tentative step after another, he started walking. Darkness had fallen, and he needed to find a place to rest. Any shelter would do. At least he still had his bag; he could use it as a pillow. At the end of the road was a shop doorway with bills posted on the windows. The shop looked vacant, so there'd be no risk of being moved on early in the morning. He sank to the floor, wincing at the chill of the tiles against his legs.

Burrowing his hands into his pockets for warmth, wishing he'd brought a pair of gloves, his fingers touched the piece of jet. 'You'll find a way to survive,' Grace had said. But how? He'd only been here a couple of hours and he'd already made such a mess of everything.

His eyelids fluttered. He was exhausted, freezing cold, and sore where the punch had landed. He rolled over, turning his back on the street. Please, let sleep come.

'Oi! Whadd'yer think you're doing on my patch?'

William stirred and cried out at a sudden sharp pain in his back. He shuffled round, to see a tramp swinging his leg back for another kick.

'No!' he shouted, putting his hand out. He scrambled to his feet as fast as he could, and stood in front of the man, trying not to recoil from the stench of alcohol. He grabbed his bag and shuffled sideways to get past.

'Lookin' for a thick ear, are yer? No one takes my place, right? No one. If yer don't want a bloody nose, get yerself off.' The tramp raised a fist.

He backed away. 'I'm very sorry. I didn't know.'

The man's tone changed as he peered at him. 'New 'ere, eh? Bit young to be outside for the night, ain't yer?'

'I've had my money stolen. Is there anywhere else I can sleep?' For the first time in his life, he was aware of his voice being different. But in a desperate situation, he had no choice, and this man must have more idea than most. He frowned as he tried to make out the semi-coherent instructions for finding the river, then escaped as soon as he could.

This wasn't the way he envisaged spending the night. Oh, to be back in his own bed, with a soft mattress and plenty of blankets. But no, that could never be. His bedroom was now a scene of sorrow, of trampled canvases and a shattered box, the end of his dream.

The track took a downwards turn, and the houses became sparse as he approached the river, watchful for anyone who might do him harm. What a strange way to be, after a life spent trusting everyone he met. But look where that had got him.

Slipping and sliding on the muddy bank, at last his feet found the path. He glanced along the river, the darkness amplifying the sound of the water lapping against the bank. In the distance, he could make out a bridge. That must be where the tramp meant. He made his way towards it, clutching his bag and listening for voices. There was a faint murmuring sound, then a raucous laugh that made him stop.

Did he really want to do this? Of course not, but what was the alternative?

As he approached the bridge, he tried to make out the

vague shapes under the arch. He hesitated for a moment then walked on, the echoing of his footsteps announcing his arrival better than any brass band could.

Three heads popped up.

'Eh now, we've got company, lads.' An elderly man with a long scraggy grey beard raised his head. 'Who are you?'

William cleared his throat. 'Today's my first day in the city and someone's stolen my money. I met a man in a doorway, and he told me to come here. Can I stay for the night?'

'You can if you've got whisky.' The second voice was as rough as gravel, and the laugh that followed it was punctuated with a rasping cough.

The first man gave a snort. 'Like you haven't had enough, Ed. Looks too young to drink, if you ask me. Come nearer, posh lad. We don't bite – there's not enough meat on you.'

He took a few steps forward, while they observed him. It was just like Papa's inspection before church, but he had the distinct impression they were assessing his clothes to decide whether they could fit into them. They'd be persuading him to part with some of them next.

The third man made a grunting noise and muttered to the other two, his accent defying any understanding. It seemed an age before the grey-bearded man moved, shedding a holey blanket as he stood. He limped towards William. 'Looks like these two have no objections. But only one night, mind you. We've fought for this spot; we don't want no new beggars turning up if they think it's easy to join our party, if you know what I mean.' He turned and settled back into his spot.

There was no problem in agreeing to that; he had no intention of sleeping outside for more than one night. William placed his bag against the arch and eased himself to the ground, curling into a ball and wrapping his arms round himself to keep warm. But sleep evaded him, even in his exhaustion.

How could he let that woman fool him? Elizabeth. She would have given a false name, of course. But she was right; he'd been a stupid naïve boy, so easily taken advantage of. He'd have to be smarter than this to survive, become more suspicious of people. It wasn't a happy way to be, but a necessary one. All the lessons he'd learned were of no use: the poetry he'd been forced to recite, the mathematical calculations, studying the Bible... What he most needed was a way of knowing who he could trust.

Trust. That word was heavy with pain now. The lies burned into his mind like flames licking at the family photograph on the mantelpiece in the drawing room. Papa had insisted on having it taken as a way of impressing his business colleagues. But it was built on a pretence. The people he'd called his family were liars, no better than that Elizabeth woman.

William rolled over, wincing. Every movement reminded him of his injuries, his muscles stiffening with the cold. What if the men were waiting until he was asleep, before taking whatever they wanted and throwing him in the river? No one knew he was here, and no one would miss him. What a lonely place to die.

He started to make plans for tomorrow to help him stay awake, listening for any talk or any movement from the other men, ready to grab his bag and run off if needed. An early start was best. He'd wear the remaining change of clothes from his bag; he could use the water in the river to wash himself, to remove any trace of dust or dirt. No one would employ someone who looked and smelled like a vagrant. He'd have to accept the first work he was offered, to get money for lodgings. There'd be time later to look for a better job.

At last, the men's conversation settled into a quiet hum and the river noises subsided into a gentle rhythm. William fought to keep his eyes open, but it was no use; he kept nodding off, then jerking awake, as all the images of the last twenty-four hours taunted him.

It was like a carousel of tableaux from the school performances: Mama in her rocking chair by the window, sobbing as she prayed for his return, Grace sitting by the fire with her sewing, and Papa stamping on the canvases. Round and round they revolved, blurring into one another. Then he was running through the streets of York, chased by Papa, dodging people, trying to find a gap between the shops where he could dive into an alleyway to hide. He tripped, and Papa was upon him, putting his hands round his neck, squeezing...

William woke with a cry. The night was as black as tar, confusion lying thick upon him as he struggled to work out where he was.

'Ah, belt up, will yer,' Greybeard said.

'Sorry,' he said in a small voice. The cold was eating into his bones. Should he put on another layer of clothes? Better not. He needed to be presentable in the morning to look for work. If he could bear the discomfort for this one night, God would provide everything he needed.

A scrabbling noise began, then a snuffling, echoing under the canopy of the bridge. Every nerve stood to attention, his senses alert. Then something scuttled across his ankles. William shuddered and let out a scream.

'For God's sake man, give it a rest,' the man next to him shouted. 'We're trying to sleep here.'

'But a rat ran across my legs,' William said.

'So? We get them all the time. They're in the same boat as us: hungry, cold... all beggars together.' He let out a rueful laugh.

'Wassa marrer?' Another voice echoed under the bridge, muffled and rough.

'Only your old mate Ratty, come to see the new lad,' came the answer.

'Sod it, I was dreaming I'd got a job at the distillery. Didn't want waking up… He'll 'ave to go.'

'I'm sorry.' He didn't want to upset them; it would be even more scary sleeping out in the open, and the night smelt damp, signalling the possibility of rain. 'I'll be quiet, I promise.'

'Last warning.' There was a veiled threat in the words.

William pulled his coat closer around his neck, dipping his chin to muffle any sounds he might make, hoping sleep would come without the faces of those he'd left looming over him.

CHAPTER 5

As soon as dawn broke, William stirred from his fitful sleep. Every muscle ached and every move brought a stab of pain as he struggled to his feet, his body frozen to its core. First, he needed a wash, even if it was only to freshen up his hands and face. He shrugged off his coat, leaned over the edge and scooped up a palmful of murky water, gagging at the pungent smell. He opened his fingers to let it run out, stirred the water and plunged both hands further into it. It wasn't much better. As he splashed his face, the chill shocked him. He hadn't even thought about how he'd get dry. After a moment's thought, he took off his waistcoat and used it as a towel.

At least he hadn't lost his bag. A change of clothes was vital to his search for a job, he mused, as he swapped yesterday's dusty garments for his only fresh set.

With a last glance at the bundle of tramps still snoring their cares away, he set off to walk along the river bank. The ducks stood by the water's edge preening their feathers, quacking with laughter at him. If there'd been any chunks of stale bread ignored by the birds, he would have taken them.

Never had he known such a hollowness in his stomach, not even when he'd been ill in bed.

The shops wouldn't be open yet; the owners must be setting up, making sure their stock was at its best for the start of the week. They wouldn't appreciate being interrupted this early by a job-seeker. No matter; finding food was his first priority. But how could he do that, with no money? He couldn't bear the idea of begging, so he made his way towards the main streets, looking at the floor in the hope of finding a coin someone had dropped. Or a note; that would be a triumph.

At the end of a busy street, he stopped and stood watching for a moment, trying to imagine he was part of the crowd, going to his first proper job. After yesterday, he must deserve a bit of luck. All this noise and bustle was so different compared to home. No, not home; he had to stop calling it that.

But it was hard to dismiss all his memories, the times he used to stand at his window early on a morning when he couldn't sleep, watching the fishermen hauling in their catch and the ruddy-faced labourers setting off for their day on the farms. Today, Grace would be clearing out the ashes from the grate before she sat down to eat a slice of bread for breakfast, then she'd be helping her mother get the boys ready for school. He couldn't bear to think of her sorrow when she realised that he'd gone.

William tried to find a bright side to his situation. If he hadn't overheard the truth, he'd be preparing to join Papa's business like every middle-class son. At least now his future was in his own hands, even if that thought scared him. There must be opportunities here. But what sort of job? He only knew he didn't want to be in an office, not after spending time at Papa's company.

He soon found the shops. A clockmaker's caught his eye;

he didn't have a watch, and he would need one to get to work on time. Ah, but he didn't have a job yet. First things first. He surveyed the shop signs: a general dealer, butcher, boot and shoemaker, undertaker… None of those appealed.

It was strange having to make a decision, instead of Papa ruling over his every move. Dare he follow his dream and seek something creative? He spotted a bookseller's shop on the corner; if they gave him a job, he'd be able to read all the art books he wanted in the quieter moments of the day. Imagine building a collection of work, ready to be discovered. He chided himself for being unrealistic, then stopped. No, he had to get rid of Papa's words from his head, always criticising and dampening his desires, otherwise what was the point of his freedom?

The display in the book shop window drew him closer. Straight away he saw it, his favourite book. Around the World in Eighty Days, with Phileas Fogg and Passepartout. Oh, to think of the adventures they'd had. Mama used to read it to him, sitting beside his bed until he fell asleep.

Now he knew she was not his real Mama.

It was too much to bear. She loved him as if he were her own child, that much he knew; but it wasn't enough to make her tell him the truth. Did she have an excuse, living under constant strain, fearful of being found out, or of his real parents turning up one day to claim him as their own?

The shop owner was staring at him, so he turned away and continued walking. First things first: food, a paid job with someone willing to advance him a small sum, then a room to live in. Everything else would follow on from there.

Shreds of paper from discarded food wrappings tumbled along in the wind as a street sweeper tried in vain to brush them into a heap. A glint in the gutter caught his eye, but it was only a fragment of glass. The rumbling in his stomach made him press on, alert and watchful, focusing only on the ground, until he reached the end of the road and stopped at a church. At the foot of the steps lay a coin, almost invisible in the dust. He bent to pick it up and rubbed the dirt away with his fingers. A farthing. His spirit lifted; one find might lead to another.

He spent an hour wandering the city, one street at a time, switching between looking for coins and checking the shop windows for cards that might advertise a job. No luck with either.

The next row of shops was called Stonegate. His nostrils twitched at the irresistible smell of newly baked bread, the same aroma that emerged from the staircase early on a morning when he woke, accompanied by the clink of crockery from the kitchen as Cook prepared breakfast. That was another world now. A world he didn't belong to.

He traced the smell to a baker's shop, with a window display of wicker baskets filled with bread rolls, smooth and rounded. When he pushed at the door, a bell jangled, the tone reminiscent of the grocer's shop on the sea front where Mama had an account. A piece of bread would sustain him while he searched for work.

William took his place in the queue and examined the goods on the counter, imagining the crunch of the crust and the softness of the inside of a loaf, the comforting taste satisfying his hunger. But was a farthing enough? Would they sell an individual roll? He had no idea about the cost of things. A small ticket was poking out of a basket of rolls, but it was partly hidden. He had to wait his turn.

The bakeress brought a big crusty loaf to the counter, wrapped it in a sheet of brown paper and handed it to a customer. She wiped floury hands on her apron before taking the money and putting it in the till. A smile transformed her round, rosy-cheeked face as she said a thank you and goodbye. Then she tucked a stray wisp of hair back inside her white cap before turning to the next customer. Her kindly expression reminded him of dear Cook, who used to let him taste her biscuits if he wandered down to the kitchen when his governess took a break.

'Now then, Mrs Bennett, I'll have one of your best beef pies please,' said the lady. The queue shuffled forward, and William moved nearer the counter. The aroma of warm bread and pastry was torture. He craned his neck, trying to see the price tag on the basket of rolls. A farthing wasn't enough; you had to buy half a dozen. What was he to do?

He swayed as a light-headed sensation came over him. The bakeress looked sympathetic. If he did faint, would she give him a drink and a piece of bread? He couldn't be sure. With a busy shop to run, she'd probably either ignore him or push him back outside.

From deep within him came a voice he hadn't heard before. So many bread rolls; they won't miss one.

But stealing is wrong, said Mama's voice inside his head. He pictured the vagrants under the bridge, devoid of hope, dulling their pain with drink, barely surviving from day to day on nothing more than scraps of food. Mama would have given a beggar a piece of food left over from dinner if they'd asked her. It wasn't as if he would hurt anyone to get a roll.

Still he agonised.

The queue moved forward again; soon it would be his turn. No one stood behind him, and he was level with the basket of rolls now. His hand came out of his pocket, letting the farthing come into view, and he arranged his fingers to feign a hint of more coins in his palm, as if ready to make a purchase.

It was now or never. The lady in front was placing her order and the bakeress had turned her back to get it. William reached out and grabbed a roll from the top of the basket with his other hand.

The customer had seen him. 'Hey!' she shouted.

He picked up his bag and darted away from the counter towards the door, as the bakeress' cry of 'Stop, thief!' rang in his ears.

CHAPTER 6

Tinny Bennett tipped the tray of bread rolls into the basket, inhaling the yeasty aroma as she arranged them. Making sure that everything was neatly presented helped to distract her from the tiresome routine of her days in the shop. Oh, to be one of those young ladies in the novels she read, who could sit and read, sew or play the piano all day. Think of the things she could learn.

She said a silent prayer to God, to show she was sorry for complaining. Working alongside her mother was better than being a pauper in the workhouse.

'Tinny! Where's them rolls?'

She jumped as Mam's voice broke into her thoughts.

'Coming!' she replied, picking up the basket to take it through to the shop.

She placed the basket on the counter and tidied the cloth around the edges to make sure it looked nice. There were only three customers in the queue, two ladies and a boy of about her own age. Another quiet day. Mam was already worrying about the takings. It was a real dilemma – they had to keep the shop well stocked, otherwise customers would go elsewhere, but the baking was too much for only two of them to manage.

It hadn't even occurred to her that they'd struggle like this once Lizzie had left to get married. She'd been so happy to have Mam all to herself, instead of feeling like she was in the way whenever Lizzie started talking about her sweetheart. Their evenings were lovely and quiet now, but Mam was always fretting about whether the landlord would put the rent up.

She moved away from the counter and started lining up the loaves on the back shelves. There was a sudden commotion and a cry from Mam. As she turned her head, she caught sight of the boy rushing towards the door, a bread roll in one hand. How dare he?

She dodged around the corner of the counter and gave chase, inwardly cursing her layers of petticoats for getting in the way. Too late; a customer was coming in, holding the door wide open for him. Indignation rose in her chest. He mustn't escape. Gathering her skirts, she sprang forward, just as the boy stumbled and collided into a man.

Thank goodness it was someone she could rely on to help. 'Mr Johnson! Hold him; he's a thief.' She was breathless, though she couldn't tell if it was through exertion or a strange excitement.

'I've got him, don't you worry.' Johnny Johnson gave her a triumphant smile and addressed the boy, who was taking bites out of the roll as though he hadn't seen food for a month. 'You're in trouble, young man, and no doubt about it. Now then, we're going back into the shop so's you can face up to what you've done. Mrs Bennett will have a few harsh words for you, I'll be bound.'

Tinny held the door open for him as he marched the miscreant back inside. She turned to the little gathering of eager onlookers. 'Please come back in about five minutes; we need to sort this out.' She shut the door and changed the sign to 'Closed'.

The lad was standing in front of Mam, chewing the bread frantically. She stepped forward and grabbed the roll from his hand. 'I'll have that. Stop eating the evidence.' She tossed it on the little table by the window, trying not to think about the germs on it. But when she got a proper look at him, he didn't seem dirty, only a little dusty. That was a leather bag on the floor, and his shoes were polished to a shine that the grime from the street couldn't hide. The material in his clothes was a good quality weave too, better than anything they could afford. She'd love to sew material like that. But why would a toff thieve from them?

Mam came to stand in front of the counter. 'Johnny! Thank goodness you were here.'

Mr Johnson swung the boy round to face her. 'You'd better apologise to Mrs Bennett. Unless you'd prefer a policeman to sort you out? I'm sure there'll be one some-where round here.'

'I'll go and find a constable,' Tinny offered. She didn't want to miss hearing the lad apologise; he was nothing like the usual ragamuffins that darted in trying to steal a piece of bread. But a crime was a crime, and he needed to be punished. She stared at him, unable to fathom why he'd done it. His shoulders had slumped, and he was looking at the floor as if wishing it would open up into a tunnel for him to escape into.

Mam wiped her floury hands on her apron. 'No you won't. Let's just listen to what he has to say.'

Tinny gave a sigh of frustration as her mother faced the thief. What was she thinking? He needed to be taught a lesson. That was the trouble with Mam; she was always too kind and trusting.

'Well?' Mam was standing with her hands on her hips, waiting for an answer.

At last he lifted his head, his cheeks crimson and his eyes full of shame. 'I'm very sorry,' he said. 'Someone attacked and robbed me last night. They took every penny, so I had to sleep outside, and I'm starving.'

'A likely story,' said Johnny. 'Can you prove it?'

Tinny exchanged a glance with her mother, knowing she was thinking the same thing. That posh voice... it was obvious he wasn't from round here.

Mam put her hands on her hips and stared at him. 'What's your name, and how old are you?'

'William Harper, and I'm fourteen.' He pushed back a lock of hair that hung over his forehead, in a gesture of annoyance.

Tinny frowned. He was the same age as her, and he'd slept on the streets last night? She'd have been terrified.

'And you're on your own? Not in a gang of thieves?'

The boy straightened up, as if offended. 'Certainly not. I'm from a respectable family.'

Ha, she was right. Then he would have heard the commandment 'Thou shalt not steal'.

'But how have you stooped so low, lad?' asked Mr Johnson, as if reading her thoughts. 'Where are your parents?'

'I... I'd rather not say, sir. I've had an awful shock.'

Tinny saw Mam raise her eyebrows at Mr Johnson. She knew that expression; it was an unspoken signal that she was taking charge of the conversation.

Mam stepped closer to the boy. 'This is Mr Johnson, and I'm Mrs Bennett. Sarah Bennett.' She pointed in Tinny's direction. 'And this is my daughter, Christina.'

Tinny refused to look at him, to make a point that she wouldn't associate with his kind. Go on, Mam, she thought.

Make sure he's punished. Good family or not, he's still a criminal.

'This is my shop, and I work hard for my living. Then you come along and try to steal goods that I should be selling to my customers. Do you understand why that's wrong?'

'Of course I do. I never meant to steal. I hate lies and wrongdoing, but I got in a pickle and didn't know what to do.'

Tinny gave him a sideways glance. He sounded like he meant it, but it could all be an act. The question was, would Mam fall for it?

His hands were buried in his pockets, searching them. 'Here,' he said, offering a farthing. 'Will that cover it? It's the only coin I have. The sign said you had to buy half a dozen rolls, but I didn't have enough for that many.'

Mam had folded her arms. That was good; it meant she wouldn't be swayed.

'That's not the point. You stole from me instead of asking.'

'No, I can see that. I'm sorry, but I was desperate. Can I eat the rest of the roll now please?' He darted across to the table and grabbed it back, then bit into it, chewing as fast as he could.

Mr Johnson laughed. 'I don't think she'll be wanting it back now.'

'It's not a laughing matter, Johnny.'

Tinny could tell her mother was struggling to keep a serious face. This wasn't going as it should. So much for keeping the evidence. The boy finished the roll and wiped his mouth with the back of his hand.

'I only took it because I felt faint. Yesterday was my first day in York, but the people who attacked me took all my money, so I couldn't pay for a bed for the night. I'm looking for work, honestly. I'm not a thief.'

Tinny couldn't help herself. She had to know. 'So where

did you sleep?' She looked into his eyes, defying him to tell a lie.

As he explained how he'd slept under a bridge with the tramps, she stared even harder, willing herself not to show any reaction. If he thought they were being taken in by his hard-luck story, he'd try to escape.

'Look at this, if you don't believe me,' he said, and lifted his shirt and waistcoat to show them a purple bruise spreading across his stomach. Tinny swayed at the sight of it, and looked away, while Mam made a sympathetic noise.

'Sit over in that chair by the window,' Mam told him, turning away and beckoning Johnny to follow her. 'Tinny, stand guard.'

That wasn't fair. Why couldn't she be involved in the decision? She scowled, as much for her mother's benefit as the thief's. Mam and Johnny moved to the rear of the shop and stood whispering, flicking glances in the boy's direction. Tinny could see more customers gathering outside, looking through the window in a cheeky pretence of examining the display.

At last Mam came back. 'I've made a decision, young man. I had a girl assistant, Lizzie, but she left a couple of weeks ago to get married, and I haven't filled the position yet. You can work for free, to repay your debt.'

'Mam, no!' The words escaped from her mouth unbidden. 'You can't... How can we trust him, after what he's done?'

'Christina, don't question my judgement. Remember, God expects us to be forgiving.'

She blushed at the rebuke, knowing she wouldn't win the argument. Mam only used her Sunday name when she was either nostalgic or annoyed. Forgiveness was one thing, but having him working in the shop was too much. What on earth was her mother thinking? She'd better not let him anywhere near the till.

'Really?' the boy's expression was incredulous, as if it was the last thing he'd expected. 'How long will it take me to repay you?' he asked.

'Smart lad, this one,' observed Mr Johnson. 'It was only a bread roll.'

'That's not the point,' Mam replied. 'It's the principle of the thing. There needs to be an element of punishment.'

Tinny said a silent prayer that he would soon work out he couldn't accept the offer. If he wasn't getting a wage, he wouldn't be able to afford to rent anywhere. And even if he found a fool to take him in, he'd still need to find a real job when Mam decided she'd had enough of him.

Johnny must have been thinking the same, for he said it wasn't going to solve all of William's problems. 'Of course, over at the police station he'd be fed, and have a cell to sleep in.'

Oh no. She recognised that tone of voice, the one he always used it when he wanted to wheedle his way round Mam. And by the look on her face, it was working.

'You're a cheeky old so and so, Johnny Johnson. You know full well I have two spare rooms upstairs. They're more like cupboards, but...' She tailed off, giving an exasperated sigh. 'Go on then, he can stay here; it will make it easier for him to do the early starts.'

Tinny felt hot tears welling up. No, it couldn't be... invading their home as well? What was Mam up to? It would completely disrupt the cosy togetherness that they'd only just got back, and she wouldn't be able to read her beloved books or do her embroidery in peace. She couldn't bear it.

Mam went closer to William. 'You can eat with us, but you'll have to work for longer to cover the lodgings and food. I'll ask the knocker-upper to tap on your window on a morning until you get used to waking up before dawn.'

'I'm very grateful for your kindness, Mrs Bennett.'

'Hmm. Don't think you can take advantage. I'll be watching you carefully. One wrong move and you'll find yourself hauled off to the police station.' She smoothed her apron. 'You can call me Sarah; I don't go in for formality.'

William gave a little bow. 'I promise to work hard to make amends for my bad behaviour. I don't know what came over me, except I was so hungry that I didn't think about what I was doing. It's the first time I've ever taken anything that wasn't mine, I promise you. I had a horrible day yesterday, but you've restored my faith in people.'

Was that a blush on Mam's cheeks?

'Well, my Bert always said everyone deserved a chance. I try to live by his principles. It's hard, being a woman in business, but I have a good set of friends. And Tinny here keeps me going, don't you, love?'

Tinny couldn't bear it any longer. 'It's not right… You've ruined everything,' she said, hoping they both took her meaning. She ran out, stumbling through the back room and up the stairs to her bedroom, where she threw herself on the bed and sobbed.

CHAPTER 7

W hat on earth was that? The sharp rapping on the
window broke into William's dreams, throwing him
into a panic at his strange surroundings. For a moment, he
thought he was back in his old bedroom, scrunched-up
canvases raining down on him while Papa stood with a cruel
smile on his face.

Then he remembered where he was. Who woke the
knocker-upper, he wondered? Even the birds weren't
chirping yet. The darkness wrapped itself around him like a
shroud and he shivered, tempted to burrow under the covers
and hide. But that wasn't a good idea; he had to make a good
impression on his first day. He eased himself to a sitting
position, groaning as the soreness around his stomach
reminded him of the attack. In a painful move, he pushed
back the covers and moved his legs round to sit on the side
of the bed.

Last night he'd planned ahead, setting his clothes out on
the chair and filling the water jug. But now, in his sleepy
haze, he couldn't remember where the gas lamp was. Once
he'd found it and achieved a dim light, he poured the water

into the bowl and washed, dried and dressed himself as fast as he could to stop his shivering.

Sarah and Tinny were already in the kitchen, stoking the oven and measuring out the ingredients for the dough. It might as well have been the middle of the night; the lamps were lit and flames flickered in the fireplace, warming the kitchen.

'Good start, William,' said Sarah. 'You've managed better than Lizzie. She wasn't keen on the early mornings. I've started the fire for the ovens and the first batch is in. We have two strong young men, Paul and Arthur, who come in much earlier to prepare most of the dough in a big tub in the outhouse. It takes several hours. My Bert always used to do it.'

She steered him over to a workbench. 'The first lot is in and baking nicely. We do a few small batches ourselves each morning, mainly my secret recipe for a lighter loaf. It's popular with the customers, but we don't make many. They sell out every morning.'

'Why don't you make more?' he asked.

'My Bert always used to say scarcity was the shopkeeper's best friend. We need to attract lots of customers first thing when the bread is fresh. It's no use bringing people in later, when everything's sold out. And we don't want to be losing money by throwing out good food when the day's done. Besides, as you'll find out, it's hard work. You're here to repay your debt, not to mess around, and don't you forget it.'

She reached for his hands. 'Are they clean?'

He nodded. 'I've had a wash.'

'Right then,' she said. 'Watch carefully while I show you how to mix this together.' She pointed to a heap of flour on a big marble slab. 'This is a mix of flour and salt. First you make a well in the centre of it with your hand.' William rolled up the sleeves of his shirt and pushed his fist into the flour.

'Pour in half of the milk from this jug. I boiled it earlier.' He could sense her watching him. 'Now add the ale-barm. You might know it as yeast; I get it from the brewery.' William took the mug she handed him and poured in the foaming contents.

'Now put your hands in and bring the flour into the middle, a little at a time, then mix it all together.' He could sense her amusement as he tried to stop the liquid running away.

'Always keep a ring of flour on the outside,' she said, scooping up a handful of flour to fill a gap. 'It'll start to form a dough. As it gets stiffer, add more milk from the jug. You'll soon get the idea.'

She let him get so far, then stepped in. 'You're doing well for your first time. Just let me test it out to get it to the right consistency, then I'll show you how to knead it.'

Sarah rolled the dough between her hands, added more milk and gathered together the remaining pieces of dough on the worktop, shaping them into a ball. 'Try to get into a rhythm. Don't be frightened of it. You need plenty of air in it, you see?' She pummelled it, folding the dough and turning it over, before standing aside to let him try.

He was so intent on getting it right that he was barely aware of Tinny working away in silence at the other corner of the kitchen. After a while, he glanced in her direction and saw her cutting dough into small uniform pieces for the bread rolls, shaping them then setting them out on a tray. Her hair was the colour of a cornfield, piled into a bun with wispy curls around her ears. She suddenly looked his way, and he felt the directness of her ice-blue eyes glaring at him before she returned to her task.

The repeated motion of rolling, stretching and kneading

the dough was making his arms ache and his shoulder was stiff. It was harder than it looked. At last, Sarah handed him a piece of metal. 'Here, use this to divide it into loaves. They all have to be the same size,' she said, cutting one to show him. They worked together to put the dough into tins, covering them with cloths. 'How long does it take to rise?' he asked.

'Until it's doubled in size,' she said, putting the tray next to the range. 'We'll make the pastry for the pies while that's doing.'

The time passed so fast that William scarcely noticed dawn had broken until Sarah extinguished the lamps. The irresistible aroma of bread filled the kitchen as Tinny opened the oven and pulled out a tray of freshly baked loaves.

Now the next batch was ready for baking: mounds of risen dough spilling over the top of the tins, rolls of varying shapes and sizes, and meat pies standing in rows. Sarah showed him where to put them in the oven to suit the varying temperatures.

At last it was time for breakfast. William soon finished his boiled egg and single slice of bread and butter, not sure when he might get the next chance to eat. He thought of the overflowing breakfast table at home, spread with poached haddock, bacon, eggs, fruit and a big rack of toast with plenty of butter and jams to spread on it. Mama would quiz him about what he'd learned in his lessons with Miss Lawson the day before, while Papa hid behind his newspaper.

He silently scolded himself for daydreaming as he realised Sarah was explaining how they ran the shop: their busy periods, what goods they served, and what the customers liked best. There was so much to think about. He hoped she wasn't planning to test him on it later.

Tinny didn't say a word but sat nibbling her bread with her gaze fixed on the table. This was more than shyness; resentment oozed out of every pore. It was understandable, considering he was a stranger in their home. He studied her while she wasn't looking. She had Sarah's fair colouring, but her face was oval rather than round, and her features were daintier. It was a pity her expression was so full of annoyance.

He wasn't used to this treatment. If he ever irritated Grace, she'd give him a push and tell him off, not hold a grudge. Ah well, at least there was no risk of Tinny asking about his past. He would bide his time and look for little ways to help her and Sarah, in the hope that they'd soon enjoy having him around. He'd do anything to increase his chances of staying, at least until he'd found something better. If he proved himself to be a good God-fearing Christian, it might count in his favour. But he'd been in such a rush to leave, he hadn't even packed his Bible.

After breakfast it was time to open the shop, even though it seemed as if he'd done a day's work already. By lunchtime, his head was spinning with instructions, trying to remember all the strange names Sarah used for the bread rolls and loaves. But there was no sign of them closing for lunch. He couldn't ever remember spending this much time on his feet; when would he get a rest? Had he jumped from the prospect of one unsuitable job to another? Well, he'd just have to cope with it.

In the middle of the afternoon, he dropped a tray of rolls. Tinny gave a despairing sigh and Sarah took him aside. 'I can see you've never worked at this pace before. You'll have to do better tomorrow; there's no slacking here.'

He hung his head in shame. She might add more to the debt to cover the cost. At this rate, he'd never be free.

She pointed a finger at him. 'You're no use to me if you're half asleep. Go in the kitchen and make yourself a cup of tea and eat a piece of bread and jam. A small piece, and be quick about it.'

He sat alone in the back room with his meagre meal. He must try harder. If he learned everything as quickly as he could and worked hard, surely Sarah would warm to him? And Tinny... Well, that might take a bit longer.

Grace would be coming home from school around this time, to help her mother with the laundry or other housework. If he'd been at home, he would be taking afternoon tea with Mama while Miss Lawson reported back on his work. Oh heavens. Miss Lawson. He hadn't given her a thought. Once they realised that he wasn't coming back, she would lose her job.

He'd be in so much trouble if he went back to Seaton now. All the more reason never to return.

CHAPTER 8

It was December already; the last couple of months had flown by. It hadn't taken him long to get settled into the rhythm of their days, chatting to interesting customers and feeling more useful than ever before. Today was the first time he'd been allowed a weekday off. He should be able to do something different from his Sunday routine of church with Sarah and Tinny, followed by a wander along the river bank in the afternoon. There was a whole city to explore.

Tinny still didn't say much to him. Perhaps she never would, but in time she might get used to him being there. No one could sulk forever, could they?

He couldn't help but smile to himself as he hurried along, his hands pushed deep inside his pockets to keep them warm. Sarah had told him he had repaid the debt and he could stay. She'd even given him a wage packet with a few coins inside. How grown-up that had felt.

The swirling wind made him shiver and tuck his chin into his coat. He needed to find a set of cheap clothes from a second-hand shop soon, now that the weather was turning much colder. But first he wanted to find Johnny Johnson and say thank you for the part he'd played in persuading Sarah to give him a chance on that first day.

The Ouse was calm, lapping gently against the banks. But it was boring. William yearned for the sea, missing the way it filled his senses and made him forget his troubles. He could still recall the crash of the waves against the rocks, the salty smell of seaweed washed up in inky-green strips along the pale sands, and the texture of the pebbles that littered the shore like a mosaic.

More than anything else, he missed the thrill of the lifeboat rescues, dashing out with the whole village to cheer on the crew at the launch and waiting anxiously for their return. There were very few incidents here by comparison, only the odd drunken man falling into the river on a dark night, or a boat taking in water and limping to the shore with its only slightly alarmed passengers.

Whenever a customer left a newspaper for Sarah, he read the reports of shipwrecks along the north east coast, wondering if Grace had needed to search the trunk for clothes to help any other sailors. But his thoughts always strayed to the wreck that he'd lain in, an innocent baby separated from his parents. If only he could contact Grace to tell her about his experiences so far, to reassure her that he was safe. He owed her that much.

He wandered along the bank, trying to find the boathouse that Sarah had described. There was a ramshackle old timber building that looked a likely candidate. It was reminiscent of the lifeboat house back in Seaton, but a lot smaller.

Then he spotted Johnny, leaning over a boat with a pot of paint in his hand, engrossed in his work. William strolled over.

'Hello Mr Johnson,' he said.

The old man's face lit up. 'Well, look who it is. How are you, lad?'

'I'm fine, thank you. I wanted to thank you for persuading Sarah to take me on. Most people would have called the police.'

Johnny shook his head. 'Nay, lad, that's not how I do things. No need to make it official, not when I could see you needed help.' He put down the paint tin and brush. 'Come and have a mug of tea.' He beckoned William to follow him into the boathouse. It was full of timber and tools, and the musty smell reminded him of Jacobs the gardener's shed at home, a similar treasure trove of discarded knick-knacks that held the promise of being brought into use one day.

Once William had told him his good news over a mug of the strongest tea he'd ever drunk, Mr Johnson told him how Sarah had taken on the bakery after her husband's death. She'd had a hard time being accepted by the other traders, he explained, but the customers loved her.

'Aye, she's a fine woman that one,' he mused, 'one of the best. She's worked hard to keep the business running, with a daughter to look after.' He stretched out his legs and rubbed them. 'Goodness me, the damp must be getting into my bones. How do you fancy a stroll along the river?'

As William walked alongside Mr Johnson, his thoughts returned to Grace. He needed advice, but he wasn't comfortable asking Sarah, and mentioning it to Tinny was out of the question. He cleared his throat. 'I was just thinking about a friend who I haven't seen for a while. I was wondering about writing to her.'

'You should. There's nothing nicer than getting a letter. It means someone is thinking of you.'

'There's just one problem.' William tried to put on a matter-of-fact voice to hide his nervousness at where this conversation might lead. 'I don't want her to have my address. Not yet.'

They had reached Lendal Bridge, where a beggar was

sitting on a dirty piece of cardboard laid on the path. 'Any spare pennies, gentlemen?' he pleaded. William searched in his pocket and produced a farthing. Every time he saw a homeless person, he couldn't help but think that he could have been reduced to begging if it wasn't for Mr Johnson and Sarah.

After they had passed the bridge, the boatman turned to face him. 'Why are you hiding, son?' He raised his eyebrows and William felt his wise old eyes searching his soul. 'When we first met, you didn't explain how you came to be alone in York.'

William turned towards the river, studying the reflection of the trees in the shimmering water, trying to decide what he could share.

The old man cleared his throat. 'You can trust me, you know. That day we met, I could see you needed help, after the shock of being attacked. I won't tell anyone, if that's what you're worrying about.'

William shrugged. 'It's hard to talk about it, Mr Johnson. I haven't come to terms with it myself.'

'Please, call me Johnny. Everyone starts off with a family, and it's nearly Christmas. Shouldn't you be somewhere else?' He patted William on the back. 'I'd give anything to have my dear wife back with me at this time of year. It's hard to imagine not wanting to be with my nearest and dearest.'

'I'm sorry about your wife,' replied William. 'She obviously made you happy and you have good memories.'

'Yes, I do. Don't you?'

William hesitated. 'A few,' he admitted. 'But everything went wrong. I had to get out.'

'All right lad, I won't push you,' said Mr Johnson. 'But it isn't good to bottle things up inside you; it can make you maudlin. Anyway, you said you wanted to write to someone?'

'Yes, a friend from schooldays. She helped me a lot, especially when things were difficult for me. I didn't have a chance to say goodbye to her, and I'd like to tell her I'm safe, with a job and people who look out for me.'

The old man nodded. 'You and your friend have done better than many, going to school.'

He nodded. 'The vicar started it, so that every child in the village could go, even if their parents couldn't afford it.'

'Good for him, I say. What's the problem about your address, then?'

William fidgeted as the icy wind whipped around his feet. 'If her mother or father sees my letter, they might tell my parents where I am.' His lip quivered at the thought of being found and dragged back.

Johnny pulled his scarf more tightly around his neck. 'Well, if it's a lady friend, how can I resist, eh?' His eyes twinkled with amusement. 'Fair enough. You can give her my address,' he suggested. 'I'll pass on her letters if she replies.'

'You would do that for me?'

The old man chuckled. 'Of course. I don't get much excitement nowadays. This is all very intriguing. And it's good that you're thinking about the people you've left behind. Look, any time you want advice, just ask for it, won't you? I've had many more years than you to mess things up; in fact, I'm an expert at it. I bet there's nowt you can say that would shock me.'

He searched in his pocket and brought out a leaflet and a stub of a pencil. 'Turn around,' he said. He leaned on William's back to write down his address, then handed him the piece of paper.

William put it in his pocket. 'Thank you.'

'Glad to help.' They walked further on in silence, then Johnny stopped. 'I've just thought of something else. Have you bought Sarah and Tinny a present for Christmas?'

'Oh… no, I haven't. Do you think they're expecting something?' It had never occurred to him.

'Well, lad, you just think about it. Why else would Sarah have given you a day off?' His eyes crinkled in amusement. 'She's not above being a little bit crafty, you know.'

William thought for a moment. It would help him show his gratitude at least. 'Do you have any idea what sort of things they like?'

'Oh, just some little trinkets, I'd have thought. They won't want you to waste your hard-earned money. It's the thought that counts. Tell you what, let's get ourselves over to the market and see what bargains we can find.'

William nodded, and off they went. Under Johnny's guidance, he chose a handkerchief for Sarah. For Tinny he found a length of hair ribbon, and an embroidered bookmark. The stallholders took great care to wrap them for him.

As they made their way back through the streets, the signs of Christmas were everywhere. The irresistible smell of roasted chestnuts filled the air, and doors were decorated with sprigs of holly interspersed with red berries and cascades of colourful ribbons. It seemed a long time since he'd created the flower stands for the harvest service, in a different time and another world.

They parted at the end of Stonegate, and William returned home, the packages hidden in the inside pocket of his coat. He hoped he'd bought enough, but it was better than nothing.

As soon as he got upstairs, he found a single sheet of paper and a pencil in the drawer. They would have to do. He sat on the floor and used the top of the blanket chest as a desk.

Dear Grace,

He hesitated, not wanting to make any mistakes. How

could he start it? He chewed the end of the pencil, trying to imagine her face when the letter arrived.

I am sorry for not writing sooner. I hope you and the family are well.

Get to the point, he told himself. She'll be desperate for news.

I wanted to let you know I'm safe, and that I've found a job and somewhere to live. Please don't be angry with me for leaving without telling you. Something terrible happened at home, even worse than Papa destroying my pictures, and I had to get away. You and Mama are always in my thoughts. I hope she's not too distressed.

What a stupid thing to write. Of course she'd be distressed. But he couldn't start again and crossing it out would make it untidy. He sighed. This was harder than he expected.

Please write back. But I beg you, don't tell anyone where I am, not even your Mam and Dad, and definitely not my Mama and Papa. I am happy here, happier than I thought possible. Remember how I told you I didn't fit in at home? Well, here it feels just right. No one must find me, otherwise my happiness will be ruined.

That sounded melodramatic, but it would appeal to her. Now, how could he explain giving her Johnny's address? He gripped the pencil while he thought.

I will tell you more later if you write back, but for now you must promise to keep my secret. Don't show anyone the letters. Use the address on the back of this page. It belongs to a dear friend who will pass your replies on to me. We can both trust him.

That was enough, he thought. There was no point in saying any more, in case someone else opened the letter; he couldn't take any risks. He copied Johnny's address carefully on the reverse of the paper. Now he needed an envelope. Sarah wouldn't mind if he took one from the drawer in the back room. Then later he would make an excuse to go for a walk, so he could post it. Even if Grace didn't reply, at least he had done his duty.

~

A PANG of regret came over William as he took his place in the pew and looked around at the crib and the other decorations, so familiar yet not quite the same as those he'd seen every year of his life that he could remember in Seaton Carew. Why had he agreed to come with Sarah and Tinny to the Christmas Eve service? Moments of silence and reflection brought back the most vivid memories.

As he bowed his head and closed his eyes, an image of Grace appeared, full of reproach for not telling her he was leaving. It was followed by one of Mama, exhausted from her constant vigil at the window or in his bedroom, her senses alert for any noise that might suggest he was coming home. The images merged into one, smothering him.

William opened his eyes to dismiss the vision, focusing instead on the grain of the wood in the pew. It was a rich oak, like the box that Papa had smashed. A splinter of it might as well be lodged in his heart, for all the difficulty he was having in thinking of a prayer. Where was his faith when he needed it?

The organ puffed out its first notes, and everyone stood as the clergy took their places. It was hard to sing the words of anticipation and mean them.

How different the Advent preparations would have been at home. He imagined Grace performing at the school Nativity, her clear voice ringing out as she sang a solo. What if he never saw her again? Would she reply to his letter? He'd taken a huge risk in telling her where he was, but he was confident she'd keep the secret. She wouldn't want to be responsible for Papa turning up and dragging him back to work in that miserable office.

How he missed her friendship and her encouragement of both his passion for art and his dream of making a career out of it.

But he'd wasted his time and hers. What a fool he'd been, believing that running away would give him the freedom to paint. There was no chance of that now, not when he was up before dawn, serving customers all day and in bed by eight o'clock. Besides, he didn't have any money to buy materials. He put his hand in his pocket and rubbed the piece of jet, smooth and cool under his fingers. It had become a touch-stone for times like this, when the sense of everything he had lost overwhelmed him.

Absorbed in his thoughts, he jumped as Sarah nudged him. The hymn had finished and everyone else had sat down, ready for the first lesson. He took his seat, trying to focus on the reading, but the words drifted through the air like the sand blowing off the dunes on a windy day. The vicar started his sermon, a message of redemption from sin; it could have been meant for him. He certainly needed forgiveness for deserting Mama and Grace, the two people who loved him most.

William bowed his head for the prayers, not daring to close his eyes again, and studied his fingers, long and slender. He'd thought he'd inherited them from Mama, but now he knew that wasn't possible. It was just one of the beliefs he'd always held, now proven false. It was impossible to go back. He might as well look forwards instead, to find a way of following his dream, no matter how long it took.

CHAPTER 9

Christmas Day arrived, bringing a rare chance to lie in bed until the pale light peeped through the gap in the curtains. William pulled the covers around himself and tried to enjoy the cosiness. But before long, his mind wandered again, picturing Mama waking to her first Christmas without him. So much for his vow last night. He had to stop the memories crowding in; if he got upset, it would only make Sarah ask him what the matter was.

With a sigh, he took the packages from a drawer and went downstairs to place them under the tree that Tinny had persuaded Sarah to buy. They hadn't realised how big it would look in their small room, and he'd had plucked up the courage to tease them about it.

They were already busy in the kitchen. His insides churned with worry over having to spend the whole day with Tinny, without the distraction of the shop. Would she resent him even more for being there on this special day? But she did seem to be making more of an effort to be civil to him nowadays. Best not count on it, though; she was unpredictable at the best of times.

Maybe it was time to indulge in a bit of fun. He crept up on them, then shouted 'Merry Christmas!', making them jump.

'Gawd, me heart's all a-patter,' said Sarah. 'You could scare someone to death doing that. Let me finish preparing the goose, then we can have breakfast. I've been saving for a year to afford this bird. It'd better be a good 'un.'

William set about making the porridge. When they'd finished eating, Sarah produced a present for him.

'Thank you so much, Sarah. You didn't have to,' he said. He ripped off the paper, revealing a pair of woollen gloves. 'Thank you. They're perfect,' he said.

'That's a relief,' said Sarah. She handed a present to Tinny.

'Thank you. The wrapping is so pretty, and I can reuse this ribbon.' She opened it to find a shawl, embroidered with dainty flowers. 'Oh Mam, it's beautiful! Did you do this?'

Sarah nodded. 'I was convinced I wouldn't finish it in time. Why do you think I've been telling you to get to bed early every night for the last three weeks?' As they hugged, William bent to retrieve his presents for them from under the tree. He'd never seen Tinny as animated as this. What would she think of his gifts?

'Happy Christmas!' he announced. Thank goodness for Mr Johnson's help; by their reactions when they opened them, he'd struck the right note.

Then it was his turn to be surprised, as Tinny brought out a present from under the tree and shyly handed it to him. He opened this one with a little more care, sensing she had taken trouble with the wrapping. He was astonished to find a packet of sketching pencils and sheets of paper. Was this a peace offering?

'Tinny, it's just what I wanted. Thank you so much. How did you know I enjoyed drawing?'

She blushed. 'I saw you copying a picture out of a book

the other week, and it was such a good likeness. I thought you'd appreciate a set of proper pencils.'

It transported him back to the evenings in his bedroom, and the times when Papa was away on business, when he would sit by the window sketching. His fingers itched to open the packet of pencils and use them at once. They were more than a gift; they were an opening into his dream, a small step, but one that could set him back on the right path. How could he even begin to tell Tinny how much this meant to him?

'I… It's brilliant,' he said, trying to stop the emotion welling up. At last, he had the means to practise and improve.

'Time for church,' urged Sarah.

Soon they were joining the procession of people heading for St Helen's, exchanging greetings in the crisp freshness of the morning. One place was much like another, William thought, with everyone following the old traditions as the rhythms of the year rolled by, all centred on the church.

William took his place in the pew and tried his best to concentrate on the lunch he was about to have, instead of the melancholy scene he could imagine in his former home.

There was one more surprise as lunchtime approached. Johnny arrived in his best clothes, beaming at the prospect of spending time with them. 'Sarah, I can't tell you how grateful I am for the invitation.' He sniffed the air with exaggerated delight. 'Mmm… something smells delicious.' He presented them with fudge and toffee from the market.

William savoured the food and the friendship, so different from the formal way Papa presided over the occasion. He joined in their games and Tinny even laughed at his terrible jokes. Then they relaxed in the quietness of the afternoon until Johnny's contented dozing turned into a loud snore. Even their laughter didn't wake him.

After a while, Tinny went into the kitchen to make a pot

of tea. William sensed the atmosphere changing as Sarah rose from her chair and came to sit beside him on the sofa.

'Have you enjoyed today, then?' she asked him.

'Oh yes,' he answered. 'The meal was delicious.'

'I didn't mean that. You were quiet during dinner.'

William kept his head bowed and said nothing.

'You can tell me anything, you know. You've been troubled over the last week, haven't you? I want to help if I can.'

'I'm fine, honestly.'

She patted the top of his hand. 'Everyone has a family in their life. I don't want to pry or make you uncomfortable, but if you have any sadness in your past, it's far better for you to talk about it than keep it all to yourself.'

That was just what Johnny had said. But it would be disloyal to tell a virtual stranger about Mama and Papa's secret. Could what they'd done count as a crime? Forgiving Papa was too much to contemplate, but to have the police come and arrest him... Well, that would cause Mama even more distress. His hand reached into his trouser pocket for the jet pebble, as if it were a magic lamp able to produce a solution if he rubbed it hard enough.

Before he could reply, he caught a movement out of the corner of his eye, as Johnny stirred and rubbed his eyes. 'Hmm... Oh dear, I've disgraced myself, haven't I?' He sat upright. 'Would you believe me if I said it was a compliment to your cooking, Sarah?'

'You can get round anyone, you old rascal. It's been lovely to have you here today.'

Johnny struggled to his feet. 'Well, I won't need to eat for another week. He gave a satisfied yawn as he rubbed his stomach. 'I'd better be going. Thank you for a lovely time. I've spent too many Christmas Days on my own, so this has meant a lot to me.' His attempts to rise from the chair made William chuckle.

As Sarah started to move, Johnny held up his hand. 'Stay where you are, my dear. William will show me out.' He collected his coat from the hook on the door, gave a wave to Tinny and kissed Sarah on the cheek.

William followed Johnny to the door, grateful for the chance to escape Sarah's interrogation.

The old man rummaged in his pocket and pulled out an envelope. 'Didn't want to give you this with those two watching,' he whispered as he handed it over.

William took it, unable to hide a smile. Grace had replied!

WILLIAM PUT the letter in his pocket, locked the door and returned to the back room. 'Can I help you tidy up?' he asked, praying that she would refuse.

'Bless you. That would be such a help.'

He silently cursed himself for suggesting it.

'Your face…' Sarah shook her head and laughed. 'You're so easy to tease. It's fine, Tinny's just finishing the last few dishes. There's a pot of tea here if you want a cup?'

'No, thank you. It's been a lovely day, and the meal was delicious. But I'd like to rest for a while.'

Alone in his room, he trembled as he took the letter out of his pocket and traced the rounded handwriting with his finger. She'd held this envelope in her hand, thinking of him as she addressed it.

He could picture her sitting in bed writing it, her dark curls tumbling over her shoulders as she bent her head over the paper, her tongue flickering at the corner of her mouth as she concentrated on the words. Would she understand why he'd had to leave? He hadn't given her much of a clue as to the reason.

He ripped open the envelope, unfolded the paper and prepared himself for her news.

Dear William,

You can't imagine how relieved I was to get your letter. I've never had one before, but I recognised your writing on the envelope. Mam looked curious, so I told her it was a school project and we'd had to write to our Member of Parliament with questions about what they were planning to do for the village.

Mam, Dad and the boys are well. I've got a job as a maid at Chambers House, doing menial jobs for Mrs Dixon the house-keeper. I'm not sure how it happened – Lady Forbes asked for me. The vicar's wife might've put in a good word. It doesn't pay much, but it's better than doing mending jobs. I get a uniform and dinner – they call it lunch like you do – every day. The place is full of antiques, besides the owners, I mean.

He gave a chuckle. Typical Grace, irreverent and funny. How he missed her.

I imagine you've been there and seen the ancient paintings, but it can be creepy when it's dark, with all those eyes watching me. I have to be there very early to clean the grates out and set the fires, so I'm in bed by 8 o'clock at night – you will laugh at that.

The Nativity was hilarious this year. Mary dropped the doll and one of the little 'uns yelled She's killed baby Jesus! and started crying.

He couldn't help smiling as he imagined Grace convulsed in giggles and the teachers trying to keep a straight face. Thank goodness she'd found a decent place to work. Lord Forbes was a kindly solicitor who would make sure his staff were treated fairly. Chambers House was warm, and at least she wasn't cooped up in a busy kitchen all day.

That night was horrible. Mrs Dodds from next door came in to say you were missing. That was all she could tell us; I had no idea if you were dead or alive.

He swallowed hard, caught unawares by the sudden

change of tone. It was painful to see his cruelty to her written there, as if he hadn't tortured himself enough with it. He needed the chance to explain he'd had no choice. Would she understand?

Then later on, your parents came here. I was asleep, but Mam woke me up because they wanted to ask me about it. We told them we'd seen you earlier, and that you left about half past three. Your Mama stayed here while my Dad went out with your Papa to look for you. They persuaded just about every man in the village to join in the search, but you'd gone. I couldn't sleep after that for worrying about you and praying you were safe.

Papa had gone out looking for him? After everything he'd said when he was arguing with Mama, why should he change his mind? Mama must have been in such a state, to make him join the search. Did they suspect he'd overheard their conversation? He could imagine them pretending to the whole village that their beloved son had no reason to disappear. And Grace had stayed awake the whole night too, praying for him. She must love him. Trying to hold back his sorrow, he continued reading.

As I was leaving church after the Nativity service, your Mama called me over and asked if I knew where you were. I said no, but the way she looked at me, I'm not sure she believed me. She looks completely lost when she comes to Chambers House to visit Lady F, and I know you love her so much that it must have been a terrible thing that made you leave. I promise not to tell anyone where you are, but in return I hope you'll tell me everything.

It sounds as if you've fallen on your feet. I told you everything would work out fine, didn't I? But I miss you something rotten. Please write again. I want to hear what you're doing there. Give me your address in code - remember the one we used to use for notes at Sunday school?

Love, Grace.

He re-read the letter three times, then stood by the

window, turning her words over and over in his mind. How he missed her smile, her laughter and the cheeky way she talked about people in the village. If only he could have her confidence, born of the knowledge that her parents loved her. It would have been selfish to ask her to come with him, and doubly difficult for them both to make a living here. No, he must manage alone for now.

One day, when he had found his real family, and was working as an artist, he would go back to see her. Papa wouldn't be able to force him to do anything against his will, and he could marry Grace and take her with him on his adventures.

William rubbed his eyes. If he gave in to the tiredness that hung over him, he'd sleep for hours, and that would be impolite, after the lovely day Sarah had given him. Besides, he was desperate to try out his new sketching pencils. He left the envelope on the table and folded the letter into half, tucking it into his trouser pocket. Then, leaving his memories and regrets behind in his room, he made his way downstairs.

CHAPTER 10

Tinny flopped down in the armchair, glad that the busy part of Christmas Day was over and grateful to spend time alone with Mam at last. She'd known it could never be the same as their family celebrations when she was little, with Dad cracking jokes and putting peculiar things in her stocking to amuse her. But having William and Johnny there had made it more enjoyable than she'd expected. She hadn't even thought about it from William's point of view; he had no family at all, and that must be hard, whoever was at fault.

The hair ribbon lay on the arm of the chair, the exact shade of her Sunday best shawl. How thoughtful of him to try to match the colour. He obviously had an artist's eye; she couldn't imagine any of the boys at church even thinking about such a thing. She wound the ribbon round her fingers, feeling its silkiness and admiring the way the light reflected off it. The bookmark was just what she needed, too. She would use it in place of the old tattered one in her Bible, to mark the position for the next day's reading.

Mam came in, wiping her hands on a towel.

'Sit down, Mam, you look exhausted. You deserve a rest after doing the cooking.'

'Aye, if I say so myself, it wasn't a bad spread. Your Dad would be proud of us if he was watching, wouldn't he? I think that was one of the nicest days we've had since…' Her voice faltered and she brushed the back of her hand across her eyes.

'I'm sure he's watching,' Tinny told her. These were her favourite times, just the two of them, closer than ever, remembering.

Mam patted her shoulder affectionately. 'You'll be glad now that I made you give William a present, I expect?' She flopped onto a chair at the table.

'Yes, you were right. As usual. It would have been embarrassing if I hadn't, especially after the care he's taken in choosing my presents. I'm sorry I was so mean about it, but I just couldn't stop thinking about him stealing the bread roll.'

Mam gave her a knowing look. 'You'll find it easier if you forget about that and take him for what he is now.'

She gave a sigh. 'How do you forgive so easily, Mam?'

'Years of practice, my lovely. I just try to put myself in the other person's shoes. Most people have a reason for behaving badly. And in William's case, he'd just had a big shock, sleeping out there. It was the only way he could think of to stop his hunger. You're a kind person, and you'll get there in the end.'

Tinny looked up in dismay as William came back into the room. He could have given them more time together.

'That was a quick rest,' she said, immediately chiding herself for sounding disappointed that he was back. She said a silent prayer, for Jesus to show her the way to be kinder and remember that he must be feeling awkward too. If only she could be as sympathetic as Mam was.

'I couldn't doze off. I kept thinking about my present.' He fingered the bag of pencils. 'Do you mind if I try them?'

'Of course I don't mind; that's what they're for. What are you going to draw?'

'I'm not sure. I used to like doing seascapes best, but a rural landscape might be interesting, or a railway scene.' He sat at the table, laid out the pencils and opened the packet of drawing paper.

Tinny studied him as he sat there in silence, observing the room. He seemed to be struggling for ideas. Maybe she could help. 'I'll have a look in my books for some illustrations; they might give you a start.' She went over to the bookcase in the corner and pulled out a few volumes. If she was more civil to him, it might persuade God that she wasn't completely full of sin.

She studied the spines of the much-loved books from her childhood. Dad's face appeared in her mind, his face ruddy from the heat of the kitchen, sitting on the edge of her bed as he told her to be quick and choose a bedtime story. She remembered his hands, rough from the day's labour, tucking her in and stroking her face. The bed used to sink as he sat on it to read to her, pointing out the characters in the pictures and putting on funny voices for each of them to make her giggle. How she missed him.

No wonder Mam liked William; he was quick to obey and keen to please. Maybe he'd had a stricter upbringing. What had happened to make him come to a strange city alone? Had he committed a crime? Despite that first encounter, it seemed unlikely. Now she'd got to see him every day, she couldn't fault his hard work, and there'd been no sign of dishonesty.

She gave a sigh. If she hadn't consumed all her energy on hating William for invading their home, she might have got on his side by now and found out what had brought him here.

She pulled out a few books and flicked through them, searching for a suitable scene for him to draw. Best be quick, or he'd make a start on something else. She chose three and took them over to him.

'Sorry to take so long. I didn't realise I had so many books.'

Sarah raised her eyebrows. 'Oh really? I was thinking of putting a notice up to say we had a public library here. The city could do with one.' She turned to William. 'You wouldn't believe how many she won as prizes at school and Sunday school.'

William smiled as he took the books from Tinny. 'This will be a great help, thank you.' He started flicking through them.

Sarah reached for one and started opening it at random pages. 'I bet you could draw this scene,' she said, turning the book towards him.

Tinny leaned over to see it. It was a lake with trees all around it, overlooked by a mountain range.

'That's ideal, thank you,' William said, taking the book and laying it on the table in front of him.

Out of the corner of her eye, Tinny saw the paper bag from the pencils flutter to the floor. She reached for it. But it wasn't the bag; it was a letter. She held it out to him, trying to read the writing on the envelope.

'You've dropped something...'

'Give me that,' he snapped, grabbing the letter and pulling at it.

Taken by surprise, she didn't let go soon enough. She cringed at the ripping sound as the corner of the envelope came away in her hand.

'Look what you've done!' he shouted.

A flush rose in her cheeks. Why was he so angry? She was only trying to help. It wasn't as if she'd opened the letter and tried to read it.

'William!' Mam didn't sound so forgiving now. 'There's no need to raise your voice like that. What on earth's got into you?'

Tinny didn't care whether he apologised or not. The address on the envelope had caught her attention. What was William doing with a letter belonging to Johnny? Had he stolen it from his pocket today, when she and Mam had been in the kitchen? Who was this boy, and why was he here? After all her efforts to forgive him, to trust him... now it seemed her first instincts were right.

She only half-heard William's mumbled apology. If she recounted what she'd seen, Mam would only make more excuses for him. Instead, she resolved to watch him even more closely in the coming weeks. There'd better be a very good reason for this, if she was going to change her mind about him.

CHAPTER 11

After the long dark winter days full of ice and snow, the spring flowers were blooming, cheering William as they always did. Inspired by the variety of scenes in the city, he had filled the pages of his sketchbook and had saved a little money to buy another one. Sarah had agreed that he could have the afternoon off, and on his way to the shops, he decided to visit Johnny.

The river was running faster today, and the trees and bushes were in bud, providing a fresh burst of green amid the tangle of branches that framed the riverside path. After he'd bought the paper, he'd have to go back for his pencils and return to capture the changing scene.

Johnny was outside the boathouse, taking a break with a mug of tea in his hand. 'Well, look who it is. I was just thinking of coming to the shop to see how you were getting on.'

'Sorry, it's been busy. But it eased off at lunchtime, so Sarah said I could come out for some fresh air. I'm on my way to buy some more sketching paper. How's business?'

Johnny drained his mug and put it on the ground. 'Oh,

you know, the seasonal lull and all that. Everyone's just getting their boats out before it gets busy with visitors for the summer. They'll soon find out what repairs they need, and then I'll be complaining there's too much work. Anyway, how are things with you and Tinny? Has she accepted you yet?'

'I don't think she ever will. She probably sees me as a silly boy.'

'Aren't you about the same age?'

'She's exactly six months older than me.'

'Ah right. Well, girls grow up sooner than boys. Don't worry about it.'

William pointed at the empty mug. 'Any chance of a drink round here?'

Johnny chuckled and went into the boathouse to make him a mug of tea.

The ducks were bobbing on the river, so carefree. Why did humans make life so complicated? He thought about Grace's second letter, reacting to his confession about why he'd left. He'd been so sure she would have understood.

Finding out they weren't your real parents must have been a shock. But you didn't have to leave. You had a warm, comfortable home with a Mama who loved you. She still loves you, and she's heartbroken. Your Papa saved your life when he found you in the wreck. It would have been better to stay and talk to them about it. At least then we'd still be able to spend time together.

He'd imagined her saying it so many times that he knew the words off by heart. Just when he'd thought he was settled in his new life, she'd pulled him back to the past again.

'You look troubled, lad.' Johnny handed him a mug. 'Drink this. Tea makes everything better.' He tidied up his tools then sat on an upturned boat and patted the space beside him.

William climbed up to sit alongside him, fixing his gaze on the river. 'I've had another letter from Grace.'

'Well that's good, isn't it, getting a letter from your lady friend?'

He was about to protest that there was no romance in it, but thought better of it. It was none of Johnny's business. Anyway, her letter was far from romantic; it was a right telling off. She was being selfish, wanting him to be there for herself, not for his own sake. He couldn't bear to be in the same village as Papa, let alone in the same house. It simply wasn't possible to forgive the destruction of his paintings and the years of lies. No, she was asking too much of him.

A sigh escaped his lips. 'I don't want to talk about it.'

'Mebbe you should. I told you last time, it helps to talk about things. If you've run away from something bad, you need to let it go. But you can't do that if it's still swimming around in your head. D'you understand what I mean?'

William drank his tea, savouring the strong taste. 'Papa always told me never to complain, but always to get on with things. I can tell God though. And I do, in my prayers at night.'

'Strict, was he, your Papa?'

He nodded.

'Describe him to me.'

Where to start? No one had ever asked him a question like that before. He hesitated.

'If you were painting him, what would he look like?'

That was easier. 'Tall, always holding himself straight, with his chin up. He has dark brown eyes, so dark that you can't read his thoughts when he stares at you. His hair is always short, neat, and he has a thin moustache. No beard. He can't abide mess.'

He fell silent, picturing the shreds of canvas and paintbrushes scattered across his bedroom floor, surrounded by the splinters of wood from his precious box.

'What's his temperament like?'

'Unpredictable. It's easy to make him angry.' He rubbed at his eyes, the memories rising like stinging nettles.

Johnny patted him on the back. 'I'm getting a good picture of him.'

A pair of geese flew overhead, then coasted towards the river with wings outspread, skimming the water with their feet as they landed. How wonderful to have such freedom.

'You've a real talent for sketching. That doesn't come without a lot of practice. Did you used to paint as well?'

'Yes, I did. Until Papa found my canvases.' The words tumbled out, a strange release, using his voice to paint a picture of that day's events.

'Please don't tell Sarah or Tinny,' he said as he finished.

'I won't tell, don't you fret.' Johnny let out a puff of pain as he climbed down from the boat and stood facing William, grimacing.

'Oh, my back... I'm getting too old for this lark. Now then, William, let me give you a bit of advice. Never think that you have to be strict or be a bully to be successful. There are plenty of people who are admired for their gentleness and the way they encourage others. I'd like to think you will be like them.'

William looked at the elderly boatman, his face lined and leathery with years of working outdoors, and his eyes twinkling with kindness. How different he was, compared to Papa's view of what a man should be.

'Thank you, Johnny.'

'Anything else I can help with? That letter from your young lady, for instance?'

'You've helped me with that as well; I know how to reply

now.' He handed the mug back to Johnny and eased himself off the boat. 'I'd better get to the shop before it shuts.'

'Don't leave it so long next time, lad, or I'll have to come by and spend my money, and that will never do.' With a bellow of laughter he waved William on his way.

William wandered through the streets, mulling over Johnny's advice. It made sense; he had to stop treating his past as shackles around his legs, holding him back. It was time to look for new opportunities. He found the shop Tinny had told him about, and he was soon heading back home with a new packet of paper under his arm.

The shop was still quiet. At least he wouldn't be expected to serve. He waved to Sarah and Tinny, climbed the stairs and took a seat at his desk to write the letter.

Dear Grace,

At first your letter upset me. I thought you didn't understand how awful it was to find out I was an orphan, that you didn't think it a bad enough reason for me to leave. But then I realised you couldn't understand, because you've had nothing but love from your parents. They've never lied to you, or hidden secrets from you, so you can't imagine the betrayal I felt that day. It will be a long time before I can forgive what Mama and Papa did, and I can never forget it. Please trust me.

That struck the right note. He was making her blameless. Now he would get to the heart of his request.

I realise you have said this out of love, and that you want us to be together. Please believe me when I say I want that too. But I can't return home, not yet. One day I will become an artist, able to make a living, and I'll come back for you. I miss you, and your letters mean everything to me. I love hearing what you are doing, but I don't want to hear about Mama and Papa. Can we start again please?

If you can find any way of getting to York, I would love to see you. I know it's difficult, and I would send you some money if I

*could, but I'm struggling myself. Please try to think of a way to
come.*

He signed the letter, placed it in an envelope and sealed it.
There was just enough time to catch the post.

As he came out of the post office, the bells rang at the
Minster, tempting him to walk that way. He stood in front of
its vast, majestic facade and wondered how many stonema-
sons must have laboured to create the sculptures. He went
inside, found a pew and said a prayer that Grace would
accept what he'd said and continue to write to him.

As he stood up to leave, the rose window in the south
transept caught his attention. Its central sunflower was
surrounded by a continuous pattern of red Lancastrian and
red and white Tudor roses, spinning round and round in a
never-ending circle, just like his thoughts. To find peace, he
needed to break the pattern and free himself from the
torture.

Now he knew Johnny was right; his future lay in his own
hands. If he wanted to find his real family, why hadn't he
started before now?

True, the shop filled his days and his evenings were spent
sketching. But that didn't stop his brain from being active.
He could ask Johnny, or one of the businessmen at church,
how to go about finding records of shipwrecks.

A picture of the chart on the schoolroom wall in Seaton
came into his mind, with Papa standing in front of it,
coaching him in the cargo ship routes. Think of all the shipping registers in the office. Why had he never wondered if
the same system existed for passenger ships?

The task stretched in front of him, like a sea of jigsaw
pieces floating by, frustratingly out of his reach. Somewhere
out there were the records for vessels that had smashed into
the rocks at Tynemouth around that time.

CHAPTER 12

Tinny stirred in her sleep. What was that? A noise, at the edges of her consciousness, not quite there, echoing… But where? Was it someone calling out? Who? Her eyes fluttered open. It must have been a dream. The darkness was like a blanket around her, smothering her senses.

'No, go away! I'm never coming back home, never, never, never…!'

She stiffened as the words seeped through the wall between them. It wasn't a dream; not hers, at any rate. It had happened before. Three times this week now, and twice the month before. Thank goodness Mam's room was far enough away for her not to be disturbed by it. Then there was a thud against the wall. She hesitated. It wasn't right, going into a boy's room in the middle of the night. It was shameful.

She turned over and covered her ears with the blankets to dull the noise. It was his own business; he was probably still asleep. But what if he hurt himself? She eased back the covers. One more noise and she would have to check on him.

He shouted again, a jumble of groans and confused cries.

It was still dark, and she could barely make out where everything was in the room, but she managed to find her flannel dressing gown and tie it tightly before slipping out to the landing to listen in at William's door. The squeak of the bedsprings and the clang of the bedstead as it hit the wall suggested he was thrashing about. It was no good standing here. She turned the doorknob and peered in through the gloom.

'William?' she whispered, as she padded in and closed the door behind her.

'Get off! No, leave me alone, I'm staying here!' She'd never heard him raise his voice like this before. He was panicking about something, that was certain.

Her own heart was thudding now. He might shout at her, or even worse, tell Mam she'd been in his room. She could imagine what a telling off she'd get then.

'William, it's all right, it's only a dream. I'm here...' She moved forward and knelt by the bed so he could see her when he opened his eyes.

'What?' He stopped moving and turned his head towards her, his eyelashes fluttering open. 'Grace?'

'It's me, Tinny,' she whispered. 'Calm down, take your time.' Gradually, she became accustomed to the darkness. His hair was damp with sweat and his eyes were wide open now, searching her face. Who was Grace? Was he frightened of her? Why was he so determined not to go back home? He must have remembered something terrible, to be this frightened.

'What are you doing here?' He started to prop himself up, and she averted her eyes to give him time to pull the covers over himself.

'You were shouting out. I've heard you before, but this time you were hitting the wall and I was worried you might hurt yourself.'

He groaned. 'I'm sorry. This is so embarrassing. Does Sarah know?'

'Don't worry about that,' she said. 'Mam won't have heard; she can sleep through a thunderstorm. I wouldn't usually come in. I never have before. But you were making the most awful shrieking sound, and when I peeped in, you were lashing out. I was worried you might hurt yourself.'

'Thank you. For your concern, I mean.'

'I shouldn't be here. It's wrong.' She put her hand on the edge of the bed, ready to get to her feet, but he put his hand over hers.

'Don't go.' His words hung in the air between them, his eyes still full of fear. 'Can I tell you about it?'

'Of course you can.' She sat as comfortably as she could on the floor, tucking her legs in to make sure they couldn't be seen.

'Sometimes I'm convinced it's happening when I'm out in the street on my day off.'

'What's happening?'

'That he's come to find me, to take me back and force me to work in the office.'

Not Grace then. 'Who?'

'Papa.'

'Your father?'

'No.'

That made no sense. Was he delirious? She didn't dare touch his forehead to test for signs of a fever. It was bad enough that she was in his room in the dark. God would never forgive her for this. But it wasn't as if she had any impure thoughts; she was just concerned for William, not wanting to see him upset. Jesus went to places that others didn't approve of, so this wasn't so different, was it? But that didn't stop her discomfort.

Tinny tried to speak in a calming voice. 'Take your time. If you want to talk, that's grand. If you don't, fair enough.'

'What time is it?'

'About two in the morning.'

'You need your sleep.'

'And you need to talk. It's fine. I won't be able to rest if you're still disturbed.'

He seemed to relax at that; his shoulders dropped, and he tilted his head to one side. 'Papa used to frighten me. He disapproved of everything I did. I had to hide the fact I was painting from him, because he would have punished both me and Mama...' His voice faltered.

'Are your nightmares always about him?'

'Yes. I keep imagining he's come to take me back. But it's worse than that...'

'Worse? In what way?' She knew she shouldn't pry, but he'd said he wanted to talk, and it might help him.

'He always tells me the same tale, that Mama is hurt and he needs me to go back. And I don't know what to do. All I can think of is that he must have gone too far. Mama used to get upset about him taking me out of school, away from my friends, and they used to have fearsome arguments over it.'

'She must have loved you very much.'

A frown passed over his face. Had she said the wrong thing?

'She always told me she did. And I loved her. She was always on my side. But one day, Papa was cross about an order that had gone astray, and he couldn't find out who'd made the mistake. He couldn't have solved it by the time he got home the following day, because he picked an argument. Mama should have known to stay quiet. When she tried to persuade him not to employ the governess, he flew into a rage, rushed towards her, and raised his arm as if he was going to strike her. I stepped in front of her, to stop him.'

She couldn't help noticing he was trembling. 'That was a brave thing to do. What happened?'

'I thought he might hit me instead. Then he stopped, his face so close to mine that I could feel his breath, and he slowly brought his arm back to his side. But the pure hatred on his face stayed in my mind. It's what I see when I have the nightmare.'

Tinny bit her lip. That must be the reason he left. 'I'm glad you came here. We'll look after you,' she promised.

'Thank you.' His head drooped further to one side, as if he was starting to doze. She watched him for a few moments, to make sure he was settling. There was more to him than met the eye, certainly.

'And I'll try to stop being selfish about wanting Mam to myself. You were in need and she came to your rescue. I can see that now.' She got to her feet and walked to the door. 'I hope you can get some sleep. Goodnight,' she said over her shoulder, and left before he had a chance to reply.

CHAPTER 13

The early mornings weren't getting any easier, even though he'd been doing this for nearly eighteen months. William pulled on his work clothes and splashed his face with ice cold water. But he had the comfort of a routine, counting down his daytime hours in the shop and yearning for the evenings when he could sketch. He was feeling more a part of the business, too, proud that Sarah had approved of his idea to change the window displays more often, using different themes.

He went down the stairs, expecting another ordinary day in the shop, with a never-ending queue of customers. But there was no sign of Sarah and Tinny. That was unusual; they must still be getting ready. He'd better make a start on the dough.

Just as he reached for the flour jar, there was a rustling sound. He turned round and saw they'd both appeared in the doorway, with presents in their hands. A chorus of 'Happy Birthday, William!' echoed around the kitchen.

'What on earth… how did you find out?' He'd never given them any clues. It might not even be today, come to think of it. Imagine having to pick a random date for your son's birth. They beckoned him into the back room.

'That's our secret. Here, open these,' urged Tinny, handing him a parcel and an envelope. 'I hope it compensates for the fact we missed it last year.'

'I don't know what to say. Except thank you.' He turned away, pretending to struggle with the ribbon around it, so they wouldn't see him becoming emotional. As he opened it, a set of oil paints and brushes tumbled out.

'Oh my goodness! I don't believe it. This is the best present I've ever received. Thank you so much, both of you.' He turned over each of the tubes, checking the colours. 'I hope they didn't cost too much.'

'Never you mind that; our profits have improved since you started the new displays,' Sarah said, as she turned to retrieve something. 'You'll need this as well. You won't get far with just a set of paints.'

She thrust a larger parcel at him and he almost dropped it in his excitement. He tore the paper off and uncovered a set of three blank canvases, staring at them in disbelief.

'They're just perfect. Thank you, Sarah.'

She reached behind a chair and pulled out a pair of trousers. 'These aren't a present... I mean, I didn't buy them. Yours are getting short, so I've altered a pair of Bert's. You don't mind, do you?'

'Not at all. I was wondering how I could afford some new ones. Thank you.'

'I had to take them in at the waist. A lot. If they fit, I can do the same with a couple of others. I think we need to feed you up, so you can grow into a fine strong man like he was.'

'Somehow I don't think that will happen.' If he hadn't been the smallest boy in the class, the school bully and his followers mightn't have picked on him so much. But that didn't matter now; he'd prefer to use his talents instead of his fists any day.

What an incredible thing to have his own paints again, new ones this time instead of the old tubes from the attic at home. It meant he could attempt the seascapes he loved. Once he'd practised, his first task would be to recreate the scene with the schooner, Grace's favourite, which Papa had destroyed in his fit of temper. He would dedicate it to her, a silent revenge against the man he had feared for so long.

But for now, there was baking to be done, followed by a hasty breakfast so they could open the shop on time. How hard it was to concentrate on serving the customers and forget about the gifts that were waiting for his attention.

At lunchtime, Johnny arrived, struggling through the doorway with a huge bundle disguised in newspaper, and at last William realised how they'd known.

'You crafty old thing. You got me to tell you when my birthday was, didn't you? All that nonsense about how much of an age gap there was between me and Tinny.'

'Now then, lad, you would have been upset if we hadn't wanted to celebrate it, wouldn't you? You might be sixteen, but you're not quite there in the brains department yet. You young 'uns think you're the brightest, but we can fool you, can't we Sarah?' He winked at her.

William had already ripped off the paper, uncovering an easel and a palette.

'I made both of them with my own hands,' Johnny said with pride. 'The wood comes from an old boat I had to break up because it wasn't seaworthy any more. This is as good a use for it as any.'

'Thank you so much. It means a lot.'

'And Johnny's responsible for the last one too,' Sarah told him.

'That sounds intriguing,' he replied, almost overwhelmed at the thought that there could be anything else.

Johnny shrugged. 'It's not exactly a present. I just had the idea, and I helped clear out… Go on, Sarah, you tell him.'

She was grinning from ear to ear. 'We've emptied the spare room on the landing. You can use it for a studio. If you want it, that is.'

'Honestly? That's just wonderful. I had no idea. Thank you, thank you so much.' A room set aside for him to paint in? This was the best day he'd had for a very long time.

'I think someone will want time off this afternoon,' said Sarah. 'I'm sure Tinny and I can manage in the shop. We'll call you if it gets busy.'

'Are you sure?' he asked. 'I don't want you to think I'm slacking.'

They both nodded. 'Don't give it a thought,' Sarah told him. 'Go and see what we've done with the room. Quick, before I change my mind. I'll set aside a pie in the kitchen for our tea, and you can put it in the range half an hour before closing time. Do you think you can remember to do that?'

He nodded, keen to gather his presents in his arms and take them upstairs. He reached the landing and nudged the door open with his foot. It was a tiny room, but the light was bright now the heavy lace curtains had been removed, and there was a table in the middle where he could lay out his brushes. He put the bundle of presents there and retrieved the sketch books from his bedroom. As an afterthought, he reached for the fragment of the wooden box from the drawer. He would put it on the table as a reminder of how he'd triumphed over Papa. At last, he could practise his art without fear of discovery.

He sorted through his sketches, looking for ideas. Now then, where was the scene with the boats on the river? It was a nice simple one for a first attempt.

He set out the paints, placed a canvas on the easel and readied himself.

Could he remember how to do it? His mind wandered back to the times he'd spent in his bedroom experimenting. He grabbed a pencil to make a quick sketch, a faint outline of the boats and the bank of the river. Then he chose a brush and transferred a few dots of paint to the palette, mixing and testing out different shades. Why was he so nervous? Tentatively, he loaded a brush with cerulean blue, mixed in a touch of white to lighten it for a summer sky, and daubed it on the canvas. Soon he settled into a rhythm, building up layers and adding details.

He'd missed having this freedom to express himself, mixing colours to achieve a mood, creating a scene with the sweep of his hand as if by magic. He was so absorbed that the knock on the door made him jump.

'Are you enjoying yourself?' Tinny asked.

'Very much,' he replied. 'I thought I might forget how to do it, but it's coming back.'

'It's a good job I remembered to put the pie in the oven, isn't it?'

'Oh gosh, is it that time already? I'm sorry, I didn't realise. You must think I'm stupid.'

She shrugged. 'I wish I cared about something so much that I could block everything else out.' She stepped forward and peered at the picture. 'That's incredible. I wouldn't have any idea where to start.'

'I could always teach you,' he offered.

'That's kind, but I don't think I have an artistic bone in my body.'

'Well you have to start somewhere; if you don't try, you'll never find out. How do you think I began?'

'How would I know? You haven't told me much about your past life.' A tinge of pink came to her cheeks. 'I'm sorry,

I didn't mean it to come out like that. I'm sure you have your reasons.'

She was right. He'd let her think it was all about Papa's temper and left her to wonder about the rest. It wasn't fair on her. 'Don't apologise. It's just that...' How could he even begin? 'I suppose I've found it easier to stop remembering the worst bits.'

He'd already embarrassed himself in her presence when he'd had the nightmare. What would she think of him if she knew the full story?

'I had to make a clean break. I thought that if I threw myself into a new life, I could bury the things that had caused me so much distress.' He turned back to the painting, dabbing on a darker colour at the edge of the bank.

'You don't have to talk about it if you don't want to,' she said. 'I'm not one for prying. You've obviously worked out a way of coping with it.'

How could he explain the knot of anguish that still twisted inside him whenever he thought about the lies? 'Thank you for being so understanding. But I'm fine, honestly. This is my life now, and I love it. I dread to think what might have happened if I hadn't found you and Sarah.'

'And you've made a difference to us. It can be tedious spending all our time in the shop, and it's nice to have another person to talk to. I'm sorry if I seemed to resent you moving in.'

'You had every right to; I'd have been the same in your position. I'm glad Johnny's part of it, too. It's obvious he was lonely before he started coming round here so much. I do believe he's keen on your mother,' added William, glancing at her.

Tinny's eyes widened. 'Do you think so?'

'Definitely. He's always talking about her when I go to the

boathouse to see him. "She's a fine woman, that one", he mimicked. 'But don't you dare say anything to him.'

'I won't – I'm more worried about what Mam might say. She's too devoted to Dad's memory.'

She moved away from the painting and opened the door, beckoning him to follow her. 'Right, Mr Artist, tea will be about ready; come on, let's eat.'

$\sim$

'WE'LL DO the washing up – get yourself back to it,' said Sarah, as they sat around the table, their plates cleared.

William didn't need telling twice. He took the stairs two at a time and entered his room, setting aside the first canvas. Why not try something completely different: a portrait? He pulled out a sheet of paper for a rough sketch, found a soft pencil, and sat for a moment trying to bring Grace's features to mind. The shape of her face, her hairline… He frowned. Maybe that wasn't the best place to start.

His hand hovered over the paper. What about her eyes? Gentle brown eyes, framed with long dark lashes. The words didn't translate into an image. Concentrate. He shut his eyes and tried to imagine her at the Harvest Sunday meal, offering him a plate and telling him to eat as much as he could. That was no good either; the image of Papa shouting at Mr Robinson crowded out everything else. What about her glance at her mother when she had to put another log on the fire for the rescued sailors?

He pushed back the strand of hair that fell across his forehead. Nothing. How could he forget her? Why did Papa appear in his dreams, as clear as if he was in the same room, yet he couldn't conjure up an image of the girl he loved? What did it mean?

Temper gripped him and he hurled the pencil across the room. Call yourself an artist? Can you only copy what's in front of you? Sarah, Tinny and Johnny had been so thoughtful with their gifts, but they'd wasted their money. He was useless.

He looked out of the window; it was getting dusky, and the light wasn't right. He had to stop feeling sorry for himself; a walk would clear his mind. The streets were full of people walking home for the evening and he might find inspiration.

As he wandered, he reached the end of the Shambles, where ancient houses were squeezed into the narrow space. On the corner he spotted a flower girl, clutching a few bunches of daffodils and primulas. Tattered clothes hung loosely from her thin frame, and even at this distance he could see a bare toe peeping out from a hole in the top of her shoe. She lifted her head as a gentleman passed by, stretching out her arms, imploring them to buy a posy. He moved nearer to take a closer look. She had the same dark eyes as Grace, but they were circled with purple shadows.

When had she last eaten, he wondered? It would never have occurred to him before he came to York, but now he'd experienced the ache of an empty stomach. If it hadn't been for Sarah's kindness, he could have fallen into this sort of existence. He searched inside his pockets, but they were empty. Tomorrow evening he would bring a bit of left-over food from the shop.

A man came around the corner. The flower seller shrank back, as if she was trying to blend into the wall. William followed her glance towards the cardboard box on the floor; it was almost empty. The man approached her, collected the few coins that were in it and put them in his pocket, then grabbed hold of her arm, shaking her.

William sprang forward. 'Get off her!' he called out, hardly aware of what he was doing.

The man turned towards him. 'Mind yer own bloody business,' he growled, and pushed William out of the way. He turned to the girl. 'You'd better earn more than this tomorrer, or you'll be out on yer ear.' He marched off.

William rushed over to her. 'Are you all right?' he asked.

She nodded, but her eyes said otherwise.

How he wished he could do something. 'He shouldn't treat you like that – it's not right.'

'You can't help.' She dismissed him with a slight shake of her head then reached for a flower, stepped forward and offered it to a passing gentleman. Her voice cracked as she pleaded with him to give her a farthing for it.

William shook his head in despair. She must be sleeping outside, judging by the state of her. That bully would take all the money, except for maybe the odd halfpenny that she needed for food, if she was lucky. If only he'd had a coin on him, he could at least believe she might survive the night.

He turned away and made his way back home, thankful that he could rely on Sarah for a roof over his head and three meals a day. That was more than some people had, it seemed.

CHAPTER 14

I t was the start of another year, fresh and new. What would he do with it? William checked in his drawer to see if he had enough money for another canvas. No such luck. That meant he'd have to drag out the time he spent on this last painting and drop plenty of hints for his birthday. He crossed the landing into his studio where all the paintings he'd done over the last ten months were propped against the wall. As he stood trying to view them with a critical eye, he thought back to his earliest attempts when he hadn't even realised he needed to prepare the canvas before starting to paint.

He'd been so frustrated at the shortage of materials, he hadn't thought about how it had affected his work. Looking at the canvases now made him realise it had done him a favour, making him slow down and take more care over them. Whenever he'd gone wrong, he'd had to paint over his mistakes instead of tossing the picture aside and starting again like a successful artist might.

The lifeboat crew painting made him smile at the memory of Johnny bringing his friend Simon, chairman of the local art club, to see how he was getting on. He'd asked if William wanted to join the club, but that was too daunting. Besides, he'd have to produce more paintings to keep pace with them, and that would mean spending more money on canvases. It was a dream for another day.

It had been such a surprise when Simon had singled out this painting for praise, one that brought together all his memories of countless trips to the beach, watching the lifeboat being launched on a mission, and the tales Grace told him about her Dad's part in the rescues. Then there was the time he'd been hiding in the lifeboat and it was called out. Without a doubt, that had been the most exciting thing that had ever happened to him.

He studied the crew in the painting, clad in their grimy yellow oilskins, straining to control the oars as they held the lifeboat to its course amid the fierce waves rising and crashing over the bow. Simon's compliments had made him feel like a real artist.

But the portraits he'd attempted were a different matter altogether. Why couldn't he master the proportions between the mouth, nose and eyes? He needed to go back to sketching, to experiment more. As for choosing the correct colours to portray skin tones – well, he couldn't work it out at all.

What if the lifeboat picture was an isolated success, never to be repeated? Was he wasting his time pursuing his dream? He might spend years creating art and never get the chance to earn a living from it. It was stupid to think a humble shopworker could become a working artist. He needed someone important to discover him, and that was about as likely as being invited to the palace to meet Queen Victoria.

William turned towards the window and watched a silky black cat curling up on the top of the yard wall. Tinny was showing an interest in his art nowadays. While she didn't have Grace's confidence and sparkle, there was a contemplative air about her expression which might be interesting to portray.

He wandered downstairs and found her alone, absorbed in a book as usual. He gave a little cough.

She looked up. 'Oh, hello. Have you finished another painting?'

He shook his head. 'I've been looking at my portraits. They're much more difficult than the seascapes. I need more practice.' If he didn't seize this chance, he'd never pluck up the courage. 'Can I ask you a favour?'

'Hmm?' she murmured, turning over another page.

'I'd like to paint your portrait, Tinny. Would you pose for me?'

A dimple appeared at the corner of her mouth. Was she going to laugh at him? He should have known better than to rush in with the suggestion.

'You don't have to, it was just an idea.'

She laid aside her book and looked at him, her blue eyes as bright as a spring morning. 'If you want me to, I will.'

For a moment he thought he'd misheard. 'Really?'

She nodded.

'That would be wonderful. Thank you.'

'On one condition.' She gave a mysterious smile. 'We keep it a secret, and you give it to Mam as a birthday present.'

'That shows a touching confidence that I'll produce a good likeness. I wouldn't be too sure.'

'You shouldn't be so modest. I've seen how well you're doing, and I'm sure it will be perfect.'

He could sense a flush building at the unexpected praise. 'Is Sarah out?'

'Yes, she's gone for a walk with Johnny. And before you say anything, it's only a walk.'

'I wouldn't dare. In that case, if you don't mind, can I do a sketch now, while she's out?'

As soon as he saw her nod, he dashed back upstairs to get his paper and pencils.

'Where do you want me to sit?' she asked, as he returned.

He assessed the light in the room. It was brighter at one side than the other, so he experimented, moving a chair around until he found the best position, and readied himself to make a start. How strange it was, drawing a person when they were right in front of you. The light wasn't ideal, but at least he could try to capture the details of her face in a few rough sketches, just enough to allow him to develop the portrait in his spare time.

Tinny was sitting up straight, tense and uncomfortable. It would be hard to capture her features properly if he could only take quick glances. How could he watch her for longer without making her feel self-conscious? Perhaps talking to her might help.

'Now that Sarah's let me organise the window displays, do you think she'd mind if we suggested a few changes?' he asked.

She relaxed instantly, looking amused. 'What are you planning now?'

'Oh, nothing in particular... I was just thinking, we produce the same things every day.'

'Yes, because that's what the customers like.' Her eyes met his, as if waiting for him to explain.

'Stay like that a moment; don't move, keep looking at me please.' He gazed at her, concentrating on the curve of her eyebrows and the flick of her lashes. His hand swept across the paper, only glancing at it when he moved from one feature to the next. 'Our customers think that's what they like. But what if we introduced something different?'

'How different?' She tried to speak the words without moving her lips, like a ventriloquist, and William burst out laughing.

'You can talk, you know,' he spluttered.

'Don't laugh. You told me to stay still, so I did,' she said, with a flash of indignation. Then, catching his eye, she gave a smirk which turned into a giggle. In no time at all she was helpless, sliding off the edge of the chair.

If they carried on in this vein, he'd never get his sketches done. 'Oh my word,' William chuckled. 'That was funny, but we'd better get on before Sarah comes back.'

Tinny calmed down and settled back into her pose, as he explained his ideas for the shop.

'I was thinking about trying sponge cakes sandwiched together with fruit soaked in maraschino, biscuit cones filled with buttercream, and bath buns. It was Johnny that gave me the idea. Last time I went to see him, he'd been talking to a worker from Terry's. The cakes go well there, the fancier the better. We might attract customers who have more money to spend.'

A shadow passed over her face.

'What's wrong? Don't you like the idea?'

She shrugged. 'It sounds fine, if you can afford the ingredients. We're struggling to pay for the flour as it is. Mam's even talked about mixing chalk into it.'

He frowned. What did she mean? 'I don't understand.'

'It's an old trick. Lots of bakers do it. I've told her she'll lose her best customers if she follows suit. And that's the best that could happen; they can fine you if you're caught. But she just asked if I'd rather we were out on the street.'

'I thought we were doing well, with the window displays bringing in more customers?'

She shrugged. 'We were, for a while. But times are hard, and they don't spend very much. And we're having to pay a lot more for the ingredients lately.'

Why hadn't he realised Sarah was struggling to pay the rent? The landlord didn't look like a man with much patience. He'd have to think again about how to improve their range of goods without spending too much money.

The sound of the key in the lock made them both jump. 'This is a great start, thank you,' William told her, gathering together his pencils and paper. 'I'll work on the canvas this week. Do you think Johnny could persuade Sarah to go out again next Sunday, so we can have another session? I need to make separate sketches of details like your eyes and mouth, to help when I'm painting without you in front of me.' He ran upstairs before Sarah came in.

The painting soon started to take shape in the early evenings after they'd eaten. He spent so much of his spare time painting nowadays, Sarah didn't suspect anything when he left the dinner table and went to his room. One Sunday afternoon, Tinny was more tired than usual and struggled to hold the position he wanted. William put down his pencil and sat next to her. 'What's wrong?' he asked.

'It's the anniversary of Dad's death,' she said, her voice cracking. A single tear dropped onto her cheek.

The only thing he could think to do was to pull out his clean handkerchief and offer it to her. She took it and dabbed at her eyes.

With a slight hesitation, he put a hand on her shoulder. 'You should have said. I heard Johnny mention it was this month, but he didn't tell me the exact date. I wish I'd asked now. If I'd known, I wouldn't have expected you to sit for me today.'

'I'm sorry,' she said. 'For Mam's sake, I usually manage to stay brave, at least until I get to bed. I miss having a father so much.'

'I understand,' he said.

'Do you?'

'One day I'll explain, but now isn't the right time. Would it help to tell me about him?'

She nodded and began to describe the awful days when her father became ill, crying with the pain as the cholera ate into him, his skin cold to the touch. He pictured Sarah nursing Bert as he got weaker. It wasn't hard to imagine her despair as Tinny caught the disease, lying in bed for several weeks, forced to miss her father's funeral. There'd been so many burials of victims in Seaton Carew. It was easy to understand how it had torn Sarah apart.

Tinny broke down and sobbed.

William put his arm around her and let her lean into him, sensing a bond he dare not disclose: both of them had lost a father. But he hadn't known his real Papa. How much more painful it must have been for her to lose someone she had loved, laughed with, hugged and kissed.

Once she had stopped crying, he put his sketch pad and pencils away and returned to sit with her until Sarah came back, looking equally emotional. Johnny must have felt as helpless as he did. Sarah shouldn't have gone out; it would have been better for her and Tinny to sit quietly with their memories for the afternoon.

Glad to escape the gloomy atmosphere and hoping he'd done his duty, he returned upstairs and continued working on the portrait, trying to capture the sense of pride and love he had seen in Tinny's face when she spoke about her parents. He couldn't wait to present it to Sarah.

CHAPTER 15

William stood in his studio in the early hours of the morning, exhausted through lack of sleep yet unable to resist the pull of his latest painting, the wreckage of the ship on the Black Middens rocks. In his mind, this was the stormy night when his life had changed. It stood there taunting him, as if mocking his anguish. How could one painting create such a deep sense of loss and longing as he worked on it?

Why did he torment himself like this? He'd been in an optimistic frame of mind while painting the portrait of Tinny, humming to himself and thinking of ways to make her and Sarah happy. His birthday had brought the hoped-for blank canvases, and he'd been eager to start this scene, but as it had developed, he'd become moody, hiding in this room every evening, determined to finish it, trapped in his obsession.

He stared at the canvas, realising he had no idea whether it was accurate or not. It was merely a representation, his own interpretation of how it might have happened. His memories were false, every single one. His past wasn't his own. It meant nothing now, tainted with a cruel deception.

Who were his real parents – not just their names, but their souls, their way of being? What did they look like? What did his father do for a living? Did they laugh together, sing, read, or take long walks in the countryside? He didn't even know where they'd lived, or where the ship had sailed from. He had so many questions, and no means of finding out the answers, unless he could escape from his day-to-day life.

A baby would travel with its mother, but his father might still be alive, going about his daily business. What must it be like to live like that, assuming both his wife and son had perished?

He could be the one to bring wonderful news. A surge of hope raced through him, filling his whole being, giving him a new energy. He must act on the promise he'd made to himself to find the shipping records. The first step was to discover the name of every ship wrecked at Tynemouth near the time of his birth. What then? He didn't know his real name, so a passenger list was no use. This wasn't going to be easy.

Perhaps he should write to Grace and see if she had any bright ideas. But she hadn't written for ages. There wasn't much in the way of news for either of them to share, not when he'd forbidden her to mention Mama and Papa. Had she found somebody else? If she loved him, she would have written every month, wouldn't she? And he could have found things to tell her about, to keep the correspondence going, sharing his progress with his art, telling her about the window displays and the awkward customers. Was the distance too much to overcome?

He stood back to assess the canvas. That smudge of green wasn't right. As he reached for a rag in the wicker basket that held his materials, his hand brushed against the carved fragment. He picked it up, inhaling the scent of the oak, and ran his fingers along the carved acorns and leaves. The curves created by the craftsman's knife were smooth with age and use. How had the box got into Papa's loft? Who had owned it, and what had they used it for?

With his eyes shut, William let his fingertips travel along the contours, sensing the warmth of the wood, and tried to imagine who had made it. Was it an artisan, travelling from place to place with his belongings thrown in an old knapsack? Or a master craftsman in a workshop, with professional tools? It was impossible to tell. Perhaps a sailor had spent his spare time whittling wood salvaged from a wreck with a rough knife.

Whatever the answer, he had a deep-seated affinity with the creator. To have a passion for crafts, and the persistence to execute an item, went to the core of a man. He was starting to understand how all-consuming it might become. If only it was his proper job.

One thing he'd learned from experimenting was that he needed to know when to stop adding to a painting. But it had been a hard lesson to learn, particularly with Tinny's portrait, which now rested inside his wardrobe, wrapped in brown paper. As he counted down the days to Sarah's birthday, he'd become more and more anxious about whether she would like it. And even more worrying was the question of Tinny's reaction.

But today was the day, so he'd soon find out. William waited until he heard the sound of footsteps on the stairs, then collected the painting and headed for the back room.

'Happy birthday, Sarah,' he said, offering the parcel up to her.

'What on earth is this?' She ripped off the paper, and her eyes widened. 'Oh my goodness…' She held it at arms' length, staring at it in astonishment. 'Look at this, Tinny.' She gave a chuckle. 'Why am I saying that? You'll have seen it.'

Tinny shook her head. 'I haven't, except during the first few days. As soon as I made a tiny comment about the shape of my eyebrows, he decided he couldn't take the criticism and told me I'd have to wait until he finished.'

'Typical artistic temperament,' teased Sarah. 'Honestly, William, I've never had such a wonderful present in my entire life. My darling daughter captured for posterity by my favourite young man. You've caught her expression so well.' She gave a sniff. 'Oh, now look what you've done – you've turned me into a quivering wreck.'

William sensed the blush creeping up his neck, secretly delighted not only by the praise of his painting but also at her confirmation that she was fond of him. She gave the canvas pride of place on the mantelpiece and told him he would have the job of hanging it on the wall later.

This was what he'd dreamed of, having the power to move people with his art. The anticipation of this moment had kept him going when he doubted himself, and the reality was even better than he'd hoped for. Oh, to do this every day.

WILLIAM SIPPED at his cup of tea in the back room as he took a quick break from serving. The Easter weekend couldn't come fast enough, bringing two extra days off. The special window display that he and Tinny had put together had attracted a few new customers. But the prospect of being at church wasn't as appealing, bringing back memories of Mama sitting at the piano playing her favourite hymns.

He brought out the piece of jet, turning it over in his fingers and recalling Grace's expression as she gave it to him. That had been the last time he'd seen her, the last time they'd touched, both unaware of the story that was about to unfold when he reached home.

Why could he bring her face into his thoughts now, and not before, when he wanted to paint her? It was all there: her mischievous expression, and the way she flicked her hair back and roared with laughter. He was torn between smiling at the memory and yearning for her. It must be the time he'd spent last night re-reading her letters, tracing her signature with his finger and wondering how she was getting on, working in the big house every day. Did she have time to appreciate the lovely artwork, china and furniture?

He put the jet back in his pocket and returned to the shop. Grace wasn't here, and he had to accept she never would be.

But Tinny was part of his daily life. As he stood in the doorway watching her serve, he realised he'd grown fond of her. She was gentle, caring and full of admiration for his artwork. They'd come a long way since her initial suspicion of him.

On the Sunday before Easter, after a tasty lunch, William suggested a walk. 'I've set aside some money to get us into the museum gardens,' he told them. He'd been thinking about it for a while, desperate for a change of scenery. With a bit of luck it might provide inspiration for a picture.

It didn't take long for Sarah and Tinny to change into their best dresses. Soon they arrived at the gardens, where the beds of vibrant spring flowers provided a colourful contrast to the stone ruins of the abbey. From time to time Sarah stopped to talk to either a customer, or a family from church. Tinny said a polite hello but stayed close by William's side.

Sarah became absorbed in a detailed conversation about the stalls for the Easter fayre with the verger's wife. She nodded to William and Tinny to go ahead.

At last, he had a chance to talk to Tinny alone and test out his plan. Would she realise he was so nervous about asking her? Even though he'd practised the words in his room, he was still sure he'd mess it up.

He walked alongside her as they toured the gardens, admiring the flowers and shrubs. She started to tell him about the latest book she was reading, describing the characters in great detail. Then he gestured at a bench near the abbey, and they both took a seat, watching everyone stroll by in their finery.

'Tinny,' he began, 'you know we're closed on Easter Monday?'

She nodded, watching a lady in an elaborate outfit. 'Hmm? I wonder if I could make over one of my old dresses like that?'

'I was just wondering… could I take you out for the day?'

She smoothed her gloves over her hands and adjusted her hat. 'Where were you planning to go?' she asked.

Typical, he thought, she wants to get to the practicalities. But that was one of the things he liked most about her. 'I was considering Whitby. I've never been before, but I've heard a lot about it. Have you ever been?'

'No, I've never been outside York. But I'm told it's lovely. The harbour's full of fishing boats and there's an abbey right on top of the cliffs, but you have to climb a hundred and ninety-nine steps to get to it. St Hilda lived there.'

'St Hild, actually,' William commented, putting on his best school teacher voice. She gave him a dig in the ribs.

'I hope Mam doesn't mind,' she said. 'I'd need to ask her for a bit of money for lunch.'

'Don't you dare; this is my treat. Call it an early birthday present. I've been so busy painting, I've been able to save most of my wages.'

'I'd love to,' she said, smiling. 'But you must bring your

sketching things. It's supposed to be very picturesque. I think you'd enjoy trying to capture the harbour.'

'What are you two plotting?'

They both jumped at the sound of Sarah's voice behind them. 'A trip to Whitby. On Easter Monday. You don't mind if I take Tinny, do you?'

'By the look on her face, I'd say she's already said yes,' said Sarah, with a glint of mischief in her eyes. 'Of course I don't mind. It will do you both good.'

He hoped so; a change of scenery might chase away the ghosts of the past.

CHAPTER 16

As she opened the curtains on Easter Monday morning, Tinny said a silent thank you to God for the thrill of a bright day for their special trip. What an adventure, leaving the city for the first time.

'Are you ready?' he asked, once they'd cleared away the breakfast table.

'Oh yes,' she said. 'Have you packed your sketching things?'

'I have.' He pointed to his bag. 'There's a surprise in there for you.'

'For me?' She opened it and found a new book, the next one in a series she'd been reading. How thoughtful. 'Oh William, thank you so much. I thought I'd have to wait ages for a copy to come up at the church fayre.'

As they walked to the railway station, Tinny couldn't help worrying that he'd used up all his money on the train tickets and the book. Johnny must have helped him; Mam didn't have the means to contribute. But she wouldn't dream of mentioning it; he looked in his element, doing such a grown-up thing. 'You have no idea how special this is,' she told him as the train arrived.

'Oh I do,' he said. 'I remember the day I had my first experience on one, coming to York. But I was too worried about what I'd do when I got here, so I didn't enjoy it as much as I should have.'

Ah, he thought she only meant the train. She took his hand to steady her as she climbed into the carriage and they chose two seats by the window.

As the train chugged along, Tinny studied the scenery unfolding on their way towards the coast, exclaiming as the steam billowed past the window. The fields looked like patchwork quilts of green and gold, with sheep dotted around in the distance. It was like another world, so different from her relentless routine. She couldn't find the words to tell William how much this meant to her.

At last, the town came into sight. They alighted from the train and William produced a map of the town, telling her he'd borrowed it from Johnny. 'I've made a list of the main sights,' he told her.

She sniffed at the air. 'Can you smell the salt? Come on, let's go straight to the harbour.' She reached for his hand, not caring that it was a forward thing to do, and pulled him along, laughing as he feigned reluctance. 'We've plenty of time to do the rest later.'

On the quay, fishermen were unloading the boats, the nets straining with their catch. William and Tinny wandered to the market, where the silvery fish were weighed and loaded into crates. The stallholders offered delicacies such as crab, cockles and mussels, presented in paper cones.

They strolled further along, where there was an elevated view of the harbour and the abbey on the opposite side. Tinny pointed to a bench. 'Let's sit down there, and you can do a few sketches of the fishing boats. I just want to look out at the sea; there's so much going on.'

They took a seat and William pulled out his sketch book and pencils. Tinny spent a while gazing out towards the sea, watching the boats come and go. Then she watched the activity around the harbour. In the dry dock, workers were patching boats or painting them in traditional colours. Johnny would love it here, among his own kind. At the far end of the quay, a group of women were sitting on boxes mending fishing nets, their needles flying in and out, no doubt sharing gossip and scandal as they worked. What a sense of companionship they must have; her life seemed very small in comparison.

She turned to watch William drawing. What a wonderful skill to have, to create your own version of real life with a simple pencil and a piece of paper. He was concentrating on the lobster pots piled against the harbour wall, trying to capture the intricate criss-cross pattern of ropes. How fascinating, seeing the picture develop from a few tentative lines to the final image with its shadows and patches of light.

'How about trying a long-range view from the harbour towards the abbey? It's very dramatic. Just imagine the colours you can use.'

'I can stop now, if you'd rather do something else.'

'Heavens, no. I've been so busy watching everyone going about their business that I haven't even read any of my book. This is such a lovely place.'

'It is, isn't it? But there's still so much to see, and I don't know about you, but I'm getting hungry. Let's find a place to eat.'

Did he have enough money for a meal? It wouldn't be proper to ask. She resolved to eat as little as possible, just in case.

It didn't take long to find a café for a simple lunch of

sandwiches and tea. Tinny cast a critical eye over the produce, then admitted it looked just as good as Sarah's. 'I wonder if we could make more of serving tea and cake in the shop,' she mused. 'I'd love to run a tearoom one day.'

'Really? I had no idea,' he said.

'How could you? I haven't told anyone, not even Mam. It's just a pipe dream.'

'Don't say that. I bet you could do it. Look at the ideas you've had for the window displays, not to mention those new biscuits you tried out a few weeks ago,' he said.

Would he think her silly if she shared the plans she'd made inside her head? 'Can I tell you about it?' she ventured.

As soon as he said yes, the words flowed out of her, bringing to life the image she had held in her mind for so long. A cosy place where customers could feel comfortable, with colourful sturdy crockery they wouldn't be afraid of breaking, and where children were welcomed. There'd be tasty cakes and scones, and an endless supply of the best tea.

She finished and waited for his reaction.

'What a wonderful idea. If I ever earn any money with my painting, I'll be proud to invest in it.'

It was hard not to hug him there and then. Instead, she thanked him and promised she'd remind him of that, *when* he earned his first commission, not if.

They left the café and walked along the edge of the harbour, watching the water lapping against the brightly coloured boats. The sight of the sea seemed to give William a burst of energy.

'I saw a sign for pleasure boat trips,' he said. 'Would you like to go on one? Johnny gave me some money for a treat.'

She nodded. 'That was kind of him. When I was younger, he used to take me out on the river, to give Mam a break.'

They found the mooring and climbed on the boat, joining a well-to-do couple. Tinny was sure they were looking down their noses at them. The cheek of it. The captain unravelled the rope and pushed the boat off with his foot, jumping on at the last minute, and they sailed out of the harbour, bobbing and dipping as the seagulls wheeled overhead with noisy cries.

A wind was gusting; Tinny shivered, wrapping her shawl around her. She smiled to herself as William's arm crept around her shoulders, drawing her closer to him to help keep her warm. A little thrill rippled through her and she snuggled into him.

As they travelled further out to sea, the wind grew stronger and the waves buffeted the little boat. Tinny felt William shudder and shift his position. He was gripping the bench in front of him with both hands.

She turned towards him. 'Are you all right?' she asked.

His face had turned deathly pale. The water splashed over the edge, making the boat rock and lurch from side to side.

She leaned in to him and whispered. 'You don't look well. Put your head down for a while, so's you don't faint.'

He pulled away from her, and leaned over the side of the boat, retching.

'Is your lad all right?' asked the captain.

Tinny shook her head. 'I think he's seasick.'

She put her hand on the back of his neck. His skin was clammy. 'I'm sorry – is it possible to go back?' she asked the captain. The other couple were muttering, but she gave them a good stare. How dare they make William suffer? Soon the ride became smoother, as the harbour came back into sight.

'I'm sorry,' he muttered, sitting with his eyes shut.

'Don't worry,' said Tinny. 'Not long now, then we'll be back on dry land.'

It seemed to take forever, but at last they arrived back at the harbour. William stumbled on to the quay and she steered him to a stone block so he could sit with his head between his knees to banish the dizziness.

After a while, he straightened up, took a few deep breaths and said he was better. A seagull pecked at the remnants of a fish on the quayside.

'Have you been seasick before?' Tinny asked.

'No, but I've only been on a boat once, and I was fine then. My favourite hobby was watching the lifeboat crew setting off on a rescue mission. I wanted to be part of it so much that one day I climbed into the lifeboat to inspect it. Nobody was there, but then the alarm sounded to summon the crew. If they'd found me, Papa would have been furious. So I hid inside while they launched it.'

'Gosh. What did your parents say?' At last, he was giving hints about his home life.

'They never knew. Mama was attending church and Papa was at work. My governess was ill, and I was certain Cook and Ada wouldn't miss me.'

That gave her more clues about his status. How hard was it for him to live their life, serving in a poky shop, relying on scraps of meat and left overs from the shop for meals, after being in a fine house?

She listened to his tale, of hiding below deck as the boat hit the water, then panicking and emerging through the hatch just in time to see two sailors being rescued. She'd never imagined he could be so daring.

His face brightened as he described the moment the crewmen pulled the sailors into the boat. Now she understood the passion behind his seascapes. No wonder he'd suggested coming here; the sea must have been calling to him.

She patted his arm. 'How strange that you went through that without being affected, but today you were sick. I wonder why?'

A shadow seemed to pass over his face, such a contrast from his animated expression of a moment ago.

'When I said I'd only been in a boat once before, that wasn't exactly true.' He was looking straight ahead, toward the far wall of the harbour.

'When was the other time?' she asked, keeping her voice soft to encourage him to talk.

'I don't remember it, because I was only a baby. The boat I was in hit the rocks at Tynemouth and broke up. I was the only survivor in my family, as far as I know. Papa stole me from the wreck, but they kept it a secret. They moved away, so no one would guess I wasn't theirs.' He wiped his eyes with the back of his hand. 'Please don't tell your mother. Not yet. The fewer people that know, the better.'

'Mam wouldn't say anything to anyone. You shouldn't keep secrets, it's only one step away from a lie.' She cringed as she realised how harsh she sounded.

'You don't need to lecture me about secrets. It was the worst day of my life, finding out they'd kept it from me for so many years. Especially Mama; I always thought she was on my side.'

'I'm sorry. I didn't mean to preach.' She should be gentle with him; he needed understanding, not criticism.

'I know you didn't. You weren't to know the real reason for my nightmares. The worry about Papa finding me... it was about him dragging me back to go into the business. I never want to see him again.'

'He couldn't make you go back, could he? If he isn't your real father? Anyway, if he did turn up, we'd help you deal with him. A few words from my Mam and he'd soon turn around and head back home without you.' It was best to make a joke of it, to erase her earlier cruel words.

He ran his fingers through his hair. 'I have to stay hidden. You won't betray me, I know, and Sarah might not mean to, but she knows so many people. One slip, however accidental, could cause so much trouble.'

She fell silent, not knowing what to say. What a thing to find out. She tried to imagine it. What if Mam and Dad had taken her aside one day to tell her they'd adopted her? She would be devastated, confused and possibly angry. Would it make a difference to her love for them? She hoped not. But there wasn't much point in speculating; today was meant to be full of fun and adventure. She needed to dispel the shadow that had been cast over it.

She pointed to the ancient abbey, its ruins towering over the harbour like a king on a throne surveying his lands. 'We'd get a beautiful view from up there.'

'Do you think you can manage all those steps?' he asked.

She gave his arm a playful push. 'Of course I can. I'm stronger than I look, you know. Unless you aren't feeling up to it?'

'You're not going to let me forget the boat episode, are you?' His rueful smile told her he was back to his usual self.

They crossed over the harbour bridge and found the path to the abbey. Climbing the steps was harder than it looked, and they needed to take several breaks on the pretence of stopping to enjoy the view. Tinny watched William closely each time. His gaze swept the coast then settled northward, a troubled look crossing his face.

She was starting to piece it all together. The nightmares when someone had been chasing him, trying to force him to return home, the death of his parents... he had demons to slay, just like the heroes in the adventure novels she loved to read. The drama of it might have been exciting, if she didn't sense the real agony deep inside him. Would he let her get close enough to help?

They reached the top of the cliff and stood in front of the abbey, the ruined walls looming over them. She shared her knowledge with William, retelling the story of Bede and Aidan, and how St Hild moved from Hartlepool to Whitby. 'Just imagine it, a woman presiding over the monastery. I don't understand why people disapprove of Mam running a shop.'

At last it was time to head back home.

'I've had such a lovely day, William,' Tinny said as they waited on the platform. She hugged him, and for a moment was tempted to kiss him on the cheek. No, she mustn't; it wasn't right, and it would embarrass him. Better to act as a close friend and wait for him to tell her why he'd left a good home with two people who cared enough to adopt him. There was definitely more to his story.

CHAPTER 17

The summer day seemed extra sunny as William emerged from the church after Holy Communion. 'My first commission,' he told Tinny. 'Unpaid, but I don't care. It's an honour just to know that Reverend Jones thinks my work's good enough to donate a painting.'

'I'm glad you agreed,' said Sarah. 'He didn't tell you that the cost of the restoration is much more than we'd expected, did he? I think it's an ideal prize. You never know who might put in a bid, and if they like it enough, they'll spread the word.'

'Or even ask to buy more of your work,' added Tinny.

He laughed. 'Now then, don't get too excited. I'm having enough trouble keeping my feet on the ground.' But a tiny part of him hoped it might lead to someone discovering his talent, someone who could show him how to progress.

As they walked home, Tinny chattered on, making suggestions as to which of his works he should give to the church. Together, they agreed the lifeboat rescue was the best, or if he couldn't bear to part with it, one of his schooner paintings. There wasn't time to create a new one. Not with the plans he was making for the next stage of his life, which he was about to share with them.

As soon as they finished lunch, William decided it was time to broach the subject. 'I have a favour to ask you, Sarah.' He chewed his lip, wondering how to start.

'Ask and it shall be given, eh Mam?' Tinny directed a cheeky smile at her mother.

He cleared his throat, ready to make a start. 'You both know I ran away from my family.' He looked at Tinny, willing her to be supportive. 'I've told each of you different parts, but I want you both to hear the full story, before I ask you for your help.'

Choosing his words with care, he explained what he'd heard as he sat outside his parents' bedroom after Papa had destroyed his paintings. As he finished, an uneasy silence descended.

Sarah was the first to break it. 'What a terrible shock it must have been, finding out after all that time. You poor boy. I've often wondered what made you turn up here alone, and at such a young age too.'

Tinny turned to William, her eyes full of sympathy. 'I'm glad you've decided to bring it out into the open. I can understand why you wanted to get away.' She reached across the table to put her hand over his.

Without thinking, he curled his fingers round hers. 'Can you?'

How different her reaction was to Grace's. Perhaps Tinny understood him better, but then she'd also known the loss of a father. He couldn't admit that he'd already revealed his secret to Johnny; they'd be offended that he hadn't told them first. Unless Johnny had said something to Sarah. Was she pretending? No, she looked genuinely shocked.

'So why confide in us now, William?' Sarah brushed away

the crumbs from the tablecloth, then traced an embroidered rose with her fingertips.

'Because I was hoping you might help, by giving me a bit of advice about what I want to do next.'

Tinny gripped his hand. 'You're leaving us?' Her voice cracked.

'No, nothing like that.' Did she care that much? He felt his cheeks flush. 'I love being here with you both. Don't worry, you can't get rid of me that easily. It's just that now I've settled here, one thing keeps preying on my mind. I've been wondering if one of my real parents might have survived.'

'That's only natural,' said Sarah. 'From what you've said, I'm surprised you haven't got round to it before now. But how likely is it? You were a baby, only a few months old. I'd be surprised if you weren't with your mother; I wouldn't have attempted a sea voyage so soon after giving birth to Tinny, not without Bert.'

'You've never been on a boat, Mam, so how could you know?' asked Tinny.

'I can remember how scared I was about taking you anywhere at that age. I'm just trying to put myself in his Mama's shoes.' She turned to him. 'You said you had no brothers and sisters. Perhaps she had the same trouble as me, losing other babies. But I suppose one of your parents, or both, might have survived the wreck. They could've had a bump on the head, or been seriously injured. By the time they recovered... if they recovered, they'd have assumed you'd died.'

William fell silent. They were the same thoughts that had buzzed around his head for weeks. He'd spent almost three years avoiding confronting the possibilities, but now a strange determination had gripped him, a desperate need to find out the truth. Imagine living for years thinking your son was dead, grieving for him, then everything turning into joy when he arrived at your doorstep one day. But how could he prove his true identity?

Sarah folded her hands and let out a sigh. 'Of course, it's just as likely that they didn't make it, I'm sorry to say.'

'But there could be brothers, sisters, cousins, aunts and uncles…' Tinny tailed off.

'True. You might have a full set of relatives you don't know about,' Sarah added. 'I'd start by trying to find out whatever you can about the wreck. If you know where the ship started out, that might give you a clue about where the family lived.'

'But that's my problem,' William explained. 'Where do I start? I don't even know the name of the ship, nor which route it was taking, only that it sank at Tynemouth. I used to read the newspapers when Papa had finished with them, and there were lots of stories about ships running aground on the Black Middens rocks.'

Tinny lifted her hand from his. 'I'll make some more tea,' she said. 'We need to think about this properly.'

William felt the burden of his secret lift from his shoulders. Why had he waited so long to tell them? He should have known they'd want to help.

But as the afternoon passed, he realised he had expected too much. He couldn't fault their willingness to help, but they knew so little, with their world confined to the house and shop, the church and an occasional walk around the city. The only alternative was to visit the vicar tomorrow afternoon, the most learned person around, and ask him where he could find the shipping records for that area. It was time to find out where he truly belonged.

He thanked Sarah and Tinny for their help and went up to his room, where he could be alone with his thoughts, pondering the decision he'd taken to leave home, nearly three years ago. Had it been the right thing to do? Or should he have pretended he hadn't overheard the secret? Then Papa would have taken him to the office the following Friday as usual, and he could have asked the clerk, Mr Wainwright, how to trace a passenger ship.

But deep down, he knew it wouldn't have worked. He couldn't have feigned innocence of what he'd overheard, and even if he could, Mr Wainwright's loyalties lay with Papa. He'd be bound to say something about his curiosity. No, he had made his bed and had to lie in it, as Papa was fond of saying. He'd just have to hope Reverend Jones could give him better advice.

WILLIAM TRAMPED through the streets with his shoulders slumped and his head down, just as on that first morning when he was looking for a stray coin so he could afford breakfast. But this time, it was the difficulty of the task he'd set himself that weighed him down. He'd been sure Reverend Jones could help, that by some good fortune there would be local records of ships that had sailed along the coast in years gone by. He'd been disappointed; if the vicar was to be believed, his best hope was the shipping records held by insurance companies, but he could never afford a train ticket to London.

There was only one way left: to put an advertisement in newspapers around the region, asking for anyone with information about a shipwreck in 1861 near Tynemouth. But that might not even be the right year. What if Mama and Papa had guessed, or told a lie about the date of his birth, to avoid detection?

William arrived home intent on taking action. He had an hour before Sarah needed him in the shop to cover for Tinny, who was going out to help organise the stalls for the church summer fayre. As soon as he was back in his room, he took a piece of paper and a pen from the desk. How should he begin the most momentous letter he'd ever written? His hand hovered over the blank page, his skin prickling with anticipation as he tried to compose the words that might encourage a family member to get in touch.

As he focused on the event he needed to describe, he could almost smell the salty water lapping around the sodden timbers of the wreck, while the cries of drowning souls rose up from the sea. A shiver rippled through him, and he shook his head to dispel the images and return to his vital task. Would it reach the people who needed to read it? It was so long ago, a dim and distant memory for anyone who'd been aware of it at the time. His task was to present the basic facts in a way that might prompt remembrance and start a chain of mentioning that would lead to the right person. Someone out there must know.

Soon there were more crossings out than phrases left untouched, but at last he had the words.

Sir, I was a baby on a ship which crashed into the Black Middens at Tynemouth in or around 1861. By a miracle I was rescued, but I was alone. It is my dearest wish to know whether either of my parents survived. I am hoping you will print my plea for anyone with any information that might lead me to any living relations to come forward. I would be much obliged if they could write to the Editor with details of how I can make contact.

Yours, an anxious son.

That sounded like the wording he'd read in the Letters to the Editor section of the local newspapers. He copied it out as neatly as he could on a fresh piece of paper, finished with his name and address, then added a postscript:

You will understand the sensitivity of this request, and I pray for your discretion. I am seventeen years old and as I have no means to pay for an advertisement, I am falling on your mercy to ask you to publish it as a letter. Please forward any replies to my address above.

He copied it four times for his chosen newspapers, all near ports: Grimsby, Hull, Whitby and Tynemouth. As he folded each letter, he whispered a prayer that whoever opened it would understand and be willing to publish it. It was best to avoid Hartlepool; it would be disastrous if Papa were to find out about his search.

He addressed four envelopes, sealed the letters inside and fixed the stamps on them before he lost his courage. If he left by the back door, he'd escape an inquisition by Tinny and Sarah. He ran to the post box and pushed the letters in the slot before he could change his mind. There, it was done.

CHAPTER 18

Every day since placing the advertisement, William had watched for the postman's arrival, but still nothing had come for him. Nearly a month had passed, and now he couldn't even summon up any enthusiasm for the latest window display. Tinny had stopped trying to cajole him into helping with the colours and layout of the baskets and produce.

Had he wasted his time on the adverts? Even if he had any family alive, how likely was it that any of them would see the newspapers he had chosen? It was an improbable dream. But the idea of that slim chance held on to him, limpet-like, occupying his every waking moment.

Each day was painful, preparing the dough and pastry in silence, and dreading the sound of the bell as the first customers entered the shop on a morning. He was running out of excuses to stay in the kitchen. Sarah must have noticed he was avoiding talking to the customers, but she hadn't mentioned it.

In his studio on an evening he could let go of his emotions, pouring out his frustration on the canvas in scenes of shipwrecks and lifeboat rescues, in turns elated and frustrated as he tried to portray the raw power of the sea, tossing ships and fishing boats about like toys. He played with colours, discovering the impact of a dash of red or bright yellow to add depth and definition.

But as the weeks passed, the canvases became darker, intense with desperation and despair. Brooding black clouds hovered in the sky and the storms became fiercer, the waves higher. He stopped painting people into the scenes. People ruined everything, denied your existence, tossed you aside. No matter that the paintings wouldn't sell; he had neither the means nor the will to find a way of showing them to anyone. Even Sarah couldn't tease him out of his dark moods.

'No! Get it right!' he yelled, impatience getting the better of him one day in his studio. Today, everything was wrong. The colours, the texture… it was all wrong, a shapeless mess. He grabbed the canvas from the easel and slammed it on the floor, then raised his foot above it, ready to stamp it out of existence.

Then he stopped himself, shocked at what he had nearly done. Destruction, not creation? He was no better than Matthew Harper. He stepped back, suddenly aware of a rumbling noise filling his ears, growing louder, white lights flashing at the edges of his vision, as the room became a blur. His head started to spin, and he sank to the floor with a wail of despair.

～

WILLIAM OPENED HIS EYES, straining to see in the half-light. How did he get here? He couldn't remember going to bed. He lifted his head, groaning at the hammering pain in his temples.

A glass appeared at his lips. 'Drink this,' Tinny urged.

'What happened?' His voice came out as a croak. He sipped at the water, then fell back against the pillow.

'I found you on the floor of your studio last night. You were distraught. What's happening, William?'

'I don't know.' He closed his eyes, wishing he could sink into the darkness and never surface.

'We've been worrying about you for ages. Mam's upset that you never talk to her any more, and now she's blaming herself for not realising you weren't coping. Has something gone wrong with your painting? Or is this about finding your family?'

The door opened, and he heard a swish of skirts and smelt the aroma of bread from the shop. A cool hand rested on his brow.

'Stop bothering him with your chatter. He's burning up,' said Sarah.

'Who's looking after the shop?' Tinny sounded anxious.

'I've closed it for a few minutes. Stop worrying; get his flannel and douse it in water from the jug.'

William kept his eyes closed, to avoid the inevitable questions. Then he remembered, and the torment welled up inside him again. With all those people out there, someone must have known his parents, must have shared in their joy at having him. Even if it wasn't a relative, just finding a living person who remembered his family would be a start. Someone who could answer his questions. The silence was torture.

The sound of water splashing into the basin brought him back to the room. A moment later, a damp cloth was pressed against his forehead. He exhaled slowly and opened his eyes. Both Sarah and Tinny were standing over him, watching. He moved his dry lips, and a strange, cracked sound emerged. 'Thank you. Better.'

'You gave us such a shock.' Sarah patted his hand. 'Now

you need to rest. I've put a hand-bell there.' It was on a wooden chair at the side of the bed. 'Ring it if you need anything. I'll make you a light snack to eat. If that doesn't help, I'm calling the doctor.' She went out, leaving the door ajar.

Tinny remained by the bed, as if she wanted to speak.

'I'll be fine. You go and help Sarah,' he croaked. 'It must have been exhaustion, that's all. A good sleep will make it right.' He mustn't make a fuss. A doctor was the last person he wanted to see; Sarah couldn't afford one and neither could he. Besides, he couldn't bear the thought of having leeches put on his skin. He shuddered at the mere thought of them piercing his skin and draining his blood.

Sarah's voice came from the bottom of the stairs. 'Leave him be, Christina – come down.'

Tinny reached into her pocket and pulled out a letter. 'This came for you earlier.' She offered it to him.

He stared at it, not even daring to take it from her. 'For me?' He started to shake. It could be a prank like the one he'd had last week. The excitement of opening it had turned to despair when he realised it was someone mocking him for his desperation. Or it could be an editor saying they couldn't help.

Tinny put it into his hand and left without saying a word.

William shook as he opened the envelope, stamped with 'Whitby Gazette' in the bottom left-hand corner. He tipped it and stared as another envelope fell out, addressed to the editor. The postmark was smudged, only just legible. Scarborough. There was a faint scent of violets, and the handwriting was cursive and elaborate. A lady's hand, for sure. Dare he open it? Why was he hesitating, when this was everything he'd hoped for? This moment could mark the boundary between ignorance and knowledge, loss and discovery, isolation and belonging.

With quivering fingers, he turned it over, then slid a fingertip under the flap to open it. He pulled out a single piece of paper, unfolded it and started reading.

I scarcely know how to begin this letter. I have spent the last seventeen years believing that my husband and baby son both perished in a wreck off Tynemouth.

A film came over his eyes, obscuring the confident script. He rubbed his eyelids with his sleeve, desperate to read the rest.

If you truly are that baby, then this is a miracle. Please come to Scarborough so we can find out if our dreams have come true. Write back to tell me everything: what you know, where you are, and whether you can come to see me. I am often away on business, but I will find a day when we can meet. I hope to receive your letter soon.

Leah Morgan

He tried the sound of the name. Leah Morgan. Her full address was at the foot of the letter. Scarborough. So close. He scanned the letter again to make sure. Four times he read it, taking in every word, every syllable, every nuance. She was as excited as he was, envisaging a grand reunion: 'find out if our dreams have come true'. Our dreams, not just his. He loved her already, the emptiness inside him now filling up with joy, excitement... and belonging. To belong, for the first time. He could burst with the thrill of it.

To think he'd spent all this time in York going about his business, completely unaware that his mother was alive. She would have often strolled along the promenade at Scarborough, watching the tide rolling in and back out again, the same sea he used to observe at Seaton Carew, the inspiration for his paintings.

What a long time she'd spent grieving for him, and for his father, too. A double loss. How would she have heard the news of the shipwreck? Please God, let her not have read about it in the newspaper.

The letter was short, but it confirmed some of the facts. He had been travelling with his father. But Sarah had said it was unusual for a baby to travel without its mother. Why hadn't Leah been with them?

He re-read the letter. Had he assumed too much, in his haste to take everything in? She hadn't said whether she was on the boat or not. What if she'd been with them and survived? Imagine her distress, trying to find them both amid the confusion of the wreck. The images he'd painted of ships marooned on the rocks gathered in his mind. Hulls smashed into splinters, masts tipping and crashing down, splitting a boat in two. Darkness, everything a blur as the waves pounded the debris. His mother, Leah, staggering to her feet, her dress saturated, stumbling over the rocks to catch the attention of the rescuers, scared that a wave might sweep her away as she searched for him and his father.

There was so much she hadn't said in her letter, but he could understand her reticence. She wouldn't want to divulge too much until she was sure of his identity. But he had no papers, no means of proving who he was. Had he inherited any features from her? He hoped so; it would help to convince her. What did she look like? And how had she survived without a husband to support her? He scanned the letter again. She mentioned having a business. What did she do? Oh, there were so many questions.

There was no time to lose. He must write straight back and arrange a visit. His tiredness evaporated as he composed the letter in his head. He had to write it now and make plans for the journey. He was going to meet his real mother.

CHAPTER 19

As the train edged nearer to Scarborough, William sat silently watching the scenery pass by, in a world of his own, oblivious to the other people sitting in the compartment. What would happen at the end of his journey? What was he supposed to say and do, in this strange reunion with a mother he didn't know existed until last week? What might she think of him?

At last, the train was slowing at the approach to Scarborough station. William pulled his bag from the rack and waited for everyone else to disembark. They would find it easier to identify each other away from the crowd. As he reached the end of the platform, a lady appeared in a rustle of cornflower blue silk, her bonnet moving from side to side like a bird's beak searching for food. William stepped forward, and she brightened. 'William Harper?'

He nodded, unable to hide his smile as they came face to face. She stared at him with light green eyes that sparkled like dew on grass, flecked with the colour of pale driftwood. Glossy chestnut hair peeped out from her bonnet, a stray tendril escaping at one side. She had ruby lips and her skin was smooth like Mama's. Faint lines around her eyes crinkled as she smiled at him.

'Mother?' Every part of him wanted to hug her and never let go, but that wouldn't be proper. He lifted his hand to his forehead and swept the annoying tuft of hair aside. Please God, let her think him tidy and respectful.

'I never imagined this day would come,' she whispered. She leaned forward and kissed his cheek, her perfume creating a haze that seemed to bind them together. 'Let's get home for a proper reunion,' she said, and led him out into the street towards a carriage where a groom was brushing a bay horse. 'Dobson, here is our visitor.'

William handed over his bag and followed Leah into the carriage. He took his seat, fingering the piece of jet in his pocket to give him courage as the horse pulled away and they bounced along the road, the smell of the leather squabs bringing back memories of the weekly trip to Papa's office. Just as the sea came into view, the carriage turned a corner and stopped.

'Here we are,' she said. 'Welcome home.'

Home. It was the word he'd longed to hear.

Dobson opened the door for them and William leapt out. Her house was three-storied, in a terrace of grand proportions. He turned round and realised they were opposite the Grand Hotel. Papa had stayed there once or twice and his description of it had enthralled Mama.

Leah came to stand beside him and smiled. 'Impressive, isn't it? I watched it being built from here; such a fascinating process.' She gestured towards the house, inviting him to go ahead of her.

The geometric tiles reminded him of his antics in the hall at home, when he used to jump from one diamond to the other. But that wasn't his true home. His life must have begun here.

He followed her into the living room. Dobson's footsteps faded as he mounted the stairs, taking William's bag to the guest bedroom.

She closed the door and stood in front of him, smiling, her arms open. He stepped forward, and she claimed him as her own, guiding his head on to her shoulder. 'My son. After all these years. It's true, isn't it? It's you. I know it in my heart.' Her voice faltered a little.

William lifted his head, wanting to look at her. 'I couldn't believe it when your letter arrived. And I know you need to be sure I am your son.' His voice seemed small in the high-ceilinged room. He had to voice the thought that had tormented him throughout his journey here. 'I don't know how I can prove it, though.'

She gave an enigmatic smile. 'There is a way, but I'd like to show you something first.' She took his hand, and led him up the stairs, not stopping until the third floor, where his bag was waiting for him outside a closed door. He followed her into another room at the front, his eyes widening at the scene in front of him.

Paintings were stacked against every wall and two easels held half-finished canvases. An array of art materials rested on a long table in the middle of the room: paint tubes, brushes, rags, charcoal stubs and sketch books.

'This is… was… your father's studio.'

'He was an artist?'

'Yes.'

'So am I.'

It made perfect sense. This was where his desire, his dreams, his ambition had come from. She must have kept it like this for the last seventeen years, preserved just as his father had left it on that fateful day. He wandered round, trying to take everything in, pausing to study the seascapes. His father's skill was evident as he absorbed the details: the swell of the sea, waves surging then crashing on to the shore, raw with anger, lifeboats cresting the waves and abandoned shipwrecks littering the shore.

A few portraits were dotted around the room, not formal sittings but working-class men and women, their faces wrinkled and skin weathered, years of hard labour written in their expressions. They were remarkable.

He joined Leah at the window and looked out at the scene below. It was just like a toy town, but with moving figures. He turned back towards the table and picked up a canvas to scrutinise it.

'Don't touch that,' she cried.

Shocked, he nearly dropped it. 'I'm sorry. I didn't know—'

Leah came over and placed a hand on his shoulder. 'Forgive me. It was just a reaction. Let's sit.' She pointed to the chaise longue.

'You said in your letter you were keen on painting. You can see from this room that it meant everything to James. It was his passion and his life. How about if I tell you our story? Then you can share what you've been doing all these years, and by the time we've finished, I'm sure we will both know the truth.' She paused, picking at a speck of lint on her skirt.

William nodded. 'Can I show you some of my drawings first? I brought a few with me.'

Her expression brightened. 'I'd love to see them.'

He ran to the landing and retrieved the rolled-up bundle from his bag. Trying to ignore his fluttering nerves, he sat beside her and opened out each drawing in turn, explaining why he'd chosen the subject and what he'd attempted to achieve.

'These are excellent. You've conveyed depth, and the shading is well executed. I can see you have talent. James was also a natural with charcoal and pencil. In fact, I preferred some of his early drawings to the oils.

Relief coursed through William. 'I'm glad you like them. Please, tell me everything.'

She settled back, ready to tell her story. 'James was not well off when we married; I suppose he was the typical struggling artist. My father had hoped I would make a better match. But love is everything, and we threatened to elope if Pa didn't agree. It made James determined to prove him wrong, and after a lot of hard work, he created a stock of paintings. In the summer months, he worked at the hotel over there, in a menial serving job, so he could save up enough money to go round a selection of art galleries in the region to show them his work. He was lucky; a private collector in Beverley gave him an exhibition and invited a few eminent art dealers. It was a great success, and the commissions started coming in.' She smiled at the memory. 'It meant we could buy this house. You were born soon afterwards, and our lives were complete.'

William looked around the studio at the canvases. 'He favoured seascapes,' he observed. 'I love to paint them too.' He pointed at one. 'Look at the motion of those waves.'

Leah nodded. 'He was brilliant at portraying the changing colour and movement of the water. It's a cruel irony that a storm caused his death.'

She stood up and walked over to the table, running her fingers along the edge. When she turned back to William, there were tears in her eyes. 'I had no word from him for weeks. I assumed you were both at your grandmother's in Tynemouth.'

'You didn't go on the ship?'

'I was ill,' she answered. 'It was a difficult birth, and I nearly died. I was desperate to look after you, but I couldn't. We hired a wet nurse, but I still woke whenever you cried.'

'So Father took me to visit his family, to give you time to recover?'

'Yes. I told him to go. His Ma didn't like me much, anyway. The wet nurse accompanied them, naturally. She must have drowned too. My sister came to look after me while you were both away. If she hadn't been here when I received the news you had both died, I don't know what I would have done. If I couldn't be with you, I didn't want to live. She showed me I needed to carry on.'

William thought of the moment he'd overheard Mama and Papa recalling the night they found him amid the rock pools and debris. Two mothers, one joyful, the other in despair. All because of him.

Leah was staring at him. 'Are you all right? You've gone very pale.'

He nodded. 'There's so much to take in. Please, go on.'

As she explained her mission to keep James' memory alive by going into business in the art world, she became animated. He could imagine her captivating the gallery owners with her vivacious manner and confidence. How Father must have loved her.

'Was it a hard decision to sell some of Father's paintings?' he asked.

'Oh yes, but I had no option,' she replied. 'It was a case of surviving financially. I wanted to establish a fund so I could sponsor artists. My plan needed an initial investment, but if I chose well, I could make a living by taking a commission when they were successful.'

It was a clever scheme, and a world away from what he'd thought possible. How different from Mama's reliance on Papa. Leah had strength and ingenuity. Grace would like her, he was sure. He listened as she described how no one accepted her at first; she needed persistence, using James' reputation to open doors.

She gave a quiet chuckle. 'I know what everyone thought. The poor widow, desperate for a few pounds here and there… but I had the measure of them, knowing what the paintings were worth.'

So, art could be a business, and she was a natural businesswoman, that much was clear. If only Father hadn't died. How wonderful it would have been to grow up with him, both of them understanding the passion that coursed through you when you had a paintbrush in your hand to capture the emotion of a scene.

He felt the touch of her arm as it came to rest around his shoulders.

'Your turn now. You promised.' She kissed him on the cheek.

William started with the facts: the house and its servants, Papa's job, Mama's nervous disposition, and the day he was taken out of school. It didn't seem important to say where he'd lived, and she didn't ask.

'It's hard to describe the sense of not belonging. Something stopped me from feeling complete. Does that make sense?'

Leah nodded. 'It does, yes. We weren't well off to start with. We were living in cramped conditions in a rented house, with no servants. Your adoptive parents would not have wanted to associate with us. Then as James became successful, I was pitched into a world of society gatherings. They were kind people, but of a certain class. I had to learn how to behave, how to speak, eat meals with a bewildering number of courses, and pretend I was like them. After James died, I had to change my life again, to make a living. It was strange, not what I was born to do.'

'That's it exactly,' said William, animated. She really understood. 'Every time I complied with Papa's wishes, it was as if I was going against something deep inside me. But I had to obey; what child has the option to do otherwise?

Besides, they never told me I was adopted, so I didn't know any different.'

'But you're not with them now?'

'No.' This was it. He described the devastation of his paintings and the revelation he'd heard as he crouched beside the bedroom wall. It sounded like a tale that had happened to another person.

Her voice cut into his thoughts like a brush dipped into water, breaking the surface to create a swirl of marbled emotions.

'How did that make you feel?' Her hand made its way into his.

'Shocked, confused… angry.' He struggled to find the words amid the images: the wreckage of his bedroom, the torn and crumpled canvases, and the splinters from the box.

'I couldn't stay there. How could I face them, knowing that? So I ran away and found a job and lodgings in York.' He told her about Sarah and Tinny, carefully avoiding the circumstances that had led him to their shop.

'Have you had any contact with your adoptive parents since?' she asked, her voice husky.

'None. It's better that they don't find me. I want nothing more to do with them, not after all the lies. But I do feel guilty about deserting Mama. She always tried to protect me.'

William watched as she stood up and moved towards the table, circling it and stopping now and then to straighten a paintbrush or a water pot.

'I've kept these things ever since the tragedy, but I want you to have some of them,' she said.

'That would be very special. Thank you… Mother.' He paused, then put his hand in his pocket. 'Actually, I do have one memento. At least I think it might belong to him.'

He pulled out the fragment of wood with its acorns and oak leaves and handed it to her.

Her face turned a chalky white, and she swayed as she fingered it. 'This is from James' box,' she whispered. 'It never left his side. I'm sure it must be one of the last things he touched.'

Sounds rose from the street: a hum of voices, horses neighing as visitors arrived at The Grand, and children laughing as they played in the gardens. Ordinary people living ordinary lives, while his own was changing right in front of him.

Leah's voice turned into a whisper. 'Remember the proof I referred to? Well, my son had a strawberry-shaped birthmark at the nape of his neck, just above the hairline.'

William stared at her, then nodded. There was no doubt. He'd often tried to see it as a child, angling a hand mirror to catch a reflection in the looking glass on Mama's dressing table. He turned away from her and lifted his hair so she could see it. When he turned back round, she was looking at him with pure love etched on her face.

She pulled him towards her. 'My darling Thomas. I thought you were dead.' She sobbed, wrapping her arms around him as if she would never let him go.

Thomas? He'd forgotten that his name wasn't really William. He stayed in her embrace, not wanting the moment to end.

She pulled away from him and wiped away her tears with a lace-edged handkerchief. 'You are so like James, it almost scares me. It's your nose, the way your mouth turns up... the slope of your shoulders, and your long fingers. I would love to see your paintings. Are there any similarities to his?' She gestured to the canvases.

William walked over to take a closer look. 'Yes, in some respects. I'm nowhere near as good as this, of course. My subjects are very similar, though I've only recently tried portraiture. But that splash of red - I've been trying that. It works with yellow as well.'

'That's remarkable.' She searched through the canvases, pulling one out. 'Like this, you mean?'

He stared at it in amazement. 'Just like that, yes.' How strange. 'I wasn't aware you could inherit a painting style. It happened one day by accident when I picked up the wrong brush, but when I stood back and looked, it seemed to lift the tone. So I tried it out on other paintings.'

She put the canvas back. 'James was unique among his contemporaries for that technique. You can't be consciously copying it.'

He could hardly hold in his excitement. 'Tell me more about what he looked like.'

Leah placed her hand over his. 'He was striking. Taller than you, but otherwise very similar: lean, eyes a lighter brown, more like hazel. His hair would never lie flat on the top of his head, just as yours won't. I was convinced you were our son within minutes, when you ran your fingers through it. James had the same mannerism.' She lifted a hand and brushed her fingers along the side of his face. 'It seems strange to call you William, but I don't suppose you will want to revert to Thomas.'

'No, it might confuse people.' And me, he thought.

'I understand. The important thing is that you have come back into my life.' She turned away from him and collected together a bundle of items: pans of watercolour paint, tubes of oils and a collection of brushes. She set them out on the table in front of him, adding a few pieces of charcoal and several pastel sticks. 'They're yours. Use them well.'

His father had handled these. He couldn't believe it.

She looked at him, suddenly energised. 'I want to sponsor you.'

'Sponsor me? You mean persuade a gallery to exhibit my paintings?'

She laughed. 'I don't think you're quite ready for that. An exhibition will come later, if you work hard and if you're as talented as James was. Let's take it slowly. I'll pay for lessons. You can move in here... if that's what you want?'

He hesitated. 'I'm not sure. There's a lot to take in. And I don't want to leave Sarah, not so soon at any rate. She's been so kind to me.'

'Please don't worry. I rush at things; forgive me. Your loyalty to Sarah is commendable. One of my other artists lives in York, so we can see each other regularly, whatever you decide. Just let me know where you want to be, then I'll arrange lessons with one of my tutor friends.'

'I have so many questions for you, Mother. I don't know where to start.'

'We have all the time in the world. Now then, I think dinner will be ready. Go and change, and I'll see you in the dining room.'

CHAPTER 20

I t was hard to say goodbye the next morning. Leah held him close as they stood on the platform at the station.

'I'll come back soon,' he promised. All the information she'd given him was buzzing round his head like bees competing for a honeysuckle flower. How wonderful to have this close bond and to know at last how his life had begun, born to two people who loved each other so much. What a tragedy she'd had to bear, but now everything would be different, for both of them. He was an artist's son, and now he had the chance to make his dream come true.

Her lip quivered as she tried to smile. 'Don't wait too long to come back. It feels like I've found and lost you in one day.'

He picked up his bag, paused a moment then, on a delicious impulse, kissed her cheek. 'Bye, Mother,' he said, the words still seeming strange. He walked towards the train, resisting the temptation to skip with the joy of having found her. Instead, he waited until he reached the compartment before turning to give her a wave.

The gentle rocking of the train gave his thoughts chance to settle as he tried to make sense of his new situation. He'd woken early that morning and crept into Father's studio while Mother was sleeping soundly on the next floor down. The rising sun had brought a wonderful light to the room; it was obvious why Father had chosen this location. William had examined the pictures one by one, placing each in turn on the easel in the corner, and standing back to assess it, noting the composition, style and colours. It was so striking: the freshness of the brush strokes, those unexpected combinations of colour, and the way he'd placed objects or people in the scene. Father must have created some of them twenty years before. Did the art world consider them too daring at the time?

He already had a scene in mind for his next painting, based on a glimpse of the promenade at Scarborough as they'd approached the house, with the cliffs in the distance. It was such a pity he hadn't had a chance to explore it, but there'd be time for that later. He imagined it: ladies in their finery, twirling their parasols as they strolled along, and gentlemen leaning on the railings watching the fishing boats coming in to harbour. Young children played on the sands, running with kites in bright colours. It was time to experiment with other views, perhaps with more people in them doing everyday things.

In addition to Father's paints and brushes, Mother had given him a purse of money. With a pang of guilt, he thought of Sarah, Tinny and Grace's mother, all struggling to make ends meet.

He could imagine his father walking around Scarborough, gathering inspiration for his work. He should try that himself. Getting out to see different places and people might stimulate new ideas. If he gave Sarah some of Mother's money, she could find a girl to replace him while he took an occasional day off to go sketching in different locations. He could be generous, repaying them for their kindness; then Tinny could stop worrying about the takings from the shop.

Back in York, he made for home, conscious of his father's precious belongings stowed in his bag. It was like having a guardian angel to watch him grow, not only as a young man but also as an artist. He would be proud to use these paints and brushes.

As William turned the corner into Stonegate, an unexpected rush of affection came over him. After only two days, he'd missed Sarah's little shop and home. Without the encouragement she and Tinny had given him, he'd never have had the courage to persevere with his painting or the confidence to search for his family. Could he have the best of both worlds?

Sarah turned at the sound of the shop bell and gave a shriek of delight. 'Tinny!' she called. 'Look who's here!' She ran around the counter, beaming at him. 'I'm so glad you've come back. We were worried in case you decided you liked Scarborough better than York.'

'Not a chance. No one makes pies like you do. I'll take my bag upstairs and unpack, then I'll come back to help. It won't take me long.' He couldn't wait to lay out Father's materials on the table in his studio. It would give him such a thrill to use them.

'You'd better be ready to tell us all about your mother once we close.'

Tinny laughed. 'Don't believe a word of it, William. She's bursting with curiosity. As soon as it starts to quieten down, she'll be pinning you against the wall for information.'

'Don't worry, I'll tell you everything. Leah – Mother – is an incredible woman, and I found out about my father too. You won't believe it when I tell you what he did.' He looked past them and gave a cheeky grin. 'You'd better get back to it, Mrs Bennett. There's a queue forming.'

Back in his bedroom, he caught sight of his reflection in the mirror. The person looking back at him seemed older, with a hint of knowledge and confidence that wasn't there before. He'd just opened the door to a new adventure. And he had a difficult decision to make. If he moved to Scarborough, he'd make Mother happy and it was bound to help his new career. But how could he leave York, after everything Sarah had done to help him? Besides, Mother said she was often away on business, so he'd be left alone in that big house for days on end. At least he had company here.

Mother would understand he needed time to think about it. What was she doing now? Would she be in Father's studio, thinking of him? He had to work hard and convince her that he was worth investing in, so that no one could accuse her of favouritism. Whatever he achieved had to be through his own merit.

Hastily, he unpacked the bag then took the treasure trove of materials into his studio, viewing his paintings in a new light. There was definitely an echo of his father's style and subject matter. How fascinating. If only he'd known him.

He thought back to the day when he'd found the wooden box in the attic while searching for the telescope. To think of the times he'd used it, without knowing it belonged to his real father.

Why had Papa taken it from the wreckage that night? Did he think it was worth something? A scene came into his mind, a baby lying amid the debris, wailing, the box close by. He pulled the fragment from his pocket and examined it. This was with him at that crucial moment when Life chose him.

His lip quivered. How did his father die? Was it sudden, or did he know it was the end, his semi-conscious mind in torment at being torn from his son, sorrowful at the thought of his wife far away, unknowing, waiting?

He chose a brush, fingering the sable hairs. They were still soft and silky. His father couldn't have used it much; perhaps it was bought not long before his death. Was the picture he painted with it still hanging on someone's wall? The responsibility weighed heavily on his shoulders. Was he worthy enough, talented enough to do justice to his father's memory? The thought made him hesitate. He wouldn't try to use it yet. Sarah and Tinny were waiting for his news; they could share his joy at last. He put the brush back on the table, returned the piece of wood to his pocket, and went downstairs.

Trust the shop to be busier than ever. William rolled up his sleeves, put on an apron and started serving, in the hope of clearing the shop as soon as possible.

At last he locked the door and sat at the table while Tinny served tea. Soup and left-over bread rolls again. They could eat properly, now he had a bit of money.

'Well, we're all ears,' said Tinny. 'What did you find out? Did Leah Morgan prove she was your mother?'

'Yes, she did, in a way that was truly convincing. Let me test you first. Have you ever noticed my birthmark?'

Their expressions told him they hadn't.

'Well, she knew where it was, and she described the shape. Look.' He turned around and lifted the hair at the nape of his neck.

As he turned around, Sarah's expression showed she was convinced. 'I'm so happy for you,' she told him.

'It still feels strange,' he admitted. 'There was so much to take in. She told me my real father, James, was an artist. His studio is still there, intact, at the top of the house. You should see his paintings.'

Tinny's eyes widened. 'How wonderful. It means you've inherited your talent. You lucky thing.'

'I'd have been luckier if the shipwreck had never

happened,' he said. 'He would have taught me everything. There'd have been no need to skulk in my bedroom on an evening, painting in secret for fear of Papa finding out.'

'Of course. I'm sorry, I didn't think.'

William cursed himself for being harsh with her. It wasn't her fault; he had to admit it took a bit of believing. 'James was just starting to be successful when he died,' he explained. 'Suddenly Leah had to work out a way of making a living, with no training in the art world and no sense of business etiquette.'

It was hard to get the story in the right order so it made sense to them; he kept forgetting parts of it and had to go back to fill in the details.

'Well I never, this is the most exciting thing that's happened round here for ages,' said Sarah. 'But don't you go getting airs and graces, do you hear?'

William grinned. 'I haven't told you the best thing yet. She sponsors artists, so she's going to pay for me to have lessons.'

'That's incredible, William,' said Tinny, 'and no more than you deserve. You'll soon be good enough to hold your own exhibition, I know it.'

CHAPTER 21

One day could change everything, William thought as he stood in his studio in York on Sunday morning after church. Before he met Leah Morgan, he wasn't sure how to achieve his dream, but now the future was full of promise. She'd said he had talent, and she was prepared to take a risk on him. But he was no nearer deciding where to live. It was the one part of his conversation with Mother that he hadn't mentioned to Sarah and Tinny, knowing they'd want him to stay. But was that the right thing to do?

The two new canvases were ready for him now, underpainted with one of his old brushes, ready to make a start on his portrayal of children running with kites on the beach at Scarborough. The time spent sorting through his existing paintings had brought a mixture of pride and frustration, searching for any similarities to the striking features of his father's style. There were a few signs of it, but it had also made him more aware of his failings, seeing mistakes he hadn't noticed before. Thank goodness he was going to have lessons, to help him achieve the same standard of brushwork.

Was that why he been putting off the first use of Father's

brushes and paints, afraid he wouldn't come up to scratch? Such foolishness. They were only tools, and if he didn't use them now, perhaps he never would. He chose a piece of charcoal and sketched out the figures in the scene, then chose a tube of cadmium yellow paint and squeezed a blob on to a palette, mixing it with a tiny amount of turpentine. Good, it still behaved as it should. Burnt umber next, and a touch of zinc white, mixing them in different patches on the palette to create dark and light shades for the sand.

Then he selected a broad brush of soft sable, pristine and dry, sweeping it across the canvas to test it out. Good, it was light and controllable. He loaded it with colour and dabbed it on the canvas.

'William!' Tinny called out from the foot of the stairs.

No, not now. What rotten timing. Lunch must be ready. 'Coming,' he shouted, as he wiped his brushes clean.

Just as they'd started their meal, there was a knock on the door.

'Who on earth can that be on a Sunday lunchtime?' Sarah groaned.

'I'll get it, Mam,' offered Tinny.

A minute later she returned, looking awkward. 'Mrs Morgan is here to see William.'

Leah swept in. 'Please forgive me for arriving out of the blue like this,' she said. 'I had to come to York for an urgent meeting with one of my artists, and I couldn't leave without saying hello to William. I'm so looking forward to seeing his paintings.'

He rose from his seat. 'Mother, what a lovely surprise.' He kissed her cheek. 'Please let me introduce Mrs Sarah Bennett and her daughter Christina.'

Leah held out her hand. 'I'm delighted to meet you. You've been such a help to my son.'

'It's been a pleasure,' said Sarah. 'He's very special to us.

Would you like to join us for a meal? It's only modest, but you're welcome to share in it.'

William winced. Sarah obviously felt obliged to offer a meal.

'Only if you are sure it isn't an inconvenience,' said Leah.

'William, why don't you take your mother to see your paintings?' Sarah suggested.

That was clearly a ploy, so she could share out the food across four plates. Tinny took Leah's cloak, then opened the door for her.

'I'm sorry, Sarah,' William whispered as he passed her. 'You didn't have to offer her dinner.'

'We couldn't sit and eat in front of her. I'd rather eat a bit less than have a full plate go cold.'

He led Mother to his studio with a mixture of pride and nerves. She couldn't wait to come and see him, that much was evident. How wonderful that she sensed the same bond between them as he did.

Inside the room, he pulled out a few canvases and fidgeted as he waited for her to pass judgement.

'Very promising, a nice touch... you have a good under-standing of light and shade.'

He beamed.

'But your use of perspective needs work.'

'Oh.' She'd homed in on the technique he found hardest.

She gave a sniff. 'I'm sorry, I'm not usually this emotional. It reminds me of James' early work.'

'Don't apologise. It means so much to me, hearing about him.'

She gave a smile. 'I've spent such a long time bottling it up, unable to talk to anyone about him. We had a special relationship.'

'I love hearing you say that. You can tell me about it any time you like; I want to know everything about your time together. But we'd better get back to our lunch before it gets cold.' The look of longing in her eyes made him sure that she and James had known true love. Did they have special places in Scarborough, a favourite view across the bay, or a bench in a park? He couldn't wait to find out and visit them all.

He led her to the back room, where Sarah and Tinny were waiting at the table.

Leah sat opposite Sarah. 'I appreciate your hospitality. My meeting took longer than I expected, and I don't like eating alone in restaurants. I had resigned myself to doing without a meal until I got back to Scarborough.'

Soon their plates were clean. 'Tinny, give me a hand,' said Sarah, in a tone laden with insistence. They both scuttled into the kitchen and began whispering.

'I hope your urgent business wasn't too difficult,' said William, keen to hide what was going on in the kitchen.

'Not difficult for me, but it wasn't pleasant for him. It was one of my artists. He's got himself into a pickle, running up debts and telling everyone I'm arranging a major exhibition in London for him which will enable him to pay them off. I had to bring him down to earth.'

William admired her steely determination. She would protect his interests, without a doubt, even if she hadn't been his mother.

Sarah returned with the teapot and set it on the table, then turned to Leah. 'How does this sponsorship thing work, then?'

William cringed at her directness, but Mother didn't show any signs of taking offence.

'I pay for lessons, materials and so on, so William can learn his craft. When he has a body of work that is good enough to display, I contact a range of gallery owners to offer an exhibition and agree the dates.'

'Right. So, what's in it for you, then?'

'Sarah!' William glared at her. He waited for Mother's reaction. It would be understandable if she was angry.

Tinny entered with a tray of cups, poured the tea into them and handed them out.

Leah waited until they were all served before answering Sarah's question, in a calm, reasonable voice. 'It's a business arrangement, Mrs Bennett. By providing the money for William to develop his art, I'm buying a stake in his future sales. In time, I will take a commission on every painting he sells.'

'How much commission?'

'Sarah…' He had to stop this insolent questioning.

'You haven't had this discussion, have you?' Sarah looked at him knowingly. 'Have you signed a document?'

'No, but…'

'It should be a formal agreement, shouldn't it?' she insisted. 'It's only fair that you know how much of your income you will have to give away, before you accept her offer.'

'She's my mother,' he said. 'She's hardly going to steal my money.' This was getting out of hand.

Sarah ignored him and turned back to Leah. 'You said yourself it's a business arrangement. Well, you're talking to a business woman who understands these things. I've been running this shop for years, and you have to protect yourself. We both know we can lose our livelihood in a flash if anyone takes advantage of us.'

Leah sipped her tea. 'I wouldn't quite put it like that, Mrs Bennett, but I do understand your meaning. William is lucky to have someone as astute as you to look after his interests. But as he points out, as his mother, I'm in an ideal position to support him and help him develop his talent, as well as fulfilling James' dreams through our son. It's tremendously exciting.'

It was as if he wasn't there, the way they were talking about him, but he stayed quiet, glancing at Tinny to see what she made of it. Her face always betrayed her thoughts. She was observing Mother with a quiet wariness, her brow furrowed.

Leah smoothed the tablecloth over the edge of the table. 'I've been thinking it through over the last couple of days. It's best if no one knows that William is my son. He deserves to be recognised for his ability; there are jealous people out there, artists I've refused, who might claim that I was favouring him. That wouldn't be fair. As much as I love him, the fact that he's my son isn't a factor. I couldn't support him if I didn't believe he has the talent within him to succeed.'

Sarah nodded, as if reassured. 'Of course. It's wonderful that William has found you. And we're thrilled that you can help him improve his skills... aren't we, Tinny?'

'Er... yes. Yes, we are,' said Tinny, seemingly taken by surprise.

William frowned at her. She could have managed a smile.

Sarah cleared her throat. 'I'm sorry I sounded suspicious, Mrs Morgan, but this has all come as a shock to us. William didn't confide in us about his background until recently.'

She turned towards him with a look of reproach. 'I've got used to thinking of you as one of the family, you rascal. That's why I'm over-protective.' She turned to Leah again. 'I lost my husband, Bert, from cholera, and I nearly lost Tinny as well.'

Leah nodded in sympathy. 'Well then, you above anyone will understand how my world fell apart when James died. We loved each other beyond measure, and I sat in my home wondering if I wanted to carry on living. The pain of losing my baby son as well was unbearable. You will understand the loneliness, the pressure on you to make a living and stand up for yourself in a world run by men. I think we will get along fine. We both love William and want him to succeed. You must come to Scarborough, both of you, and we can spend time together.'

She made ready to leave. 'I think my groom will have finished at the inn now. Can I have my cloak please?'

Tinny ran to get it, while William kissed his mother on the cheek. Sarah and Tinny would never take up the offer of a visit, but at least Mother had made it. 'Thank you for coming,' he told her.

'The pleasure was mine. I'm so glad to have met you, Sarah, and you too, Christina. Goodness knows what might have happened if you hadn't taken my son in. And thank you for my lunch.' She fastened the cloak around her shoulders and beckoned William to show her to the door.

Out of sight of Sarah and Tinny, she held him close. He closed his eyes and inhaled her scent, trying to hold it in his memory for the coming days until he could see her again. He felt a surge of love for her, and the look she gave him as she pulled away suggested she felt that way too.

'Goodbye, my darling son. I love you so much, it breaks my heart to say goodbye. We must make sure we can spend time together, as often as my business trips will allow.'

'I'd like that,' he said with a smile. 'I'll wait to hear when you're going to be back in Scarborough for a suitable length of time. Goodbye, Mother.'

He waved her on her way, proudly watching her walk along the street, then he shut the door and returned to the table. 'Well, now you've met her, what do you think?'

'I thought she was looking down her nose at us at first,' said Sarah. 'But when she talked about your father, I could see how lonely she was. It's not easy to be a widow, let alone find a way to earn a living.'

'You always think the best of people, Mam,' said Tinny. 'I'm not so sure about her.'

'And there lies the difference between us, my love.' Sarah brushed crumbs off the table with a cloth. 'You've always been cautious about strangers.'

William nudged Tinny. 'Yes, look how suspicious you were when I arrived. It took a good few weeks before you even spoke to me.'

'Well I hope you'll be careful. She looks like she'd sell her own mother.' Tinny gave a sniff and disappeared into the kitchen. A moment later a clashing of pans and the clatter of crockery suggested she was taking her temper out on the dishes.

'She's not particularly impressed, is she?' said William.

Sarah leaned closer to him, lowering her voice. 'For a sensitive artist, you can be dim sometimes. She's been in a right mood since you left for Scarborough. She missed you.'

William stared at her. 'Did she say so?'

'She didn't have to; I can tell.'

'I need to check my paints,' he muttered, and fled upstairs to his studio.

He felt in his pocket for the piece of jet. As soon as his hand closed over it, Grace came into his mind, as if he could summon her simply by the touch of his fingers on the talisman, her bubbling laugh like a brook running over a bed of rocks, her eyes shining with passion when she saw injustice.

He must write and tell her about his discovery. It was easy to imagine how her eyes would light up, a dimple appearing in the corner of her mouth as she smiled at the news. Like him, she would see the pieces of the puzzle falling into place and understand what it meant to him, after the sadness he'd lived with. She could be trusted not to disclose it to anyone.

He couldn't imagine ever going back to Seaton now. York was his home, but even that might not be permanent. Mother had given him the choice of staying here or moving to Scarborough, whichever he wanted. But what did he want?

PART II

CHAPTER 22

William leaned against the railings and looked out over the bay to Scarborough Castle and the harbour, as the cries of the seagulls filled the sky. It was good to be out early on this bright morning after the long hours he'd spent in his studio lately, trying to prove himself to Mother. He desperately wanted to reward her faith in him, after the money she'd spent on his lessons and materials in the last eighteen months since they'd been reunited. How his life had changed in that time.

He lifted his face to the wind, inhaling the salty air that he missed so much when he was in York. The bustling resort made him feel alive, with the visitors coming and going, taking the sea air and enjoying the music at the Spa. There were constant changes in nature too: the ebb and flow of the tides, leaving different patterns in the sand, the sky with its cloud formations and varying hues of blue and grey reflected in the sea, and the trees and shrubs wearing their seasonal coats of many colours. It was easy to find inspiration for his paintings here. But it made Tinny and Sarah's life seem so humdrum that he'd taken to holding back from telling them too much about it each time he returned to York.

A girl passed by with a heart-shaped face and soulful eyes, reminding him of the flower girl in York. Was she still in her spot at The Shambles, pleading with the passers-by to purchase a single bloom, scared of a beating if she didn't earn enough? He hadn't seen her for a while, but that wasn't surprising, now he was spending so much time away from the city.

She would make a good subject for a painting. Perhaps he could draw attention to her plight, in the same way his father had portrayed the cockle pickers and fish sellers. He would enjoy pricking consciences among the upper classes about spending more money on a portion at a dinner party than would feed a working-class person for a month.

But there were more urgent things to think about, like how to handle Mother's insistence that he should move here. It was getting harder to resist; he had learned so much from being with her, and they were devoted to each other, but every time he thought he'd decided to do it, he was over-whelmed by a pang of guilt over leaving Sarah and Tinny. They couldn't survive without his money, and it would be disloyal to abandon them now, after everything they'd done for him. Besides, he'd miss Tinny too much. She stopped him from getting too fanciful about his career and she inspired him with ideas for paintings taken from the stories she loved to read.

He reached for his pocket watch, his eighteenth birthday present from Mother. Oh no, look at the time. He'd missed breakfast. She would understand though, knowing that he'd been working late last night on his latest canvas. It had taken an age to perfect the shading without spoiling the whole effect. With a sigh, he pushed himself off the railings and walked back to the house.

Mother was working at her desk in the corner of the sitting room.

'Good morning, Mother,' he said, kissing her cheek. 'I'm sorry I missed breakfast. I went for an early walk to clear my head.'

'Did you finish the painting?' she said, turning over a piece of paper and circling a figure at the bottom.

'I think so, but I'd better ask Mr Liddle if it needs any more highlights.'

'Hmm,' she said, still studying the paper. 'Knowing when to stop adding to a painting is one of the hardest lessons.'

'Yes, that's what I'm finding. I've been looking more closely at Father's canvases and I can see there's a freshness there that might have been lost if he'd over-worked it.'

'That's good, you're clearly getting the idea.' She pushed the papers aside. 'I have news for you. I've been consulting Mr Liddle about planning your first exhibition.

William's heart skipped a beat. 'Do you think I'm ready?'

She nodded. 'Nothing ventured, nothing gained. There's no doubt about your talent, and you have a good range of subjects and techniques in your work.'

'It just seems too soon. Do I have enough portraits? What if no one likes my paintings? Your reputation...' What if he embarrassed her? It was a daunting thought.

'You should have more confidence in yourself. Anyway, it's happening, so you need to prepare. I'm talking to Mary Ann Uppleby at Crescent Villa. She's recently added a large room to the house, and it would make an excellent exhibition space. Her husband was a solicitor and he led the development of The Crescent, but he died over twenty years ago. She likes to socialise. I'm sure she will be keen to hold your exhibition there and invite her friends. Many of them are wealthy.'

'If you're sure…'

'Trust me, William. I'm sure. Of course, you'll need to work harder; you must finish those canvases you've set aside. I'd like to see you here more often now. This is your job, not serving in a little shop.'

He nodded. It was best not to argue, when the prize was an exhibition. She loved him and wanted only the best for him, and after so many years apart, it was only natural for her to want to spend more time with him.

But where was the elation he expected to feel? This was what he'd been working towards under Mr Liddle's instruction. Instead, he felt a leaden weight of dread at the thought of a roomful of people passing judgement on his work. He wasn't ready for this. What if none of the paintings sold? They might hate them. Why couldn't he just enjoy putting oil on canvas, trying different things, knowing that they were only for Mother and his tutor's eyes? But he couldn't refuse; she'd invested in him as part of her business.

Breakfast didn't matter any more; he needed to be alone. He returned to the studio and stood at the window, trying to calm the nervous fluttering in his stomach. Then he knelt on the floor and began examining his paintings, selecting one canvas at a time and assessing it, then setting it aside as either yes, no or possible. Mother would have the final say, but he wanted to make a few suggestions.

If only Mama could see him now. When he'd found the box in the attic all that time ago, she could have taken it from him, but instead she'd conspired with him, finding ways of obtaining the other materials he needed. What risks she'd taken. She had shown faith in his ability, but she would never see how far he'd come. She would be his secret inspiration to make this exhibition a success.

He must write to Grace and tell her about it; she'd be thrilled for him. It might make amends for the harshness of his reply to her last letter, when she'd shocked him with her description of how sad Mama was, sobbing in church on the day of his birthday. He'd written straight back, full of anger that she should be so insensitive, and had put it in the envelope without re-reading it. It wasn't surprising that he hadn't heard from her since.

Well, now it was time to give her the good news that the second of his dreams had come true. He just had to make sure he didn't let the opportunity slip through his hands.

CHAPTER 23

The bakery kitchen was strangely silent as he entered. Sarah wasn't doing her usual humming, and the atmosphere was as frosty as the windows. She and Tinny were at opposite ends of the table, each concentrating on their own tasks. Something wasn't right.

He cleared his throat. 'I'm sorry I was late back last night. I hope I didn't wake you when I came in.'

Sarah shook her head. 'No, you didn't. It's good to have you back. How's the painting going?'

He'd wait to tell them about the exhibition. 'Pretty well; I've finished another Scarborough beach scene. What do you want me to do?'

'I think you'd better take over,' said Sarah, pointing at Tinny. 'She's beating the life out of that pastry. So much for a light touch. You need to start again.'

William glanced across; it was clear she'd been crying. 'What's the matter?' He put a hand on her arm, but she shrugged it off.

'Nothing, I'm fine,' she insisted, though her expression

told him something different. Then she rushed out of the kitchen.

'What's going on, Sarah?'

He'd never seen Tinny like this before; she was always so even-tempered. The pastry she'd left on the table was a soggy mess that couldn't be rescued. He discarded it and reached for the flour jar.

Sarah dried a tray. 'I don't think she slept much last night. She's tired, that's all.'

'I know her better than that. Is she ill?'

She heaved a sigh. 'For a supposedly sensitive artist, you're not very perceptive when it comes to people, are you?'

'Obviously not.' He measured out the flour and added salt to it while waiting for the answer. 'Well, are you going to enlighten me?'

Sarah gave a theatrical sigh. 'I've tried to tell you.' She wiped her hands on her apron. 'She's worried that Leah will take you away from us permanently.'

William rubbed the fat into the flour, but the rhythm didn't soothe him the way it usually did. He could understand that his coming and going might be unsettling for Tinny, knowing her love of routine. It had felt strange to him at first too, but he'd become used to it over time. He'd better not mention Mother's expectation that he would spend even more time in Scarborough.

'I don't have any plans to change our arrangement,' he said, swallowing down the lie.

'It might not be your decision, not when Leah starts to promote you. You must be getting to that stage, and London is the real centre for artists. Tinny would miss you more than you think.' She turned away and lifted the tea kettle from the range.

In silence, William added the water to the mix and swept

it round the bowl with his hands, pressing it together in a ball.

'Don't you have any views?' Sarah put a mug of tea in front of him and placed a hand on his shoulders to turn him round towards her. 'And I'm not talking to you as her mother, but as your friend. You are dear to me as well, and I don't want to see either of you hurt.'

'It's too much to take in,' he mumbled. 'I do care for Tinny, you must know that. I just hadn't realised she thought of me as more than a friend.'

'Granted, she doesn't give much away,' Sarah agreed. 'And you are a man, and not the most perceptive example of the species.' Her cheeky grin forced him to return a smile. 'You need to decide whether you have the same feelings for her. If you don't, you need to tell her sooner rather than later.' She started setting out tins on the tray.

He turned back to the table and started to roll out the pastry, cutting it into rounds and laying it in the pie tins for Sarah to fill with cooked meat. She'd decided to reduce the amount of filling to save money and wouldn't let him or Tinny do it. They worked in an uneasy silence until Sarah spoke.

'But for God's sake, don't make any promises unless you are absolutely sure, otherwise you'll have me to deal with.' She put the spoon down with a sigh. 'I'm sorry, William. Now I am talking as her mother. This is important.'

'I understand. But I thought we were fine as we were.'

Sarah shrugged. 'Maybe you are, and now you're back, she might settle better. I don't suppose you'd go and check on her for me, would you? I need to get a move on, and if you don't mind me saying, you're not the fastest pie maker this morning.'

William could sense his cheeks burning as he climbed the stairs and headed for Tinny's room. What could he say to her? Sarah was right about being under Mother's control; he couldn't make any promises that he'd always be here. It wasn't fair on Tinny. But Sarah's words had set him thinking. Decide whether you have the same feelings for her. Did he?

There was no reply to his knock. Was she ignoring him? A faint noise came from his studio. He peered round the door and saw her standing at the table, looking through his sketch pad.

She turned round as he entered. 'I'm sorry…'

'What for? You've done nothing wrong.' As he stepped closer, he became aware of the gentle curve of her cheek, and the way her wispy curls framed her face. He turned to look at the page. It was his sketch of the lobster pots on the quayside at Whitby.

'It seems such a long time ago that I drew that.'

'I'll always remember that day. I felt so grown-up and close to you. You gave me such a shock when you panicked on the boat. Of course, at the time, I didn't know your full story.'

He nodded at the memory. 'I was convinced we were going to sink. It was as if I was re-living the shipwreck. If you hadn't been there, I'm not sure what I would have done.'

Her physical presence seemed more noticeable somehow. She was slender yet strong in the way she stood so straight, and her apron was tied tightly around her slim waist, accentuating her shapely figure. Why hadn't he noticed she was no longer a girl, but a young woman? He felt an attraction, a desire to hold her close.

'I'd do anything for you, William; you must know that by now.'

Taking her hand, he entwined his fingers with hers and gently drew her towards him. He'd never kissed a girl properly before. He'd never wanted to, not in this way. As he bent his head towards her, she lifted her face and their lips met in a moment of tenderness, a closeness that he'd never imagined was possible.

The spell broke as she pulled away, but William held on to her hand, wanting to focus on the moment, inhaling her scent. Her eyes were bright with emotion, and suddenly he knew what he wanted.

'I have some wonderful news. Mother has just told me I'm about to have my first exhibition.'

'Oh my goodness!' She threw her arms around him, a look of wonder on her face. 'I'm so happy for you; it's what you've been hoping for all this time, isn't it?'

'It is, but now it's actually happening, it's scary.' He cleared his throat. 'Sarah said you've been worried about me lately. That tells me you care.'

She nodded. 'I do.'

'Then I have a question for you.' He held her hand, trying to steady himself as he went down on one knee. 'Tinny, I need you beside me on the journey I'm about to start. Will you be my wife?'

He would always remember this moment, the way her eyes widened with delight, as if she couldn't believe what she'd heard.

She pulled on his hand to bring him to his feet. 'Yes!' She was half laughing, half crying. 'Oh William, do you mean it?'

'No, I thought I'd pretend. You silly goose, of course I mean it.'

'You haven't mentioned the word love,' she said with a pout.

He frowned. 'I'm sure I did.'

'No, you didn't.' Her dimple appeared, and she burst out laughing.

'Oh dear, that wasn't a good start, was it?' He felt a blush come into his cheeks. 'I love you Christina Bennett. There, I said it. I love you. I love you.'

She gave a giggle. 'And I love you.' She grew pensive.

'What's the matter?'

'Oh nothing.'

'Christina?'

'Are you going to use my proper name?' She laced her fingers with his and snuggled into him.

'I quite like it, actually. Tinny sounds more like a little girl.'

She thought for a moment. 'It might take a while for me to get used to it. We'll see.'

'Well, my dearest Christina, you looked worried, and I want to know why. We're a couple, and we need to share everything, our worries as well as our joys.'

'I was just wondering whether your mother will let you stay here, seeing as she has grand plans for you.'

William wrapped his arms around her, enjoying the closeness of her body nestling into his. 'I'll be honest with you; I have no idea. But I promise I'll only agree to something if you are happy about it.'

'I might not have a say. When you are famous, we'll have to live in London won't we?'

If only he had the answer to that. 'If I'm famous. Perhaps. But that could be years away. Don't worry about things before they happen, my darling.'

She gave a tiny nod, and he felt her mood lighten. She pulled away from him and straightened her skirts. 'Can we tell Mam? She'll be thrilled.'

'I hope so.' He pushed back a strand of hair that had fallen on to her cheek and tucked it behind her ear. 'Oh. I don't have a ring for you.'

She shook her head. 'It doesn't matter. We can choose one together. You'll need to tell your mother as well.'

He frowned, thinking of Mama. If only he could share his news with her; she'd be overwhelmed with happiness if she knew he'd found love. Then he realised she meant Mother, not Mama. That was an entirely different prospect. How would she react?

'William? You've gone quiet. Are you all right?'

'Yes,' he lied.

What about Grace? A true friend would be glad he had found happiness; so why was there a knot in his stomach at the thought of putting it in a letter? He might wait a while. Telling her about the exhibition was news aplenty for now.

He reached for Tinny's hand. 'Come on, let's tell Sarah.'

They rushed down the stairs and burst into the kitchen, giggling like a pair of schoolchildren.

Sarah turned around with a look of surprise. 'Someone sounds happy. What's going on?'

'William's asked me to marry him,' said Tinny.

Sarah gave a sharp intake of breath and put a hand over her chest. 'Oh my goodness! That was the last thing I expected you to say.'

'It was a bit of a surprise to me, too,' said Tinny.

She looked from one to the other, beaming. 'Well I never! Did you say yes?'

Tinny laughed. 'Of course I did!'

Sarah reached out to gather them both to her. 'Then congratulations. I'm thrilled for you both.' She turned to William. 'It's very sudden... you haven't been spending time together behind my back, have you?'

'No, nothing like that's gone on, I swear it...' He caught her eye and shook his head in despair. 'You catch me out every time.'

She chuckled. 'When are you going to tell your mother? I hope she can take the excitement.'

'It might be best if we both go to tell her, face to face. She's in London until Wednesday, at an exhibition by one of her artists. I was due to visit on Thursday anyway, so we can go then.'

He turned to Tinny. 'I can't wait to show you Scarborough.'

'But Mam will need to organise some help in the shop,' she pointed out.

'I'll ask one of the girls from church,' Sarah replied. 'It'll only be for a day, won't it? You go off to Scarborough with your good news, and I'll be just fine here, planning the wedding in my head. I'll have it all sorted by the time you get back.' She gave a wink.

William smiled, knowing that given their financial situation, there wouldn't be much more to do than put on their best clothes and head off to church. But she meant well. 'Thank you, Sarah,' he said.

She glanced at the clock. 'Now then, I hate to interrupt this little celebration, but we only have five minutes before opening the shop, and we're behind with the pies.'

The day flew by, full of congratulations every time Sarah shared their good news with a regular customer. It caused such a queue in the shop that Tinny insisted that she stopped telling people. By closing time, they were exhausted. Sarah turned the sign round and locked the door with a sigh of relief.

'Oh my feet,' groaned Sarah. 'I never used to have this trouble. Must be old age catching up with me.'

'Just wait until I start selling my paintings, then you can retire and we'll open a tearoom,' William told her. He winked at Tinny.

'I thought you'd want me to stop working,' she said.

'Not if you don't want to. I thought it was your dream to run one?' He could tell it was the right answer by her delighted smile.

'Quite the modern gentleman, aren't you?' teased Sarah.

'You two will get on just fine. If there's one lesson I learned from Bert, it's that a couple need to encourage each other. Life's too short to argue, believe me.' She stood up. 'Well, I've had enough excitement for one day. I'm off for an early bedtime. You can clear the things away for me.'

'Very tactful, Mam.' Tinny smiled. 'But you don't have to go on our account.'

'Of course I do. You need time together to talk about your plans. You don't need me hovering over you. I really am tired out. Goodnight.'

CHAPTER 24

The shop was so busy today that William had stopped noticing when the bell rang, but there was no mistaking the hush that descended as an aristocratic-looking lady appeared, wearing a huge hat and carrying a matching parasol. Although advanced in years, her dress was of the latest style; he had taken to noticing the fashions of the day so he could portray them in his paintings. He smoothed his waistcoat to make sure he looked smart enough, and directed a smile at her, hoping it might help.

'Ah, young man,' she said, with the hint of an assumption that he was in charge. 'I see you have some delightful small cakes in the window. Could I trouble you for a box of six?'

'Certainly, Madam. Would you like to take a seat while I get your order ready?' He pointed towards the table and chairs by the window. There was a familiar look about her that he couldn't place. Perhaps she'd been in the shop before. Or could he have seen her at the Spa in Scarborough?

As she passed him, he realised. Of course, it was Lady Forbes from Chambers House, where Grace worked. She looked older and frailer than the last time he'd seen her. Papa had been cultivating a friendship with Lord Forbes, hoping to break into the elite circle of local businessmen and politicians. He wondered if that connection was still going strong.

'Thank you.' She followed him to the window, where he held out the chair for her. As she sat down, her maid came into view.

His stomach did a somersault. Grace. Here, right in front of him. It was a moment he'd imagined on so many nights when he couldn't get to sleep, until he had it to perfection. They would hug and slip straight back into their easy conversation, joking with each other and reminiscing. The reality was different; they couldn't even speak to each other. What was she doing here, a lowly house maid?

Grace looked in his direction, her eyes widening and a smile of recognition on her lips. The childish features and cheeky grin he remembered had been replaced with an air of beauty and confidence. She stayed silent, but her eyes conveyed an unspoken message: her employer mustn't realise who he was.

'I'll make up your order personally. I can serve you a cup of tea while you're waiting, if you'd like one?' Out of the corner of his eye, he could see Sarah watching, full of curiosity.

'No thank you; I am due at my dressmaker's shortly. I will just take the cakes.'

His hands trembled as he placed the cakes in the box and tied a ribbon around it. He couldn't resist a glance at Grace. She was watching his every move with a faint smile, absent-mindedly twirling a loose strand of hair in her fingers.

How could he snatch a moment to speak to her, with Tinny standing beside him at the counter? Even if he could, what would he say?

The box of cakes was ready; all he had to do was ask for payment. This was his only chance. 'Here you are, madam,' he said, putting the box on the table and placing a hand-written bill on top.

She looked at it and passed a small purse over to Grace. 'It's terribly hot in here; I need some fresh air. Pay the man and meet me outside. Be quick about it. We mustn't be late.' She rose from the chair, directing a slight nod at William. He inwardly said a thank you to God for the opportunity.

Grace spoke before he could get any words out. 'I wasn't sure she'd take my hint to come here. It's so good to see you.'

'And you. Are you all right?'

She blushed. 'I'm fine, yes. Fell on my feet with this job. I've been promoted to Her Ladyship's maid. It's long hours, but she treats me nice.'

William hesitated. He had so many questions to ask, and so little time to ask them. But he wasn't sure he wanted to know the answers. 'Is everyone at home well?'

'Muddling along as usual. Mam's tearing her hair out at my brothers. They're always in trouble, stealing apples or getting into fights.' Her gaze was steady. 'Or were you asking about your parents?'

He wasn't going to answer that. 'What are you doing here?'

'Her Ladyship has an appointment at the dressmaker's. She needs me to help her in the fitting room.' She opened the purse and counted out the coins.

'Sounds a long way to come for a dress.'

'It is, but it's for a royal visit. Never mind that. We're staying here tonight. Imagine, me in a hotel.' Her voice dropped to a whisper. 'Is there any chance we could meet?' She glanced out of the window.

William hesitated. Tinny wouldn't be impressed if she knew he was meeting a girl from his past, and even worse, one with whom he'd secretly been exchanging letters. He'd have to take the risk. 'When, and where?'

'We're at the Royal Station Hotel, which strangely is next to the station.' She chuckled at her own joke. 'I can't believe I'm staying there. It's the grandest place I've ever seen, although I'm sleeping in what looks like a cupboard with a bed shoved in it.'

'Won't Lady Forbes need you there to attend to her?'

She shook her head. 'You mustn't tell anyone, but she drinks. A lot. By ten o'clock she'll be sound asleep; even a thunderstorm won't wake her.'

Every family had their secrets. 'In that case, I'll meet you outside the hotel at half past ten.'

A knock on the window made them both jump. It was Her Ladyship; she waved at Grace to hurry.

'I have to go. I'll see you later.' She handed over the coins, letting her fingertips rest on his hand, then she was gone.

William stood transfixed, still feeling the trace of her fingers on his. He had to meet her tonight, no matter how uncomfortable it was keeping it from Tinny. He would take the back door key and slip out once Tinny and Sarah had gone to bed. They'd be none the wiser.

The rest of the day was spent remembering how Grace used to make him laugh like no one else had ever done, with her irreverent attitude and the daring things she did. She might have been angry at his desertion, but if he'd stayed in Seaton, Papa would never have permitted them to continue their friendship. They'd have had to resort to stolen moments whenever their paths happened to cross. It would have been exciting, but frustrating.

At Chambers House, Grace was surrounded by the finest things, and he could imagine her parents' pride at her having such a respectable job. But why had Lady Forbes chosen her, above others who might be more experienced? Was it a scheme, hatched between Her Ladyship and Mama, to get Grace to divulge some information about his whereabouts?

At nine o'clock, Sarah yawned and declared she needed her bed. Off she went, and William sat with Tinny for another half hour, while she chattered on about the wedding.

At last she rose from the chair. 'Well, it's been a busy day again, so I'm going up too.'

'Goodnight my love.' He gave her a kiss. 'I'll have a hot drink, then I might sit here and do a sketch.' As he straightened his trousers, his fingers ran over the door key in his pocket, the guilt weighing heavily upon him.

He sat for a while in the silence, going over his plan. What should he say if the police stopped him, wanting to know what he was doing out so late? He'd have to make up a story, something about an emergency and a sick relative. That would do the trick.

The hands on the mantelpiece clock inched their way round, until he was sure Sarah and Tinny must be asleep. The house was silent as he crept up the stairs in his stockinged feet and changed into warmer clothes. There'd be nowhere to shelter out there at this time of night. Once ready, he took some charcoal and paper downstairs. By a quarter past ten, he had completed a rough sketch of the fireplace and its ornaments, leaving it on the table for Tinny to see, in case she couldn't sleep and came for a glass of water. She'd assume he'd given up and gone to bed. He retrieved his boots from the cupboard under the stairs, his fingers shaking as he laced them.

There was a sharp chill in the air as he left by the back door. The sky was sprinkled with stars and everything was quiet, except for a dog yapping in a nearby yard. His heart pounded with the wrongness of it all, but he had to talk to Grace.

CHAPTER 25

William's boots clicked on the pavements as he paced back and forth opposite the hotel, trying to avoid attracting the attention of the doorman who was standing just inside the main entrance. Perhaps Lady Forbes hadn't gone to sleep yet. He walked a little further along the street, then turned at the sound of a door opening. No, it wasn't Grace. What if there was another door?

At last she emerged. He strode across the road, calling out her name.

She greeted him with a smile of relief. 'I'm sorry, I couldn't get away any sooner. She's been worse than usual, and I needed to get one of the hotel staff to help me get her into bed. I was so embarrassed. The things I've discovered since I started working at the big house… you'd never believe me if I told you.'

'It doesn't matter, you're here now. Can we walk?'

'Yes,' she said. Her hand brushed against his as they crossed the road. 'I can't believe we're here together. It was lovely to exchange letters, but I've been dying to see you in person. What have you been up to?'

'All in good time. I'm really worried that Lady Forbes might have recognised me. Do you think she did?'

'I don't think so. I made sure I didn't mention your name.'

'Yes, I was glad of that.' He stopped walking and took both her hands in his; how cold they were. He rubbed them gently. 'I'm happy here. It will only cause problems if they find out where I am. Imagine how it would make Mother feel.'

'You should have come back to ours that day. My mam would've let you stay until you sorted out what you wanted to do.'

'I couldn't do that. It was obvious yours would be the first place they thought of. No, I had to get away. Once I found out I wasn't their child, there was no reason to stay.'

Grace turned to him, her eyes full of reproach. 'Didn't I mean anything to you?'

'Of course you did… you still do.' Why did he always say the wrong thing?

He gestured towards a nearby bench for them to sit down. 'I meant there was no family to stay for. It tore me apart, leaving Mama. You know how much we loved each other. But I couldn't bear the thought that she'd lied for so many years. And once they were aware that I'd found out, things could never be the same.'

She sat on the bench and crossed her arms, rubbing them to keep warm. 'We'd have protected you from them. Just disappearing like that… it was awful.'

This was what he had feared, hurting those he cared about. 'I'm sorry; I wanted to come to you, but I had to get away as fast as possible. My world had collapsed. They had no right to claim me as their own that day, not without trying to find out if I had any family alive.' He sat beside her.

'If you'd stayed, you might have found your real mother sooner. Once the truth was out, your Mama would have helped you search for her. Instead, you've got nowhere. You've wasted your life working your fingers to the bone in a bakery and trying to fit your painting in.'

'It hasn't been that bad. And your gift helped when things were difficult.' William brought out the piece of jet from his pocket and opened his palm to show it to her.

'You've kept it all this time? I thought you'd have left it behind.' She reached out and stroked it.

'It's one of my most treasured possessions. You're not getting it back.'

'Knowing you still have it means a lot to me.' A tiny sigh escaped her lips. 'I'm sorry for going on like this. But you don't see the consequences of your actions like I do. Lady Forbes says that apart from the times your Mama visits her at Chambers House, church is the only place she goes.'

William bowed his head. Her criticism was even worse than his self-punishment. 'Don't judge me, please.' He glanced at her. 'I was hoping you'd tell me how the lifeboat crew have been doing. Life's a bit tame here without the chance of rushing out to cheer them on. Has your Dad been in any more exciting rescues?'

Her eyes shone with pride as she nodded. 'Oh yes. He's been given an award for bravery, for rescuing a ship's crew. Mam told him off when he came home injured, but she's forgiven him now.'

He listened enthralled as she described the rescue. With typical courage, Tom had put the safety of those he'd rescued before his own, and had almost been pulled under by a sailor who'd panicked as he was being helped to the lifeboat.

It was no good succumbing to nostalgia. He had to make the most of his time with Grace, but it was important that she understood his situation. He couldn't be disloyal to Tinny.

'I've had some wonderful news. Mother says it's time I

exhibited my paintings, and she's arranged for a well-connected lady to host my launch party in Scarborough.'

Her smile made it even more special.

'How wonderful! I told you it wouldn't be long before you had the chance to show the world your talent, didn't I?' She shivered. 'Can we walk again? I'm freezing to death here.'

'Good idea.' He stood and helped her to her feet. Saying goodbye was the last thing he wanted to do, but they were already on the edge of impropriety, or had more likely crossed it. 'We could go back to the station and shelter there. Do you need to be awake early tomorrow to go home?'

'I doubt it. With a bit of luck Her Ladyship will have one of her longest ever sleeps, to give me a chance to catch up. I always have to help her dress. She gets the shakes on a morning and can't fasten her own clothes. It's sad, but comical too; I struggle to keep a straight face.'

William smiled. 'I can imagine. You always were a giggler.' He started laughing. 'Do you remember the councillor's wife and her awful hat?'

'Oh, I was in so much trouble for that. I couldn't see the vicar, there was that much fruit on it, and when Teddy pretended to take a grape off and eat it... your Papa turned and glared, which set me off even more.'

It all came rushing back. He hadn't laughed like that for a long time. As they walked, he kept glancing at her, trying to fix her features in his mind so he could never lose the image of her again.

Her expression became solemn. 'I am glad you've done well here, you know, despite what I said.'

He nodded. 'Yes, I've been lucky.'

All too soon they were back at the hotel. He had better tell Grace the whole story while he could. It wasn't the sort of thing you could put in a letter. 'There's something else I wanted to tell you. I'm getting married.'

Grace's eyes widened. 'Married? Heavens, the surprises keep on coming, don't they? Who to?'

'Christina, Sarah's daughter.'

Grace turned away, but not quickly enough to hide a flash of disappointment. 'I see.' She pulled her coat around her. 'You didn't look far, did you?'

This was harder than he'd thought. 'You're a dear friend, Grace, but you didn't think we had a future together, did you?'

She sniffed, trying to bury her face in her coat. 'It just sounds sudden. You're too young to marry.'

'I've had to grow up fast since I came here. Anyway, it's not long since I asked her. The wedding could be a year or more away.'

'Was she the one serving in the shop?'

'Yes.'

'Plain little thing. Does she eat all the cakes?'

'Grace! Don't be so horrible; she isn't plain, and anyway, you shouldn't judge people you don't know. She's a very loving person. Both she and Sarah suffered so much when her father died.'

'It sounds more like a rescue mission. Do you honestly expect me to be thrilled at your news? That's the trouble with you, William, you don't think about the impact of your actions on everyone else.'

The barb hit its target. Was it always going to be like this with her?

'You think Christina's not good enough for me, don't you? But you're wrong, Grace. You don't know her like I do. I've spent every day with her, and I know her inside out: her little ways and her kindnesses. She works so hard and never complains. I'd have been lost without her and Sarah.'

Grace came closer and put her head on his shoulder. The

smell of her hair and skin filled his senses. It was churlish to refuse to hold her close.

'You can't blame me for reacting like that,' she said. 'You know I've always wanted to be close to you.'

He looked into those chocolate brown eyes and felt the tug of a shared soul. This was a test, wasn't it? If he could resist kissing her, then marrying Tinny was the right thing to do. A picture of his fiancée's trusting blue eyes came into his mind and he pulled away from Grace.

'I don't want to lose your friendship over this, Grace. You mean a lot to me, and if I hadn't run away… well, who knows what might have happened between us? We both wrote about loving each other, and it was true at that point. But things change. I'm here, and you're there. If you can't be pleased for me, then there's nothing more we can say to each other.'

He turned away from her, one step that felt like a hundred miles, and started walking away.

Her touch on his shoulder was like a spark from a flame. 'All right, you win.' She poked him in the chest, breaking the spell. 'But she'd better look after you, or she'll have me to answer to.'

'We already look after each other. I know we'll be fine.'

She nodded towards the hotel. 'I'd better go in. I don't know when we'll see each other again, so I'll wish you the best of luck.'

He'd known tonight couldn't last forever, but saying goodbye was harder than he expected. 'Come to our wedding. Please. I'd like you to be there.'

She brightened. 'Would you?' Then she pulled a face. 'But I'm not sure Lady Forbes will allow me the time off. I might have to tell her my grandmother has died. As long as she doesn't work out that she already has. Twice in fact. Once for real, and once so I could look after Mam when she was poorly. But that was when I was reporting to the housekeeper.' She gave the impish grin that he recognised so well.

'Don't expect anything too grand,' he warned her, 'now that you're used to the finer things in Lady Forbes' life. It will be the worst attended wedding York has ever seen. Christina only has Sarah, and I have an older friend Johnny.' He didn't mention the possibility of Mother taking it over, in which case it would be a different prospect.

'Write and tell me the date. Now I really must go. It doesn't seem so hard, now I know I'll be seeing you again.' She stood on her tiptoes and gave him a fleeting kiss on the cheek.

'Goodbye Grace.' He touched his face where her lips had brushed it as he watched her run into the hotel.

CHAPTER 26

Tinny climbed into the train and chose a seat, watching William settle next to her. Her fiancé. Her heart gave a little jiggle at the thought of the word. The carriage soon filled up, and the guard blew his whistle. They were off, on a journey she didn't relish making, as much as she loved him.

'I'm so nervous about this,' she confessed.

'Don't be. Once Mother gets to know you, she'll love you just as much as I do.' He reached for her hand and gave it a squeeze. The lady opposite smiled, and Tinny felt a nip of joy.

They watched the countryside through the billowing steam as the train increased its speed.

'I wonder what it would be like to live on a farm?' Tinny mused.

She listened, enthralled, as William told her about the boys in his class who had lived in the farmhouses around Seaton Carew, the rhythm of the seasons and the tasks that had to be done.

'There was good money to be made for boys who didn't mind hard work,' he said, counting on his fingers as he listed the different jobs his friends had done: potato picking, cleaning the barns ready to store the grain, looking after the cows, and helping with the harvest.

'Did you do any of that?' She loved hearing snippets of new information about his past. It was like opening a door into another world, piecing together bits of his experiences to better understand him.

'No, Papa would never allow it. He couldn't abide dirt, and he'd have been furious if I'd missed any lessons.'

'Didn't you ever disobey him?'

'Sometimes I used to sneak out to the lifeboat station to sketch the boat, like the day I stowed away. But I always did as I was told, as far as my lessons were concerned. I liked school, anyway, apart from the bullies. Performing well in lessons was the only way I could get any praise from Papa. But he made me leave and employed a governess to teach me. That was dreadfully boring.'

'Well I can tell you now, if we're lucky enough to have a son, I want him to have the freedom to be himself.' Why had she said that? It was the first time she'd even thought about having bairns, let alone say it out loud.

She hoped he didn't think her forward. But it was part of the marriage service: 'First, It was ordained for the procreation of children, to be brought up in the fear and nurture of the Lord, and to the praise of his holy Name.' She tried to imagine them with a clutch of boys and girls at their feet. Goodness knows how they'd afford to keep them. But God would provide. No matter; she had more immediate things to think about.

At last they arrived at the station. 'Is your mother meeting us?' she asked as they walked along the platform and out into the open air.

He shook his head. 'No, I haven't actually told her you're coming with me. I thought it would be better as a surprise.'

'Are you sure that's wise?' She couldn't imagine Leah approving of an unexpected visit.

He took her hand and gave it a squeeze. 'I want to see her natural reaction to our news. Come on, I've been looking forward to showing you round. We'll go to the promenade first. It's not very far.'

Tinny let him lead her through the streets and into the gardens near the Crescent, where he pointed out a grand house. 'Isn't this magnificent? This is where my exhibition's going to be held.'

She looked at the imposing stone frontage. 'Just think, if you're successful in years to come, we could even buy a place like that as our home.'

'I thought you were worried about moving away from York?'

A blush warmed her cheeks. 'Yes, I was. But you'll be my husband, and wherever you are is where I want to be. We'll do everything together.' She squeezed his hand.

'Naturally, but I wouldn't want to take you away from Sarah.'

'Oh, don't worry about her. She must know deep inside that one day I'll leave.' A pang of guilt arose in her stomach. She wasn't sure that was true, but it was a wife's duty to follow her husband, and a dutiful wife was what she wanted to be. Today wasn't the day to worry about it. 'Well, are we going to take a walk by the sea?'

'In a while; you'll have to be patient. First, I have a surprise for you. Come this way.'

She pestered him to tell her where they were going as they walked on, but he wouldn't be persuaded. Turning a corner, he stopped and pointed to a large sign that read 'South Cliff Railway'. He took her hand and stepped out into the road.

'Look out!' she yelled, just in time to stop him walking

into the path of a horse and carriage. They let it pass and crossed the road.

'What on earth is this?' she asked, looking at the huge drop to the shore below.

'A funicular railway,' said William, grinning.

'A what?'

'It's a carriage on a track, that takes you down the cliff to the promenade.'

'But it's so steep. How do you stop yourself from falling over?'

'Ah, that's the beauty of it. The clever thing is that it has legs holding it level the whole time, driven by steam pumps. Look, here it comes.' He pointed at a wooden carriage coming into view, ambling up the slope and groaning at the effort like an old man with creaking bones. 'Come on, let's get a ticket.' He guided her over to the ticket office, and they joined the queue.

'Are you sure it's safe?' she asked, gripping his hand.

'Yes, I'm absolutely sure. You're not frightened, are you?'

'No. I just like to understand something before I put my life in its hands.'

He chuckled. 'This is a lot safer than the boat you got me on at Whitby. Come on, I've been dying to try it ever since I saw it. The fare's only a penny.' They joined the queue and shuffled towards the booth, where he bought their tickets.

There was just enough room for them in the waiting carriage. They held on to the leather straps as it descended, and Tinny peered out of the window, entranced. 'Ooh, what a lovely view,' she exclaimed. 'The boats are bobbing about like they're made of paper. And there are so many visitors!'

They reached the bottom and stepped out on to the promenade among the crowds. In the distance they could hear a brass band, amid the shrieks of children and the busy chatter of adults. Tinny marvelled at the ladies parading in the latest fashions, holding parasols to shield their faces from the sun. Grubby children chased each other along the promenade, eager to get to the beach, and seagulls screeched as they wheeled overhead, swooping to grab the remnants of a picnic from the sand.

'I wish you'd brought me here before; it's so different to York. I understand now why you've livened up your paintings with people,' Tinny told him. 'Look at all these lovely dresses.'

'If my exhibition's a success, I'll treat you to a couple of new gowns,' he told her.

As they walked towards the Spa, the sounds of a string ensemble floated through the air.

'Can we go and listen for a while?' she asked. How wonderful it was to see a different place, just like their day in Whitby. If William hadn't entered her life, it would never have happened.

'Of course. Come on,' he said.

They stood at the edge of the outdoor area where the musicians were playing. The music seemed to drive her nerves away, letting her cares float off into the distance. She could be someone different here, instead of a humble shop assistant living a relentless routine day in, day out. One day, when William was a famous artist, she'd come here with her new friends, to while away the day, enjoy a nice lunch and tell them about his latest exhibition. It seemed like a far-off dream; she'd have to be patient and trust in God to show them the way to make it happen.

They joined in the applause at the end of the piece. Then the bubble burst as William pulled out his pocket watch. 'We'd better get along to Mother's, I suppose,' he said.

Tinny took his hand. 'You sound as nervous as me.'

He gave her fingers a gentle squeeze of reassurance. 'I'm just trying to imagine how she'll react.'

They walked over the Cliff Bridge, marvelling at the view, and arrived at St Nicholas Cliff. The Grand Hotel dominated the area, its stonework bright in the sunshine. Tinny listened in awe as William showed off his knowledge of its design, gleaned from Leah.

'I couldn't believe it when I heard the way they'd planned it: four towers to represent the seasons, twelve floors for the months, fifty-two chimneys for the weeks, and three hundred and sixty-five bedrooms for the days of the year. 'They even built it in a V shape, for Queen Victoria,' he told her.

'Yes, but are the beds comfortable?' she asked. That was far more important.

Now for the inquisition, she thought, as he led her through the gate to Leah's front door. It had a slight air of faded grandeur, with its weathered stone and tall windows with heavy curtains. William rapped at the door and walked straight in, urging her to follow. As they were taking their coats off, Leah appeared.

'William! How lovely to see you.' She leaned forward and kissed him on the cheek, then stood back. 'And Christina too; what a surprise. A day trip, is it?'

Tinny edged closer to William. 'Something like that.'

Leah asked her maid to fetch tea, and led them into the front room, inviting them to sit on the sofa.

'If I'd known you were both coming, I could have planned a nice lunch and a trip to the Spa for a concert.'

William cleared his throat. 'I didn't think I'd be bringing Tinny until a day or so ago.'

'Have you seen Mrs Uppleby yet? The sooner she approves your theme for the exhibition, the better. You need to get on with—'

'This is a personal visit. We wanted to share our news.' He paused for courage. 'We're getting married.'

Leah's face was inscrutable as she spoke. 'Congratulations.'

Was that all she had to say? That wasn't the reaction they'd hoped for. Tinny bristled. 'Are you pleased for us?' she asked.

'Of course I am,' Leah replied. 'It's just come as a shock. A surprise, I mean. I didn't realise you were close.'

'It's only happened recently,' said William. 'I was thinking about my future, and I realised I wanted Tinny to be at the centre of it.'

'Well, I hope you're prepared to move as William's career develops.'

'Naturally,' Tinny said. She wouldn't give Leah any excuse for criticism. Besides, it was her duty to support him when she became his wife.

'Let me see your ring, dear.'

Tinny got up from the sofa and extended her hand to her future mother-in-law. She couldn't stop fiddling with the ring, which they'd only chosen the day before. William had insisted that she tried several styles, and she had settled on a small opal surrounded by tiny pearls.

Leah took her hand, studying the ring. 'Hmm. Very understated, I have to say. Didn't you want diamonds? William, you should have bought her diamonds.'

Tinny pulled her hand away. 'I love it, and that's what matters.' How dare she criticise their choice? She turned towards William, seeking his support. He looked bewildered.

'I imagine you'll have a long wait to get married.' Leah said.

'We have plenty of time; we're only young,' Tinny replied.

'I suppose you have to be practical. It will take a long time for your mother to get the money together.'

'Right, I think we've said what we came to say,' said Tinny. She marched out of the room without looking at

William, trusting him to follow. When he didn't, she stayed in the hall, leaning against the wall, listening and waiting for him to tell Leah that it was unacceptable to speak to her like that.

'You want to watch her,' Leah said. 'Looks like she has a nasty temper.'

'You provoked her, Mother. I think we'd better go; we don't have a lot of time before the train home. I'll visit Mrs Uppleby next week, then we can discuss the exhibition.'

Tinny tried to calm herself ready for his appearance.

Leah's voice rang out, as if making sure she would hear. 'I was going to offer to pay a decent sum towards your wedding. But only if she learns some respect.'

At last, William emerged. She flashed a look of fury at him and ran outside, her skirts swishing as she scurried along the path.

'You shouldn't have walked out like that, my darling.' He rushed to get to the gate before her and held it open.

'Don't you take her side.' Her boots clattered as she strode along the street.

'I'm not. But you both need to learn to get along.'

'I won't put up with her saying horrible things about Mam. She works harder than your snooty mother, who as far as I can see spends most of her time at cocktail parties and dinners, charming the gallery owners. Although charming is hardly the right word for her.'

William grabbed her hand and stopped dead in his tracks, forcing her to stop walking. 'Calm down, Christina.'

She flinched at his chiding. That dreadful woman had ruined the day in a single moment. 'Don't you tell me to calm down.' She turned towards him and saw the hurt in his eyes. 'I love you, William, and I can't wait to be your wife. But I will not be talked to like that. This ring is more precious to me than a thousand diamonds, and if she can't see that—'

She groaned and stamped a foot in frustration.

'I'm on your side, you know that. Please try to be civil, for me, even when she annoys you. I'll have a word with her.' He pulled her close, but as he leaned into her, he knocked her hat off, and the breeze sent it bowling along the street.

'Oh no… quick, get it!' she called out. He ran after it, but just as it came within his grasp, a gust of wind sent it tumbling further away and he had to give chase again. It happened twice more, until at last he managed to grab it. She gave a giggle, then burst into uncontrollable laughter. William walked back towards her, unable to resist joining in.

He brushed the dust off her hat as best he could before handing it back to her for inspection. Their laughter tailed off, and they fell back into their easy companionship.

She picked at the material with her fingers, watching the light catching the opal in the ring. It was just the right size for her slender fingers. Leah had been cruel to criticise it, and to mock Mam's financial position. William needed to make his mother realise how hard it was, working in the baker's shop day after day. But she had to try harder too, otherwise she might ruin any chance of William achieving his dreams.

CHAPTER 27

Their visit to Leah had unsettled them both. William pummelled the dough one morning as if he was punishing it, afraid he couldn't hold his tongue if Tinny started to go over it all again. If only there was a way to get his mother and his fiancée together soon to agree a truce, instead of each stewing over the incident for weeks until he could take her to Scarborough again.

How could he shake off this feeling of being torn between them? One day his sympathies lay with Mother, and the next he was all for Tinny. Mother had been through so much loss that she was bound to be over-protective. She only wanted the best for him. But Tinny was the best. He just needed to make her see that.

It was time to stop worrying about it and find a solution. The two of them must have something in common besides their love for him, a shared interest. If only he could discover what it was. After the exhibition, he would work out a plan to bring them together.

The exhibition. It was his one chance to make a good impression, the chance he'd been waiting for, and he couldn't afford to disappoint Mother. There could be influential people there. Still the doubt hovered. Was he good enough?

The postman came in and handed him a few letters.

'Thank you, Mr Groves. Those bills never stop coming, do they?' William put them on the table in the back room. Among the envelopes, he spotted one with Grace's rounded handwriting. He put it into his pocket and carried on with his tasks, wishing he could open it there and then. It was a good sign that she was writing to him again, wasn't it? But was she still full of resentment that he was marrying Tinny?

He was so distracted that he miscalculated a price twice, and Sarah had to tell him to cheer up and talk to the customers. At last the queue vanished and he could snatch a moment to go into the back room and open the letter.

Dear William,

I'm still pinching myself that we had the chance to talk. In all the excitement, I forgot to say I hope your exhibition goes well, but there's probably no need. It's bound to be a big success. I shouldn't have been rude about Tinny, and I'm sorry. Disappointment made me say it. You were right: she is there and I'm not.

But if things ever go wrong and you need someone to talk to, I hope you will come and find me. Don't worry about your Mama and Papa. You are a man now and they can't control you.

Thank you for inviting me to your wedding, but I won't be able to afford it. I have to work hard and save every penny for Mam and Dad. It isn't the worst job in the world, so don't be sorry for me. I will be fine.

Your Mama came to church on Sunday and she looked so frail and miserable that I wished I could tell her you were alive and well. Don't worry, I didn't. See, I can respect your wishes even when I don't agree with them. I imagine you won't want me to write when you are married, so this will be my last letter. I hope you are happy. Just remember I will always love you.

Fondest thoughts,

Grace

Her last letter? He sat holding the paper in his hand, trying to absorb her words. She would always love him. But not enough to keep writing to him. How could she deny him the chance to keep in touch?

He put the letter in his pocket and returned to the shop, composing a reply in his head.

Time dawdled, but at last he turned the sign to 'Closed'. William ate his meal as fast as he could and ran upstairs to write back to Grace.

Dear Grace,

It was wonderful to see you last week, and I'm sorry we quarrelled. It must have been hard for you to hear that I'm marrying Tinny, and I was insensitive about it. I wish you could come to the wedding. Let's wait and see when it is. I might be in a better position by then, able to send you some money so you can come.

Please don't stop writing to me. I delight in hearing from you; it's like a window into your world and it helps me imagine what you are doing. Please reconsider. It means so much to know that you will always love me. I love you as a dear friend, and I say a prayer for you every night. Can we still be friends?

William

CHAPTER 28

'I'm ready!' Tinny shouted from the landing.

William put on his new jacket, bought with some of Mother's money, and emerged from his room, ready for their day out to the fair at Rawcliffe village. She was wearing her best dress and bonnet in honour of the occasion. How excited she'd been when he broke the news that he'd ordered a carriage to take them.

It was going to be a good day; he could feel it in his bones. After all the time he'd been spending in his studios lately, both here and at York, it was time to pay attention to his fiancée. How much longer could he persist with this dual life? It filled his thoughts as the carriage set off, only interrupted by the need to make appropriate encouraging noises as Tinny prattled on about the latest book she was reading.

Despite the tension over his choice of Tinny, the time he was spending with Mother in Scarborough was more precious than he could put into words, their closeness and shared ambitions creating a sense of belonging that he'd never thought possible. He loved the time they spent sitting by the fire on an evening, when she told him about her

203

protégés: the difficult ones who thought they knew it all, those with real talent who always seemed to lack self-confidence, and the intelligent artists who had an eye on the latest trends. She preferred the latter, because they gave her the best chance of success. The way she didn't hesitate to take financial risks for greater returns was impressive; he could never be that brave.

Why she had never re-married? When she spoke of the launch parties and the meetings she had with art dealers, her face was animated, enthused by the vivid world of colour and expression that she lived in. It was a wonder she wasn't surrounded by suitors. She must be completely devoted to Father's memory.

Yet again, William put off the decision about where to live. He would bear the constant travel back and forth, so he could be close to both Mother and Tinny, and hope everything would resolve itself after the wedding, whenever that might be.

'Look – there's the fairground!' called Tinny, bringing him back to the present as she bounced up and down with joy.

He leaned across to see from her side, and smiled at the vibrant scene ahead, full of striped awnings and bright lights. It was about time they had a bit of fun.

As they climbed from the carriage, Tinny took his hand, her ring pressing against his fingers. 'Come on, let's play!'

They ran hand-in-hand towards the fayre, eager to explore and enjoy the stalls. Music floated across the air, like a tune from the Pied Piper, inviting them to follow it. As they rounded the corner past a row of tents, a carousel came into view.

'Golden gallopers,' whispered Tinny, turning to him with bright eyes and an irresistible smile. 'Can we? Please?'

How could he resist? He bought tickets and helped her on

to the platform, lifting her on to a horse with a pink rope bridle before climbing on behind her and putting his arms around her waist. As the ride started, the horses started to move, and the barrel organ grew louder, turning the ride into a magical world where they alone existed, whirling around in their own little timeless bubble.

Tinny laughed out loud, turning her head to smile at him, making his spirits lift as the horse rose in the air. He wanted to capture this moment, so he could escape into it whenever he was hemmed in by all the people in his life who wanted different pieces of him.

The ride was over all too soon. 'Win me a prize!' Tinny challenged him, leading him towards a coconut shy. He paid for three beanbags and took a stance, ready to throw them.

The years fell away; Grace was at his side on the day of the church fayre, while he steadied his arm ready to throw. Just as he brought his arm forward, a thud hit him square in the back and he fell forward, crumpling into the barrier. Grace shouted in anger and he scrambled to his feet, only to see Robbie Brown's cruel smile and hear his mocking voice: 'Ooh, poor little Willie Harpy, needs a girl to stand up for him.' The taunts of Robbie's gang echoed in his ears.

'Come on.' Tinny's voice broke the spell. 'This had better hit the target, the time you're taking over your aim.'

He pitched the ball, but it sailed way too high. He threw the other two lazily, both falling short.

'What are you doing?' Her voice was full of exasperation.

'Just leave it. I'm sorry, all right?' He marched away from her. Sorry for everything, for believing he could make her happy, for concealing his correspondence with Grace and sneaking off to meet her late at night. It was no basis for a relationship and a marriage.

'William! What's the matter? I don't understand you sometimes.' She struggled to keep pace with him.

'I don't understand myself either, so we're equal. Things are difficult for me at the moment.'

She grabbed hold of his arm and forced him to stop. 'If something's wrong, you need to tell me. You can't expect me to guess how you're feeling all the time. You have everything you've ever wanted: a real family, the chance to paint for a living, Mam and I here to support you... But you seem so distant and I can't reach you, no matter how many ways I try. We're going to be married... aren't we?'

That was the question he'd been turning over and over in his mind for weeks now, ever since receiving Grace's letter with its air of finality. Why did she always manage to distract him with her devotion and longing for him? But Tinny's face was so earnest, her beautiful blue eyes looking into his with a plea for reassurance, that he didn't have the heart to show any hesitation. She deserved more from him, and if she thought he was having doubts, she'd be heartbroken. He couldn't do that to her. Besides, Sarah would kill him.

'Forgive me, my darling. I've been preoccupied and selfish. The exhibition's been on my mind. I can't help worrying that it will be a flop. I've been struggling with my work, and even Mr Liddle can't work out why.'

She put her arms around him and snuggled up close. 'You know what I think? You need to paint for yourself, from the heart, and forget about the exhibition.'

Why on earth hadn't he thought of that? It was obvious. Until Mother had announced the exhibition, he'd found it easy to paint. He produced his best work when he was completely absorbed, every sweep of the brush flowing from his soul through his arms and hands, right to the tips of his fingers. It made sense to carry on in the same way. Now he was convinced he'd made the right choice for his future wife.

'You're right, my clever girl. That's the solution.' He gave her a kiss. 'Let's talk about your dreams for a change. Tell me about the tearoom. How would you go about it? Do you need a different shop, or would you ask the landlord for permission to convert the bakery?' He shouldn't mention that he'd been thinking about looking for a new shop in Scarborough. Not yet.

Her face lit up. 'My original idea was to put it in the back room and create a sitting room upstairs.'

William tried to work it out. 'Would we have our meals in the tearoom then? A sitting room on the first floor might be cosier if we didn't need a dining table in it.'

'Yes, that's true. But then I reconsidered. The back room isn't very big.' She gave him an enigmatic smile. 'Not big enough for my plans, anyhow.'

He dismissed Grace from his thoughts and put his arm around Tinny's shoulders as they wandered around the fair. 'Tell me more.'

It was soon evident that she was overflowing with ideas. He listened as she described the different meals she would serve: breakfasts for businessmen, mid-morning refreshments for shoppers, and lunches and afternoon teas for the well-to-do ladies. She'd thought about using themes for different seasons and had even worked out a colour scheme. And yet she didn't believe she was creative.

'And I'll make sure that the place we choose will have lots of space on the walls for your paintings. It will be like a permanent exhibition, and you can change them as often as you like. We'll hang tickets on those that have sold to show how much your talent is valued, and if you get a batch of small posters printed, I'll put them on the tables.'

She'd thought it all out. And even better, it would be a true partnership, each supporting the other. He must make more of an effort to encourage her. So far, their conversations had only been about his plans; it was time to change that.

He hugged her. 'I love the idea. As soon as we're married, let's find a way to make it happen. Sarah could stop working; she seems to be finding it much harder nowadays. We need somewhere with plenty of space above the tearoom, for her to have her own quarters.'

'That sounds lovely. I'm not sure I want to be the one to suggest she gives up, though!'

'That's a task for me, then. A bit of gentle persuasion is in order. We both know she won't be able to sit back and do nothing, but at least she won't have to rise so early and spend the morning up to her elbows in flour in a hot kitchen.'

Tinny nodded, then looked around. 'I'm parched. Is there a tea tent anywhere here?'

He spotted a red and white stripy tent. 'That looks like one over there.'

The fair was getting busier, and it was hard to find a direct path to the tea tent, with people criss-crossing in front of them and children running about. He held on to Tinny's hand to keep her safe, then caught a fleeting sight of a man turning his head... a small moustache, a straight nose and greying temples. Papa? Here? No, it couldn't be...

The back of his neck grew clammy as the fear returned.

'Ow, William, let go... you're hurting my hand.'

Her voice pulled him away from the living nightmare. 'Sorry.' He glanced at her hand, worried that he'd bruised it. 'I didn't realise.' He looked up again. Had Papa disappeared? Was he even there in the first place? Why did the fear keep returning?

'You've gone white. Tell me what's wrong. You were happy a moment ago. What's happened?' She tugged at his hand.

'I thought I saw Papa.'

'Here? Why on earth should he come to Rawcliffe?'

'I don't know.'

'He wouldn't. You've got to free yourself from this, dearest. Lots of men look alike, but you can't keep torturing yourself, thinking it's him every time. If he ever turns up, he'll have me to deal with. I can't bear to see you tortured over what he did so long ago. You must look to the future and put every ounce of your energy into your painting. Make this exhibition a success, and then we will have the money to make our dreams come true. Together.'

'My darling Christina, how did you become so wise?'

She gave a tinkling laugh, full of merriment. 'I don't think anyone's ever called me that before. Now come on, let's get that cup of tea.'

THE CARRIAGE DREW to a halt at the end of Petergate and William helped Tinny down.

'That was such a lovely day, thank you,' she said as she straightened her skirts. 'But oh, my feet... it's a good job we're not far from home, otherwise you'd be carrying me.'

William couldn't concentrate on what she was saying. He'd spotted the flower girl was standing on the opposite corner. She was even thinner now, and her skin was so pale, it was almost translucent. Her matted hair hung in dirty strands around her shoulders and she had the same pair of tattered shoes on as when he last saw her. To think of the money he'd spent on the carriage and the stalls at the fair. It would keep this girl in food for a week. Mother's generosity was making him thoughtless. He nudged Tinny and pointed.

'She's moved here now. How dreadful she looks; see how thin her arms are? Can't we do anything for her?'

Tinny clung to his arm. 'A few coins will help.'

'I've seen her employer taking most of the money from her. The best we can hope for is that it'll stop him beating her for not earning enough. I meant we could try to do more than that.'

Tinny shuddered. 'Have you seen him hit her?'

'No, but he was threatening her, and she looked terrified. I wish I could think of a way to rescue her.'

'She doesn't look too well, I agree. But you can't go saving all the waifs and strays in the area.'

William released Tinny's arm and went over to the flower girl. 'Are you all right?' he asked. Her sunken eyes were ringed with purple shadows, and her skin was so dry and papery that she could have been a ghost. The slight shrug of her shoulders was enough to reveal her ribs poking through the shredded rags that didn't quite form a dress. He handed over a few pennies and her mouth dropped open.

'Thank you, sir, thank you.' Her voice was a whisper.

'You're welcome. Do you have a home?'

She shook her head. 'Only a spot under the bridge.'

It wasn't safe for a girl. He remembered the pitch-black night he'd spent among the tramps, not daring to sleep for fear of being tossed into the river. What might they do to her? It didn't bear thinking about. If he'd had his own house, he would have gladly given her shelter, but he couldn't ask Sarah to take her in.

He turned away from the girl and took Tinny's hand. 'I won't give up on her. There must be a way.'

CHAPTER 29

William stood in front of the easel in his father's studio, a paintbrush in his hand. Concentrating on a canvas was the only way to calm the fluttering in his stomach, the only way to dismiss the image of his paintings hanging on the walls of an empty room, where champagne bottles stood untouched on a table. Or the one where a tiny group of people were standing around making polite talk, hardly looking at his work, only there on the promise of a free drink. No tags proclaiming the sale of a painting were visible in this exhibition.

Mother stared back at him from the canvas, a half-finished portrayal of her. How difficult it was to make it distinctive, not just a copy of the versions his father had painted. He couldn't get her eyes right, and without those, he couldn't capture the captivating smile and vivacious air that were so much a part of her. This studio usually did the trick; working in Father's space, using the same brushes, was guaranteed to bring inspiration. Not tonight. His insides were churning.

He stepped away from the easel, knowing it was futile to

attempt any work now. He'd have to try again another day, when he wasn't feeling so useless. He stood at the window and watched the guests coming out of the Grand, dressed in their finery, looking as if they were going to a function. Maybe even his. For a March evening, it was fairly mild.

The house below him was quiet; was it foolish to leave Tinny and Mother alone together? If only they could learn to get along better, without exchanging biting comments and defensive retorts.

Tinny's voice rang out from below. 'Are you finished yet? You need time to get changed.'

'Almost. I'll be there in a moment,' he promised.

'No you won't; you'll tinker with that painting for ages, then it'll be a mad rush to get ready. Stop now and get yourself sorted out.'

Her huffing as she returned to the lounge and shut the door suggested she was having a hard time of it. He'd better be quick. The formal suit hung on the door, a present from Mother. It had been his first proper fitting at the tailor's. With luck, it might act as a mask, so he could pretend to be someone else for the evening.

As he arrived at Mrs Uppleby's grand house, William half wished he could turn and run back to Mother's, or even catch a train straight back to York. Coaches and horses crowded the Crescent, the guests' voices bubbling up as they convened at the front of the building. They'd all know each other, whereas he could count on one hand the number of friends here tonight. He would just have to summon up his courage.

Mother led the way, the extravagant train of her blue-green silk dress shimmering like a peacock's tail. She must be keen to impress, but he couldn't help thinking she'd overdone the glamour. Tinny, on the other hand, looked perfect in a soft silver-grey dress with a delicate lace trim on the bodice. He'd insisted on buying it for her with Mother's money. He offered her his arm, feeling very grown-up.

As they entered the room, a ripple of applause greeted them. William lowered his head in embarrassment. Then he remembered Mother's advice: act as though you deserve success and it will find you. He looked around at the crowd of guests, everyone smiling and nodding at him.

Tinny squeezed his hand. 'I'm so proud of you,' she said.

'If I were you, I'd reserve judgement until you've seen the paintings.'

'Nonsense. I believe in your talent. Now please try to relax; you're making my fingers go numb.'

'Sorry.' He loosened his grip. Mother appeared at his side, steering him away to talk to a succession of people, ignoring his plea to let Tinny come with him. He mouthed 'Help' at her, but she just smiled and gave him a wave, then turned towards the wall to examine his pictures. He allowed himself to be led away, like a puppy learning about the world.

His ears buzzed with the chatter around the room as he tried to take in what each guest was saying, in an incessant round of introductions. Was he expected to remember their names? The gallery owners, all men, fluttered round his mother like drab moths round an iridescent flame, keen to share in her limelight.

A waiter handed him a glass of champagne. He clutched it and sipped at it frequently, more to occupy his hands than anything. The faces blurred into each other, mouthing platitudes that soon faded. The room became warmer; his collar was digging into his neck, but he didn't dare loosen it. Wasn't there any food? It might settle his stomach if he ate something.

A waiter offered him another glass of champagne to join in the toast that was being given by a group of people around him. Mother was in her element, taking their business cards and placing them in her beaded reticule.

At last, Tinny appeared by his side. Once the art collector he'd been talking to turned away, he leaned towards her. 'What have you been up to?'

She stared at him. 'Have you been drinking? I can smell it on you.'

'Only a little champagne. I'm fine. What have you been doing?'

'I've been on a mission to see every painting in the exhibition. You won't believe this, but over half of your pictures have 'Sold' tags on them already!'

He stared around the room, trying to take in her words. 'You'd better not be teasing me, my love. Show me.'

He took her hand and let her guide him around the room. It was true; almost every seascape had been taken, as had several of the portraits. This was like another world, where a different William was popular, confident, and in demand. But the air was stuffy, and he couldn't bear the heat for much longer. 'I don't feel too good,' he said.

'Stay there, I'll find a chair for you.' She vanished from his side.

He would just wander over towards the edge of the room…

Without warning, his feet slipped from under him and he skidded and fell backwards. There was a muttering from a group nearby, and he struggled to his feet, apologising.

Mother rushed over, grabbed his arm and steered him into a corner. 'You've drunk too much. How could you embarrass yourself like this?'

Tinny was beside him in an instant. 'What's going on?'

'Someone must have spilled a drink on the floor. I slipped on it, that's all.'

'He's drunk.' Mother's look of disgust was clear for everyone to see.

'I'm not. I've only had two glasses of champagne. The reason I'm a little faint is that I haven't eaten.'

Tinny glared at Mother. 'If you hadn't dragged him round to meet the guests, he could have had some food, and then the drink wouldn't have gone to his head so much.'

'He's here to make a good impression and meet his potential customers. Not to enjoy himself. Don't interfere in matters you know nothing about.' Mother started to walk away, but William grasped her arm.

'This has to stop. I'm sick of you two arguing over me, like a pair of children in the playground.' He barely recognised his own voice, loud and angry.

Mother shook him off. 'You're making a scene,' she snapped. 'I suggest you go outside and calm yourself.' She hurried away from him, putting a thin smile on her face as she reassured guests nearby that it was nothing, only that William was a little tired.

Tinny was still holding on to him. 'Let's sit over there,' she said in a soothing voice. They were halfway across the room when there was a commotion. A lady, wearing an elaborate hat and a dress that wouldn't have been out of place on a theatre stage, was raising her voice. William looked round and realised she was addressing Mother.

The room quietened, and all heads turned towards the intruder.

Suddenly, Mother staggered backwards, and a gasp came from the people around her. A gentleman sprang forward to break her fall. William took a step towards them, but Tinny held him back. 'Don't interfere. Just watch.'

A murmur spread throughout the room as everyone speculated about the intruder. She was waving her arms now, shouting at the top of her voice. 'You with your fancy airs and graces, pretending to be a bountiful sponsor, helping desperate artists. Well I know your true nature, you fraud.'

She looked around the room, her lips curling into a sneer as she saw she'd secured the crowd's attention. 'A husband stealer, that's what you are, as common as a street girl.' She was still yelling as two men bundled her outside.

Mother swept into the centre of the room. 'I'm sorry about that little interruption, ladies and gentlemen. I don't like to speak of people's ailments, but I am acquainted with that lady and I'm sorry to say she is deranged. Her husband is a talented artist, but I had to stop sponsoring him, because she couldn't accept it as a business arrangement. She kept haranguing me, accusing me of having an affair with him. I assure you, nothing of the sort was happening.'

The room filled with a low hum, as the guests made sympathetic mutterings of 'disgraceful', 'shameful', and 'poor Leah'. She cleared her throat. 'That is all I want to say on the matter. My apologies, William; I hope this hasn't spoilt your evening. Ladies and gentlemen, please show this talented young artist your appreciation.'

William blushed as a round of applause echoed around the room. He'd take it, to save Mother from any further embarrassment. 'Just smile,' whispered Tinny. He obeyed as several guests gathered round, slapping him on the back and complimenting him on his talent.

At last the guests began to drift away, not before time. It had been a long evening, and the strain of being sociable was taking its toll; he'd shaken so many hands that his fingers were numb. But Mother had given him strict instructions to stay until the end. If only the remaining groups of people would go home.

'I could do with a glass of water,' he told Tinny. 'You stay here. I won't be long.'

The entrance hall was still busy with people saying their

farewells to each other, bursts of cool air blowing in as the door opened and closed. A lone figure came in, parting the flow of people going out. He turned his head, expecting it to be a guest who'd forgotten a pair of gloves or whose carriage hadn't turned up.

It was someone he'd never expected to see.

CHAPTER 30

M ama? How? Why? William was almost paralysed with the shock of it.

Her eyes met his and she rushed over, taking him in her arms and pressing him close as if she was never going to let him go.

'William, oh my darling, thank goodness! I've had such a journey, I thought I'd never get here.'

The familiar lemon scent transported him back to the times when they'd stood together at the drawing room window watching the sea. How had she managed to come this far on her own? And how could she have found out where he was?

Grace. She must have betrayed him and broken her promise not to tell. How could she? After everything she'd said about keeping her word... her disappointment at his engagement had driven her to interfere.

He looked into Mama's eyes. 'I can't believe you're here. But no one must realise who you are. Not now, at least.' He stepped to the side and steered her into a corner of the hall. 'How did you find me?'

'Lady Forbes showed me an article in a newspaper about the exhibition. I'm so proud of you. Can I see your paintings? Please… I almost didn't get here. I got on the wrong train, had to transfer to another one, change again at York, and then I was stuck at the station, trying to get a carriage.'

So it wasn't Grace that had told her. 'Of course you can see my work. You might as well, now you're here. Come through to the exhibition room. But there's something important I need to ask of you.'

'Anything, my darling. I wasn't sure how you'd react to me coming. You must be so angry at me for not telling you the truth. I need to explain—'

'Please. Listen to me. My sponsor, Mrs Morgan… she mustn't find out who you are.'

'William, my darling, don't fret. I have no intention of introducing myself. I know who she truly is.'

'Hush.' He glanced around, hoping no one was listening; Mother would be furious if anyone found out about their relationship. The last thing they both needed was an accusation of favouritism. 'How did you find that out?'

'Lady Forbes came across a letter you'd sent to Grace, saying you'd found her. Her Ladyship's been such a good friend to me; I'm sure I would have died of sorrow without her support.' She dabbed at her eyes with a handkerchief. 'I had to come; I couldn't go any longer without seeing you. Every day, I've been sitting by the window, and I wake up several times each night, imagining I've heard you coming in.' She gave a small sob.

'Don't cry, please, Mama. You'll attract attention. 'Where are you staying tonight?'

'At the Grand Hotel.'

'Good, then let's meet tomorrow morning. Unless you have to go straight back; Papa isn't at home, is he?'

'Of course he isn't. I couldn't have come otherwise. He's

on the Continent, on another of his business trips. I told the staff I needed to visit a dying relative. It was the only thing I could think of that was urgent and serious enough to justify me leaving home. I've been out so rarely…'

He snatched at an idea. 'Let's pretend you're the mother of a friend of mine. He was supposed to be here tonight, but he's been in an accident and is in hospital with a broken arm, so you came to tell me yourself. If you become emotional, people will think you're worried about him.'

'I can't talk to anyone here though. I wouldn't have a clue what to say.'

'It's better you don't talk at all, to be honest. I suppose Lady Forbes also knows about my engagement? She seems to be making it her business to find out everything about me.'

'You're getting married? That's wonderful, William. Is your love here?'

'She most certainly is.' Tinny's voice came from behind them. 'I'm Christina Bennett. Pleased to meet you.' She was looking pointedly at him.

'Oh, I'm sorry, dearest. This is Mrs Atkinson. Her son George is a fellow student of Mr Liddle. He was supposed to be here, but he's fallen and broken his arm.'

'How awful. I hope he isn't in too much pain? It isn't the arm he paints with, is it?'

William exchanged a glance with Mama, ashamed that the lie had tripped off his tongue so easily. He hoped she'd been paying attention, in case she needed to do likewise.

Tinny nudged William. 'I'm sorry to interrupt, but there are still a few guests in there you haven't spoken to. If you talk to them, they might go sooner. You're looking tired.'

'Good idea. Please tell them I'm coming.' He watched her as she returned to the exhibition space. Mother appeared at the doorway, beckoning him in. He turned to Mama. 'You can go in and have a look around, but for heaven's sake, don't talk to anyone. I'll come to the hotel at ten o'clock tomorrow morning.'

William followed Tinny back into the exhibition room and worked his way round the remaining guests, only half concentrating on the conversations. If only he could have guided Mama round the paintings, they might have been able to talk properly. It would be torture waiting until tomorrow to spend time with her.

At last the room emptied, and Mother was at his side, beaming with delight. 'Well done, William. That was one of the most successful opening exhibitions I've ever hosted. You've attracted a good deal of attention from some very influential people tonight.'

'Can we go home now?' he asked. 'I'm dreadfully tired.'

'In a little while,' she replied. 'I just need to get the list of sales from my clerk. He's been keeping a note of them. You can handle that lingerer there.' She pointed at Anna.

'I will,' he said, relieved she hadn't marched over and done it herself. But tomorrow he would find out Mama's reasons for not telling him the truth. He just needed to decide how much forgiveness was in his heart.

CHAPTER 31

The habit of waking so early was a curse. William had spent hours trying to get back to sleep, but the images of the previous evening kept crowding into his mind. All his dreams had come true: his artwork hanging on the wall in an exhibition, respected art dealers and society members applauding him, with his mother and fiancée by his side. The hard work and the hours spent worrying over whether he was good enough had been worth it.

Was it arrogant of him to feel joyful at the thought of his paintings hanging in people's homes, appreciated by families and visitors as part of their everyday life? That gave him far more pleasure than thinking of the money they had earned; he would leave Mother to revel in that part of it.

But the joy of it had been tainted by Mama's appearance, awakening his guilt for leaving her. She must have woken every day and remembered that he was still missing. Yesterday, she had summoned every ounce of her limited courage to board a train, just as he had done the day he left home. He imagined her standing outside the station, trying to work out how to make the final stage of her journey. She had done this for him; perhaps it was time to forgive her for hiding the truth from him.

Lying in bed waiting for dawn to break, he snuggled under the covers, avoiding the autumn chill in the room. Mama would be asleep in the opulent surroundings of the Grand Hotel, no doubt dreaming of their proper reunion later this morning. But Tinny was in the room below his, the first time she'd stayed in Mother's house overnight. It made for a complicated situation; what excuse could he make for going over to the hotel alone? Tinny would have to know the truth about Mama eventually, and she'd be furious when she found out he'd lied to her last night.

As the first fingers of light started to poke through the curtains, he dressed and went into the studio. He must be quiet to avoid waking Mother; she would be tired after carrying out her hostess role so well last night. Thank goodness she hadn't realised who Mama was.

The sunrise brought delicate peach rays into the room, but the early morning chill made William shiver as he searched through the paintings that hadn't been selected for the exhibition. Where was it? Ah, there. He lifted out an oval canvas and set it on the easel.

Mama's face stared back at him, in her best cherry red silk with a matching bonnet, stray tendrils of hair curling gently round her face. He had taken so much care with the tenderness of her expression, the light in her eyes showing the love he always saw when she looked at him. She was standing by the window in her sitting room beside the telescope, with the sea view behind her.

The chain of events that led to this moment had all been set in motion on the day he'd found the telescope in the attic, with the paints alongside it. Last night he had fulfilled his ambition. He would give this painting to Mama to show her she'd been in his thoughts.

Aha, there was his solution. He could tell Tinny and Mother that a guest at the exhibition had asked about a particular painting, but it had been sold, so he'd offered to take a similar canvas to him at the hotel.

But Mother pored over the accounts and was aware of every penny of sales income. He would have to take some money with him and give it to her when he came back. Taking great care, he wrapped the painting in brown paper and secured it with string.

'Are you coming for breakfast?' Tinny called to him from the foot of the stairs.

He took his seat at the table and tried his best to concentrate as Mother recounted all the conversations she'd had last night. If she kept on at this rate, he'd be late, and he must avoid making Mama anxious.

'What are your plans today?' Mother asked.

'I've got a painting to deliver to the hotel opposite,' he said, and told her the tale.

'Ooh, I'd love to see inside the hotel,' said Tinny. 'He won't mind if I come, will he?'

William just managed to stop himself from correcting her assumption of a male customer. It would divert her from his real intention.

'I'm not sure. He was a little frail last night, and he asked me to visit him in his room; it's not appropriate for a lady to do that.'

'Well, I can stay in the foyer and watch everyone coming and going.'

She was being far too insistent for his liking. 'I may be a while. He's one of those people who won't use three words where twenty-three will do. And it wouldn't be proper for you to sit on your own in the hotel lobby. You might get arrested for loitering.' It was best to make a joke of it.

'Why do I get the feeling you don't want me there? Well,

have it your own way. But I expect afternoon tea there next time we're here.' The look she gave him spoke of trouble later when they were alone.

Once the clock neared ten to ten, he put the parcel under his arm and walked over the road to the hotel. Only then did he realise the flaw in his plan. How stupid of him; Mama couldn't possibly take it home. The only option was to bring it back and say the customer had changed his mind. At least he wouldn't have to pretend to pay the money over to Mother.

As William entered the hotel, the doorman doffed his hat and gave a slight bow. Once inside, he walked purposefully to the left, hoping to give the impression that he was a guest. A wide staircase opened out in front of him, flanked by columns with painted capitals supporting a set of arches. He found the piece of paper on which he'd scribbled Mama's room number last night, and went up the staircase.

She answered as soon as he knocked on the door, as if she'd been standing behind it waiting for his arrival. He propped the parcel against the wall and let her embrace him, enjoying the moment of closeness.

'My darling, how I've missed you.'

'I've missed you too; you are always in my thoughts. I'm sorry for leaving without telling you, but once I heard you and Papa say where I'd come from, I realised I didn't belong. Things could never be the same again. Do you understand?'

She pulled away from him. 'No. I'll never understand why you couldn't tell us what you'd heard. You didn't give me or your Papa the chance to explain, to tell you how much you meant… mean to us.'

'But Papa destroyed my paintings. How could I stay, knowing he would force me into the business? And you, you didn't—'

A lump rose in his throat. He didn't want their meeting to be full of recriminations.

He pointed at the wrapped canvas. 'I wanted to show you this.' Gently, he unwrapped it, studying it for a moment. How young she looked, with smooth skin, bright eyes and an air of peace that he'd conjured up from his memory of their quiet times together. Then he looked up and saw the reality: salt and pepper coloured strands in her hair, lines around her mouth, deep creases in her forehead and a weariness in her eyes. Guilt pressed on his chest.

He turned the portrait round and waited for her reaction.

Her tiny gasp broke the silence. 'Oh, William...'

She stared at it, taking it all in. 'I knew you were talented, but... this...'

It was the reaction he'd longed for when he had painted it, holding an imaginary conversation with her while sweeping his brush across the canvas.

'It proves you didn't forget me.' Then she frowned. 'Oh, but I can't take it home. Papa would—'

'I understand; it's enough for me that you've seen it,' he interrupted. 'I'll keep it safe for you. One day...' He balanced it on the table, supported by the wall, where it sat like a second version of her listening to their conversation.

She led him to a chaise longue by the window and they sat together. 'I'm sure you want to know why I didn't tell you the truth about the shipwreck.'

'It's all right, Mama, you don't need—'

'Oh, but I do. Please let me explain.' She sat a little straighter, preparing herself for the telling. 'Perhaps then you will understand why the truth must never come out. Papa and I could be in terrible trouble.'

He couldn't take his eyes off her as she spoke.

'We weren't able to have children; we tried for years. It was unbearable. When Matthew found you, it was like a gift from God. He told me there was no one alive in the wreckage, so we had every reason to believe you were an orphan.' Her voice faded, and her fingers tightened around his own.

'Didn't you think I might have other relatives somewhere else?'

Her sigh was like a ghostly breath floating across the room. 'I used to suffer from maladies that kept me in my bed for weeks on end. The night Matthew... Papa... brought you to me, it was as if God was answering our prayers, rewarding us for never giving up. I remember taking you in my arms and staring in wonder at your tiny hands and your little snub nose. You were all we could think of.'

'But what about later?' He'd often wondered why they didn't come to their senses once the novelty of it had worn off.

'We left Tynemouth straight away. You've no idea the lengths Papa went to, closing his practice and finding a partner and new premises in Hartlepool. It was a huge sacrifice, starting again in business. He's a proud man, and he wanted you to be involved in it.'

Pride. That was the problem, the source of every argument. William felt his jaw tightening at the memory of Papa's voice booming, bullying them both into obedience.

Then he looked into Mama's eyes, full of vulnerability and love for him. It was foolish to dwell on the past. They were wasting precious time; there were so many other things he wanted to say.

'I forgive you, Mama. You had to obey Papa, I understand that now. I'm sorry too, for all the worry I've caused you.'

A wave of relief washed over him. Now he could talk freely to her, telling her about his exploits since coming to York. Anyone else would interrupt, but she simply sat there, taking everything in.

'Do you think you can come to my wedding?' he asked.

'I'd love to. But I'm not sure… Perhaps if Papa was away on business. You will tell your fiancée who I am, won't you?'

'Yes, I will. Actually, I need to get back to her now. She'll be wondering what I'm doing.' He got up from the chaise longue and wrapped up the portrait again.

When he turned back towards her, she was twisting her wedding ring round and round. It was looser on her fingers now; how thin and gaunt she looked. It was his fault, but perhaps he could start to make amends.

As he kissed her cheek, she clung to his arm. 'Don't go. Please.'

'I'm sorry, Mama, I must. Mother believes I'm showing a potential customer a painting. We can't take the risk of her working out who you are. Go back home. I'll find a way of visiting you, I promise.'

He turned and walked out of the room, clutching the portrait. As he reached the foot of the stairs and turned the corner into the foyer, he gave a start. Mother was at the reception desk, talking to the clerk.

What was she doing here? Had she followed him? Once her suspicions were aroused by something, she wouldn't rest until she had an answer. But there were many reasons why she might be here. As long as Mama stayed in her room for a while longer, everything would be fine.

Watching to make sure Mother didn't look round, he slipped out of the hotel and hurried back to the house. He'd soon find out if she suspected anything.

CHAPTER 32

Tinny jumped as the cold water splashed on to her hand from the overflowing tea kettle, bringing her out of her daydream. She poured the excess down the sink and tapped the lid into place, just as William came in.

'I've come for a drink of water. What are you doing here?' he asked.

'Making a cup of tea while things are slow in the shop. How's the portrait going? You've spent ages on this one; I hope it's worth it.'

'Pretty well so far, but I'd appreciate your opinion. You can come up and see it, if you like.' He poured himself a glass of water and returned to the studio.

Tinny put the kettle on the range and stood looking out of the window. William had been unsettled ever since the exhibition. It was bad enough having him spend so much time in Scarborough, but she didn't even get him to herself when he was here. He seemed obsessed with the flower girl portrait, spending every spare moment in that blessed studio of his.

As soon as the water boiled, she made the tea, carefully

arranging the crockery on a tray before taking it upstairs. She'd take over in the shop later to give Mam a rest.

She tapped her foot against the door and waited for him to open it.

'I thought you'd appreciate a hot drink as well, while I was making one.'

'Thank you. I'm just trying to tone down the colour of that brick wall behind her, so her dress shows up against it. What do you think?' He took the tray from her so she could stand in front of the easel.

'I'm not sure you can call that a dress. It looks like someone's cut up one of our flour sacks.'

'That's the point. You've seen how tattered her clothes are. I think I'll darken the brick by blending the burnt umber with black and a dash of this new colour Mr Liddle gave me: alizarin crimson.'

'I love the names you artists give to the colours.'

'That's because you're a reader; you like words,' he said as he poured the tea.

She pursed her lips and studied the canvas. The flower girl was wide-eyed, her lips slightly parted as she held out a single bluebell. William had chosen well: the flower signified humility and the splash of blue broke up the sombre tones.

'It's astonishing, beautiful yet heart-rending,' she told him. 'It's as if she's pleading with me to help her find a way out of her wretched life. You are so clever, my darling. It's a brilliant way of drawing attention to her plight.' She stepped back and moved towards the table to get her cup of tea. 'How have you done that?'

'Done what?'

'Her eyes.'

'Same as always. I just build up layers of paint, experimenting with the highlights until it looks right.'

'No, I mean the effect of her watching you, wherever you stand.'

He came to stand next to her. 'She's looking straight ahead. What do you mean?'

Tinny took his arm and steered him to one side. 'It's remarkable. When I came in, I thought she was glancing the other way, but now I'm standing here, she's still looking at me.'

William walked further over towards the door then paced back and forth. 'Good heavens, you're right. She's following me! I don't have a clue how I've done that. I'll have to ask Mr Liddle.'

Tinny gave him a hug. 'I suspect it's genius rather than technique. I'd love to sit and watch you for a few minutes. Would you mind? Mam's coping fine in the shop.'

'You can if you want. Just don't expect me to talk sense. You know how absorbed I get.' He reached for his brush and continued working in silence.

Tinny settled in a chair to drink her tea, alternately looking out of the window and watching him as he painted. From time to time he stepped back to examine the effect.

'Your drink's getting cold,' she reminded him.

He put his brush down and came over, leaning against the table as he sipped his tea. 'Won't Sarah miss you if you're up here too long?'

'She'll ask me if it gets busy. Somehow I doubt it will. The takings are even worse this week, and she's getting worried again.'

He put the cup back on the table and took her hand. 'I'll have to tell her not to be so anxious. Mother will be paying me the commission from the exhibition soon. I won't let Sarah get into difficulties.'

She brushed the top of his hand with her thumb. They'd

never have managed without his support. 'How are you coping with still living in two places, my dear?'

'It's manageable. I'd like to be here more, but Mother wants me to be close at hand, so she can give me the benefit of her advice. You're not worrying about where we'll live after we get married, are you?' He let go of her hand and returned to the easel to continue painting.

She didn't mind giving him the assurance he needed. 'No, I'll go wherever you go. In fact, I was wondering... If Mam can't keep the shop going, we could look for a place in Scarborough to rent for the tearoom.'

The echo of her voice faded into silence. Had he even heard what she'd said? He had that distracted look on his face that often appeared when he was trying to solve a problem.

'William?'

'Hmm? Oh, yes. No need to rush. Mama said I've come so far from the way I used to paint at home. Anyway, I need to consolidate—'

'You mean Mother.'

'Yes, that's what I said.'

She stared at him, sure she'd heard it correctly. 'No you didn't. You said Mama.'

'Then it must have been a slip of the tongue.'

She stood up and moved closer to him. A blush had come to his cheek.

'Leah doesn't know what your paintings were like at home.'

He held his brush in the air and stared at the canvas, avoiding making eye contact with her.

'She does. I took a set of sketches with me when I first met her.'

Now she was certain he was lying. 'Yes, she told me about them. Sketches, not paintings.'

An image flitted across her mind, making a connection, fragments of a puzzle coming together.

'That woman at the exhibition. The one you said was a friend's mother.'

'Yes… what about her?'

'She spoke to me at the end, while you were talking to the last few guests. She was awfully curious about you.'

'Her son's another of Mother's artists. It's only natural for her to be interested in another painter.'

It was time to sort this out once and for all. She reached across and took the brush and palette from him and placed them on the table. 'It was much more than that. She was asking where you lived and how you'd attracted Leah as your sponsor. It was quite personal.'

His silence was infuriating. She turned him round to face her. 'Honestly, William, you must think I'm stupid. I can tell you're keeping something from me; you're terrible at hiding your feelings. Why don't you try being honest with me for a change? Because if you can't be, then I'm not sure we have a future together.'

She waited again, willing him to tell the truth.

'It was my Mama.'

'Your Mama? Why on earth did you say she was a friend's mother?'

He was studying his shoes now, or the floor; anything to avoid her gaze.

'Because if Mother finds out who she is, there will be huge trouble. I told Mama to keep away from her, and she said not to worry, because she knew the truth.'

'And what exactly is the truth? I want to know. Every bit of it, right now. Starting with how your Mama found out about the exhibition.'

'One of her acquaintances told her.'

'Who?'

'Her closest friend in the village. She showed her the advertisement in a newspaper.'

'Right. But you said your Mama knew the truth. And by that, I assume she meant Leah's relationship to you. I don't understand how that was possible.' For heaven's sake, why was it such hard work to get the truth from him?

'The lady employs a girl who used to go to my school. I wrote to tell her where I was, and that I'd found my real mother. She must have been careless about where she left my letter—'

'And does 'she' have a name?'

'Grace.'

That was the name he'd called out on the night she entered his room. It conjured up something else, too. 'This is all starting to make sense now. The letter you dropped that Christmas, when you shouted at me... was it from her? Grace?'

'Yes. She's just a friend who used to help me when Papa was being cruel.'

He'd kept all this from her; it was too much to bear. She backed away and sank down in the chair. 'You've been corresponding for so long, yet you didn't think to tell me? How can I believe anything you say ever again?'

'Don't say that. You know I hate lies. You're right; I shouldn't have been secretive.' He knelt beside her. 'I regret everything. I've sinned, and I'm sorry. If I could turn the clock back, I would.'

'So would I, William. Now tell me, truthfully, have you been in touch with your Mama since that night?'

'Yes, I visited her at the Grand the next morning. But when I left, Mother was in the foyer. She might have followed me, and now I'm worried that she's worked out who Mama is.'

'There's another lie. You told me you were visiting a

potential buyer for one of your paintings. Oh, William…' She gave an exasperated sigh.

'I'm sorry. I was exhausted after the launch party, and Mama arriving turned everything upside down. How would you have felt in my shoes?'

'I can't imagine. But I thought you could trust me to understand.'

He put a hand on her arm, but she shrugged it off and stood up, moving across to the window. Dark clouds were gathering in the distance, a sure sign that a storm was brewing. What future did they have if she couldn't trust him? The distance between them seemed wider than ever. She swivelled round. William was standing at the table, his fingers stroking the carved oak fragment.

'Have you told me everything?' she asked.

He was still looking at the shard of wood, as with an almost imperceptible nod he said 'Yes.'

William woke up the next morning with a start, gripped by a new nightmare. He'd been walking along the promenade on the way to the Spa, and Papa had appeared right in front of him, bundling him into a boat to take him back to Seaton. Each day he was taken to the Hartlepool office, where he was chained to a desk, unable to do anything but write figures in the shipping registers, growing paler and thinner for want of fresh air and a chance to express his creativity.

He rubbed his eyes then tried to calm his breathing as he focused his attention on the far wall where the early light was bringing out the intensity of the colours in the flower girl portrait. He'd hung it there last night, hoping it might remind him that his problems were nothing compared to her struggle for survival on the streets. But he couldn't dismiss his inner torment that easily. The lies had unravelled like a skein of wool, and now it was lying in a tangle around his feet, full of knots that were impossible to undo.

So many women, causing so many problems. Each one had arrived as a guardian angel, one way or another, but they had turned into a writing mass of critics, accusers and judges. His priority was to make amends to Tinny for keeping so many things from her. Could she forgive him? He couldn't bear the thought of losing her; they were bound together in a promise of marriage, and every time he had to travel to Scarborough, he missed her more.

He needed to complete the rest of the paintings Mother wanted for his next exhibition. Did he dare ask her when his commission for the first one was going to arrive? It would at least delay their worries about the bakery. There was no guarantee of his future earnings, so he'd have to be careful with whatever he received. It was all horribly precarious, like the house of cards he used to build on a Sunday afternoon when the boredom of sitting with Mama and Papa got too much. Perhaps Tinny was right, and they should look for suitable premises in Scarborough, to make her tearoom dream come true.

But whenever he stood at the viewpoint on top of the South Cliff , looking across the bay at the coastline stretching northward to Hartlepool, it reminded him of the greater risk he was taking by being there. Mama wouldn't have many opportunities to visit, but Papa might travel to Scarborough on business.

He couldn't face Tinny at the breakfast table this morning. What if she'd mentioned their argument to Sarah, or if she'd decided she couldn't accept his apology? Would she break off their engagement? He couldn't live with himself if that happened.

A few minutes later, she knocked on the door.

'Yes?'

She marched in and thrust an envelope at him.

'This has arrived for you. It's from her.' The word hung in the air like an accusation in a court of law.

'You promised me you weren't writing to each other any more. Was that just another lie?'

'No. That's what we agreed.'

She was still standing there, stubbornly watching him. He couldn't wait to find out why Grace was writing to him now, so he took the letter from her and ripped the envelope open. As he unfolded the single sheet, he frowned at the rushed scribble, so different from her usual neat script.

Dear William,

I wish I didn't have to write this letter. Your Mama is ill. Reverend Wilson asked us to pray for her on Sunday, and I heard Lady Forbes say she won't see anyone. But she sent a message asking for me today, so I had to go. It was such a shock to see her. She struggles to talk and is in pain. When I took her hand, it was ice cold. I fear she may not last long, she is so frail.

Her dearest wish is that you come home. Please hurry. I'm not sure how much time she has left.

Grace

William put one hand against the table to steady himself. 'It's Mama. She's gravely ill and asking for me.'

Tinny took the letter from him and read it, then looked up at him, misty-eyed. 'You must go. It may be your last chance to see her.'

He nodded. 'I'll get the first available train.' He drew Tinny close. 'Pray for her, please. And for me. It's time to face Papa.'

PART III

CHAPTER 34

MARCH 1881: SEATON CAREW

'Next stop Seaton Carew!' the guard announced as he walked through the carriage. William put the piece of jet back in his pocket, the surface of the stone warm from the time he'd spent rubbing it between his finger and thumb as he thought about the argument with Tinny. If he hadn't been away so much, would she have been so cross with him? He'd broken the trust between them, and now he couldn't put it right until he returned. Goodness knows when that might be.

As he pulled his bag from the rack, a pang of guilt came over him. He'd barely given a thought to Mama during the journey. She deserved his attention, even if it meant seeing Papa as well. The problems back in York would have to wait. Please God, let him not be too late.

The train slowed to a halt and William disembarked, pulling his scarf more tightly around his neck to keep out the icy blast of wind that gusted across the platform. Then a voice rang out.

'William! Thank goodness you came.'

'Grace?'

She ran to him and flung her arms around him. She smelt of summer roses and her cheek was silky soft against his. William stepped back, glancing around to make sure no one was staring.

'I didn't expect you to be here. Shouldn't you be at work?' He nodded towards the path that led down the hill and started walking, eager to get to Mama's side.

Grace followed, her skirts swishing as she quickened her pace. 'I came to meet the earlier train too, just in case you were on that one. Lady Forbes is at an afternoon tea party, so I won't be missed.'

'How is Mama?' he asked, dreading the answer.

'The last I heard, she wasn't very good. Sometimes Lady Forbes asks me to go and pass on a message, usually when she's had a difficult night and can't visit her, but I haven't been since I wrote to you.'

'Her Ladyship's still drinking, then?'

'Yes, it's getting worse. But never mind that. Your Mama's the most important one right now. Can I walk with you?'

'Of course you can,' he replied, as they reached the bottom of the hill.

It all looked much the same as before: the Station Hotel opposite, and beyond that the farmlands stretching out as far as the eye could see. As they continued along the lane, the familiar large houses started to appear. Their owners had probably amassed even more wealth and influence in the six years since he'd left. Had Papa's fortunes flourished as well?

Grace's hand brushed against his as they walked. Whether it was deliberate or not, he couldn't react; it wouldn't be right.

'How did Christina react to you coming back here?' she asked.

'She understood. But we'd just had a bit of a falling out, and now I wish we'd made up before I left.'

'Well, whatever it was, I'm sure everything will be all right once you go back.'

She wasn't pressing him for information as he'd thought she might. It wasn't like Tinny's suspicious questioning. Grace trusted him to tell her in his own good time, if he wanted to. And he did.

'I'm not so sure,' he ventured. 'She found out Mama was at my exhibition and she was furious that I didn't tell her. But I had my reasons; it was important to keep her identity secret. If Mother had realised, there could have been a dreadful scene.'

'Hmm, and I suppose the longer you waited to tell Tinny, the harder it was?'

'Yes. And on top of that, she found out I've been writing to you.'

Grace gave a sniff. 'There's nothing wrong with friends exchanging letters. You've promised to marry her, for heaven's sake. Why is she so jealous?'

It was so refreshing to have someone on your side. He mumbled a few words about keeping secrets, keen to play down his guilt. Not that Grace would condemn him; she understood him completely.

'How are you doing with your painting?' she asked.

Grateful for the change of subject, he told her about the exhibition in Scarborough, his hopes for the next one, and his attempt to portray the flower girl.

'I remember you mentioned her in one of your letters,' she said. 'I can't bear the thought of her being treated so cruelly. How on earth does she survive, sleeping outdoors in all weathers? But just think, you have a real chance to draw attention to her plight if her portrait goes in the exhibition.'

She sounded a little breathless as she struggled to keep up with him.

William slowed his pace just a little, still keen to get to Mama.

'Oh, it's definitely going in the exhibition. Mother was sending a man to collect it today. I should have reminded Tinny about that.'

He fell silent, trying to match the view with his memory of the village as they walked along the track. Then he had a thought. 'I might ask Mother if it's good enough to put up for auction,' he said. Where had that audacious idea come from? Grace had that effect; she made him feel as if he could do anything.

'That's a brilliant idea,' she said, turning to him, her soft brown eyes sparkling. He'd forgotten how animated she looked when something excited her, and how her praise thrilled him.

She laid a hand on his arm, making him stop and turn to hear her. 'I've read articles in the newspapers about art auctions in the cities. If a painting goes for a big sum of money, it gets a lot of publicity. You're so clever, using your talent to help someone in need like that.'

'Don't get too enthused,' he said, shrugging off her touch and moving on. 'I didn't say it was any good.'

Her shoes tapped on the path as she caught up with him. 'Oh, it will be. I heard your Mama telling Lady Forbes about the portrait you did of her. They were taking tea at Chambers House one afternoon and I was listening in outside the door. I hear all sorts in that house; it makes the long hours bearable. Anyway, she told Her Ladyship how wonderful it was that you'd spent time thinking about her while painting it, and what a good likeness it was.'

She stayed quiet for a while, as if sensitive to his inner

turmoil about what he would find when he arrived home, especially if Papa was there.

Then at last the sea came into view. William inhaled the salty air as they turned the corner on the way to the village green. 'Will you come in with me to see her?' he asked. It mightn't be so hard to face Papa with Grace by his side.

'I'd better not. You need to do this on your own,' she replied.

He accepted her judgement and they walked towards the house in silence, then parted with a simple wave. William's hand strayed into his pocket and rubbed the piece of jet, praying for courage. No longer was he a frightened child; he'd made his own way in the world. He'd cope with anything if Mama was all right.

Two sharp raps with the shiny brass knocker brought Ada to the door.

'Master William!' she cried, disbelief written across her face.

'I've come to see Mama. Is she…?'

Ada stood aside to let him in.

He dropped his bag and looked around the hall as he took off his coat. Nothing had changed: the same portraits stared at him from the walls. He used to think the people in them were ghosts who would come alive at night. The grandfather clock continued to tick away the beats of the day, but to him it felt as if time had stood still.

He took the stairs two at a time until he reached Mama's bedroom, then gave a gentle tap on the door and entered, peering into the darkness. She was in bed, the flickering flame of a candle on the bedside table revealing the hollows in her face and dark circles under her eyes. As they entered the room, she turned her head and tried to speak his name.

'I'm here, Mama,' he whispered, taking a glass of water from the table and holding it to her cracked lips. As he tried to support her neck so she could take a sip, the heat from her fever warmed his hand.

'William, I need...' Her words faded. She lifted her hand from under the bedclothes and tried to reach over her shoulder. 'This...'

'What are you trying to do, Mama?'

'Under there... Papa afraid... could be ruined. All my fault.' She was overcome with a coughing fit.

'Steady. Don't rush.'

'He knows.' She was pointing at the pillow.

He lifted the corner of the pillowcase. A letter had been tucked underneath it. He pulled it out and held it in front of her so she could see it. 'This?' She nodded.

Did she want him to read it? There was no other reason for her to draw his attention to it, so he opened it and started scanning the contents.

Dear Mr and Mrs Harper,

I have spent many years without my husband and son, believing both to be dead. You cannot imagine how much pain I have suffered during all these years.

The discovery that Thomas – for that is his real name – survived the wreck has given me a new purpose in life. But he is torn between me as his birth mother and Mrs Harper as his adoptive mother.

You obtained my son by deception and denied him his right to be reunited with me. He could have been my only consolation after I lost my dear husband. I cannot forgive you this lost time.

It would have been much more difficult to trace you if Mrs Harper had not come to Scarborough and met William at the hotel. I know several of the staff there, so it was not difficult to find out who she was.

My son must not be distracted from his creativity by these emotional meetings. He has made a new life in Yorkshire and has a promising career as an artist. I imagine this will not please you, but your views on this matter do not interest me in the slightest. I will not let you disrupt his chances.

Therefore if you don't keep away from William, I will go to the police and report your crime. For it is a crime. You had an obligation to search for his real family, but you chose not to do so, and passed him off as your own. If he comes to visit you, I insist that you refuse to see him. I have friends in your area and have instructed them to send word to me if they hear of any contact.

I don't care what story you need to invent to explain your decision not to see William. It is evident that you are well practised in deception and need no lessons from me. You will not tell him I have had any dealings with you in this regard.

Yours sincerely,

Leah Morgan

There was a noise from downstairs. Absorbed in the letter and the effect it had had on Mama, he hadn't given a thought to Papa.

CHAPTER 35

A knock on the bedroom door made William jump. He got to his feet as Ada came in.

'Master William, Miss Simpson from next door is here. She wants a word with Mrs Harper.'

Thank goodness it wasn't Papa. 'She can't be disturbed. Please tell Miss Simpson it's not a good time.'

Ada twisted the corner of her apron. 'She says it's an emergency.'

William sighed. 'I'll come in a moment. Please ask her to wait.' He kissed Mama's cheek and told her he wouldn't be long, then followed Ada down to the hall.

'Master William?' Miss Simpson seemed shocked to see him at first, then regained her composure. 'I've just seen Mr Harper. He's on the pier. I fear he might be thinking of jumping in; he's taken off his coat, and his shoes as well. Please help him.'

He swallowed the panic that rose in his throat and thanked her for raising the alarm, promising to deal with it. She seemed glad to leave.

William reached for his coat. 'Can you sit with Mama

please, Ada? Don't say a word about this; she will only fret.' The maid nodded and ran back upstairs.

The wind stabbed at his cheeks like icy needles as he ran along the track. A mist was descending. On he pressed, his eyes watering and the ocean roaring in his ears as the waves pounded the wooden boards that were stacked against the cliff. He could just make out the low pier in the distance, and a faint figure half way along it.

At the steps, William stopped and bent over with his hands on his knees, trying to catch his breath. When he looked up, the mist had thickened. God help us, he prayed. I can't be too late. He narrowed his eyes, struggling to see. Was that him? An amorphous shape on the floor gradually became clearer. Yes, it was Papa, crouching on the floor of the wooden platform.

William climbed up the steps. 'Papa! It's me, William.' He started to stride out, then gasped as his foot slid on the mossy deck. Regaining his balance, he edged towards Papa.

'Go away. It's over.' Papa staggered to his feet.

Had he been drinking? No, surely not. He was adamant about Temperance, a savage critic of those who indulged in alcohol.

'Mama sent for me. I've just seen her.' William moved forward again, trying to keep his steps small and his body tight. Don't panic him; he might slip. 'She showed me the letter. The one Leah Morgan sent.'

Now he could see Papa's coat folded neatly on the deck, and a pair of shoes beside it. Miss Simpson had been right. 'Don't move, Papa. Everything will be all right.'

'No, go away!'

William tried to sound reassuring. 'I won't touch you, I promise, but we need to talk.'

No reply. He walked across two, three, four planks. As he took the next step, he heard a crack and the floor splintered underneath his foot. He threw his weight forward and scrambled away from the spot, turning to see what had happened. A hole had appeared, and below it the sea seethed in a foaming mass, washing over the rocks and beating against the legs of the structure.

An image of a shipwreck came to mind, with its smashed timbers scattered around the rocks. He needed to get Papa off here. Soon.

'Come away from the edge, please, Papa. It's slippery, and you could fall.'

'Better that than face disgrace and ruin.'

'Think of Mama. She can't survive without you.'

'This is all your fault.' He moved towards William.

'I've never told Mother – Leah – anything about you. I promise I'll get her to stop the blackmail. She'll listen to me.'

Papa was still too close to the edge, unsteady on his feet. His eyes were as black as night and wide with terror, or madness; it was hard to tell which it was.

'Can't stop her… deceitful witch… lose everything.'

'Why is she against me being here with you? Please, tell me.'

'… know too much…' The wind whipped away his words into nonsense. William shook his head. He sounded delirious. 'About what?'

'We lived near James' parents. Tynemouth. A family scandal, Leah… innocent.' He was wild-eyed. 'I saved you, gave Anna hope, gave you life. Was that so terrible?'

William's damp clothes clung to him, freezing and stinging his skin. As much as he wanted to run back to the warmth of the house, he had to stay, and get Papa off here. For Mama's sake. 'Not terrible at all. Yes, you saved me. I only ever wanted your love.'

Papa moved towards the edge of the pier.

William sprang forward. This could be his last chance.

'No, wait! I appreciate the risks you took for me now. I've discovered that art is in my blood, and I'm doing well, just like you have in your business. But you're right, I shouldn't have run away. I've caused too much hurt.'

All he got in return was a blank stare.

It was worth one more try. 'I'll never forgive myself if Mama dies. Please come home. I'm sure I can stop Leah. Then Mama will get better. It's such a long time ago, no one can prove that what you did was wrong. Everything will be fine.' Please let him believe it.

Papa took a few steps closer, still too near the edge, trembling.

William swept the rain-soaked hair off his forehead and looked into his father's eyes. 'Let's get home, Papa. It's cold here, and you're drenched. Mama is waiting for us both.' He held out his hand in encouragement.

'You can't stop Leah. She has spies everywhere; we can't trust anyone. You have to leave.' He rushed at William, pushing at his chest, propelling him backwards.

William stumbled, his feet sliding, body twisting, trying to stay upright. 'No! Stop it!' he cried. 'Let me help.'

Papa released his hold and stepped back, watching, waiting.

William glanced up at the sky. The mist was lifting, but the clouds had darkened as the storm approached, and a sudden flash of lightning ripped across the sky. Out of the corner of his eye he saw a blur of movement, an anguished cry, a body lunging at him. A split-second reaction, side-stepping, Papa flailing past him, slipping…

Gone.

'Papa! No!'

William rushed to the edge and looked in horror as his father's body hit the rocks and tumbled into the sea like a rag doll. 'No! Hold on…'

Could he reach him? Further along, he saw a ladder, broken at the bottom. There was no time to lose; Papa could be washed away in no time. He gripped the ladder and swung his legs over, searching for the rung, twisting, then wobbling as he descended. His hand brushed against a fragment of fishing net. Could he use it as a lifeline?

Lord… please let Papa be alive. Don't let it end like this. At the end of the ladder, he dropped down and scrambled across the rocks, all the while looking out at the waves. Was that him? No. William blinked away the spray. There… a movement, a flash of pale skin. He threw the net. No use. Try again. Fail again. Damn. Had he gone under?

There was only one way. William shrugged off his coat and removed his shoes. He overbalanced and grabbed at a jagged rock, crying out as it cut into his hand. The stone turned red with his blood as he clung on, preparing to launch himself into the sea.

It was now or never. As his body hit the water, the icy chill made him shriek, but he persisted, striking out in a desperate need to find Papa, before it was too late.

❧

WILLIAM STAGGERED into Mama's room and sank to the floor beside the bed.

She slowly turned her head towards him. 'Where did you go?' she croaked. 'You're soaked through.'

'I went to look for Papa. On the pier.' He was shivering so much that it was hard to get the words out.

'Whatever was he doing there?' She had a faraway look in her eyes, as if he was telling her they'd been out for the day.

He got to his knees and took her hand in his. 'Darling Mama, I have some terrible news. Papa was on the pier, about to jump into the sea. I tried—'

He broke down, hiding his face in the blanket to obliterate the haunting images.

'Where is he?'

William choked on a sob. 'We were talking. He seemed calmer. I thought he was going to come home. Then he rushed at me. I didn't mean to move aside; it was a reaction.'

'I don't understand. What are you saying?' Her eyes searched his face for an answer.

'He couldn't stop... he fell over the edge. I jumped into the sea, tried to save him, couldn't... I'm sorry. So sorry.'

He lifted his head at the sound of Ada approaching from behind. She dropped the towel she was holding, and her hand flew to her mouth. 'Dead? Mr Harper? Oh sweet Jesus.'

'Ada, please will you tell Cook what's happened, and ask her for a glass of brandy? It will help Mama deal with the shock.'

He wrapped the towel around himself, trying to get some warmth from it, while Mama stared at him in silence. Then she covered her face with her hands and a raw, desperate wailing sound filled the room.

It was like watching a play at the theatre, then being asked to move on to the stage and start acting out a part. The pain of recounting the scene was agonising, but if he didn't do it now, he might never manage it.

'I tried, Mama, please believe me. Papa was angry; he blamed me for the letter Mother sent. I thought I'd helped him to be calmer. But then he cried out and rushed at me. I thought he was going to push me over the edge. I didn't think, didn't do it deliberately...'

'Do what deliberately? What have you done, William?'

'Nothing... I dodged him, but he kept going. He tumbled into the sea. I climbed down and swam after him.' His failure would gnaw away at him forever. 'But he went under, and I lost him.'

The clock ticked as if nothing had happened, ignoring this silent, numb state of not-quite-being they were trapped in.

Cook arrived, tears streaming down her face. She held a small glass of brandy against Mama's lips and tipped it so she could drink.

He'd expected Mama to start sobbing and never stop. Instead, she stared past him, in a blank haze.

'Leah has done this. She killed him. I won't give you up, William, I won't. Not now I've got you back.'

'We must take this letter to the police.'

'No!'

'But Mama—'

'I said no.' Her voice rang out, clearer than before. 'They'll find out what we did. It's there in Leah's letter. The newspapers will tell our story, and people will draw their own conclusions.'

He could see the fear in her eyes. He was the only family she had now, and she needed his help. 'I promised Papa I'd make Mother stop her threats. I told him no one can prove you did anything wrong. People take in orphans all the time.'

'But everyone will say that by committing suicide, it proves his guilt. We'd be in disgrace. The shame... I couldn't bear it.' She started weeping. 'No, you have to find another way.'

Without getting the police involved? How was that even possible? But Mama needed to believe he could do it.

'I'll speak to Mother, appeal to her better nature. When she knows what's happened to Papa, I'm sure she will see sense.'

He had no idea how to even broach the subject when he next saw her, but he'd made a promise and now he had to fulfil it.

CHAPTER 36

W illiam squinted as the ray of light slipped through a gap in the curtains. It took a few moments before he realised that he was in his old room. Except for the disappearance of his wrecked paintings and the broken box, everything was exactly as he'd left it: the same counterpane, the wardrobe, the wallpaper – though faded where the sunlight had caught it – and even his old toys lined up on the shelves. The telescope was resting on its stand by the window, the brass now dull and dusty.

There, near the door, was the scratch on the wall where the box had smashed into it when Papa... Oh, Lord. The image loomed large before him, of Papa sinking as the water engulfed his lungs. Gone, and it was his fault for not saving him.

He rubbed his eyes and got out of bed to dress, remembering it all: the agony of returning to break the news to Mama, her denial, then accusing him of pushing Papa in. That had hurt; but she was mad with grief. The doctor had given her a sleeping draught and had supplied extra doses with strict instructions to Ada on how to administer them.

She needed to rest for most of today, the doctor had advised. It would buy him time to organise things, to act as a son should, even one who wasn't really theirs.

As soon as he sat down for breakfast, his appetite deserted him. He pushed his plate away and rushed out to Chambers House to break the news and ask for help.

On arrival, he was ushered into the drawing room to wait. The silence was oppressive, distracting him as he tried to decide what he could reasonably ask His Lordship to do. When the door opened, both Lord and Lady Forbes came in.

'Master William… this is an unexpected visit. I wasn't aware you'd returned,' said Lord Forbes. 'Is everything all right?'

'I'm afraid not. There's been a terrible tragedy. Papa, he died…' He tailed off, not knowing what else he could say.

'Oh, my goodness.' Lady Forbes steadied herself then sank into a chair. 'What happened?'

William embarked on the tale, trying to make it sound like a simple accident, an unfortunate slip. They were so shocked that they didn't think to ask what Papa was doing on the pier.

After the formal expressions of sympathy, Lord Forbes turned to the practical matters, giving his suggestions about what should happen next. It was such a relief to have their advice; he'd never have known what to do if left to his own devices.

'I'm very grateful for your support, Lord Forbes,' William said at the end of the conversation, as they shook hands. 'Unfortunately, I have to finish off some important business in Scarborough, so it's a great comfort to leave things in your capable hands.'

'I wish it was in happier circumstances, Mr Harper,' replied Lord Forbes. 'Your Papa and I have been friends for a long time. Knowing him as I do… did, I expect it will be very straightforward, but whatever the situation, we'll do him proud.'

'And you can be sure I will help your dear Mama,' Lady Forbes said, reaching across to pat William's hand.

He simply nodded, caught up in the realisation that Lord Forbes had called him Mr Harper, not Master William. He was the head of the household now. What did that mean for his future? Would he be expected to take up the reins of the business? He couldn't... wouldn't. But manners came first, so he dismissed the thought for another day.

'You are both very kind. I will return as soon as I can.'

He waited for His Lordship to stand up so he could follow suit.

'Your Ladyship, I have a favour to ask,' he ventured as they walked to the door.

'Of course,' she said with a nod.

'Could I have a word with your maid? Grace Robinson?'

She looked bemused, but nodded. 'Yes, I'll call her.' She reached for a bell pull. 'She should be here in a moment. I'll leave you to it; Grace will show you out.'

William gave a bow and stood waiting while Lord and Lady Forbes went up the stairs. In less than a minute, Grace arrived.

'William! What are you doing here?'

'Bringing sad news, I'm afraid.' He took her hands in his and braced himself. 'It's Papa. He's dead.'

Her fingers tightened around his. 'Oh, William. No... it can't be... what happened?'

It was painful to repeat it, but he persevered, not caring that it was improper to stand holding hands like this. As he described the moment that Papa's ghostly face faded away out of reach, she flung her arms around him, burying her face in his chest.

When she released him, her cheeks were tear-stained. 'I'm

so sorry, William. I know he was cruel to you, but it must still have been a horrible thing for you to see. And your poor Mama...'

'I keep seeing his face, mad with fear. He wouldn't listen to reason. But things were said, hints about events in the past, that I can't quite make out. I'm sure there's a clue there to why Leah wrote that letter. But I have more urgent things to sort out.'

'I'm sure you have. Does that mean you'll be staying for a while?' she asked.

He shook his head. 'Lord and Lady Forbes are going to help organise Papa's affairs and look after Mama. I need to go back to Scarborough, to find out what's behind Mother's objection to me being here. Mama won't rest until I sort it out.'

'And what about Christina? Don't you think you should go and tell her what's happened? It might make it easier for you to sort out your argument, if she's as caring as you say she is.'

He frowned. She still had feelings for him, yet she was advising him to mend his relationship with Tinny. But was that the right thing to do? What if Tinny couldn't forgive him? He could stay here instead and resume his relationship with Grace, now that Papa wasn't here to disapprove. But first he had to deal with Mother's fears over him being at Seaton.

'No, Mama comes first. I need to know whether Mother really did send that letter. For all I know, Papa might have written it, to stop Mama from seeing me again.'

Grace wiped her eyes with a handkerchief and put it back in her apron pocket. 'I doubt it. He could be uncaring, but I can't believe he'd deliberately have acted in a way that would make your Mama so ill. You're distressed, William, and it's affecting your view of things.'

He shook his head. 'Remember how controlling he was. It's possible. And if Mother did write it, then I have to find a way of stopping her from making any more threats. Mama is terrified the police will find out they took me from the ship-wreck all those years ago.'

'Well, you know best,' she said. 'I'd better go, or Mrs Dixon will be after me. She's a right slave-driver, that one; she won't accept that I answer to Her Ladyship first.'

'Goodbye, Grace, and thank you for the advice. I'll be back soon.'

She gave him a peck on the cheek and made her way towards the servants' stairs.

William put his hand to his cheek where she'd kissed it, feeling the warmth of it. Then he made his way back to the house to pack his bag for the trip to Scarborough.

CHAPTER 37

'Mother, it's me,' William called out as he went in. He put down his bag and removed his jacket.

'Darling, how lovely to see you. This is an unexpected treat.' She took his hands in hers and kissed him on the cheek.

'Not a treat, I'm afraid; I have some tragic news. Can we go into the sitting room?' He marched ahead and stood by the window, gesturing to her to sit in the chair. He wanted to see the light on her face when he told her.

She sat down and folded her hands, placing them in her lap. 'What's happened?'

'It's Papa. He's dead.' His voice cracked.

She turned towards him with a shocked expression. 'Dead? Oh, William, I'm so sorry. I mean, I know you and he didn't get along, but all the same… What happened?'

'He committed suicide on the pier. I tried to save him…'

'You were there?' She made it sound like an accusation.

'Yes. I was called back because Mama was asking for me. I thought she was dying.' He couldn't wait any longer. 'I have to ask you, Mother. Did you write that letter to Papa?'

She looked away, twisting her wedding ring. The silence seemed to go on forever.

At last she spoke. 'I did, and you must be wondering why.'

'Of course I'm wondering. You made threats that caused him to panic, to think he would be ruined. He couldn't face losing the business and his home. And Mama...' As he searched for a handkerchief, his fingers closed over the jet. Courage. Stay calm and find the answers.

'I did it out of love for you; you must see that. When I found out you'd spent time with Anna Harper, I was overcome with sadness and fear. I've lost you once, William, and I couldn't bear to lose you again.'

The tremble in her voice pulled at his heart, bringing back the memory of their reunion. Tinny was always telling him to put himself in other people's shoes. Perhaps now was a good time to try.

'How can you think I would leave you?' he began. 'After all the years we were separated... I was so happy to find you. You've given me a way to follow my dreams, to help me grow as an artist. Why can't I have both you and Mama in my life?'

She stood up and came closer. 'Because she brought you up and it's obvious you're devoted to her. I was worried that you'd agree to go back, to make up for hurting her when you ran away. Besides, I've heard your Papa's business has been doing well, and the shipping industry is growing fast. I could imagine you'd be tempted to take up your entitlement to the company.'

'You know it's not about the money. I get far more pleasure from creating a painting than seeing how much it's earned.'

She smiled fondly. 'You're just like James. He only ever wanted recognition for his talent. But if I hadn't managed the financial side of things, he'd have given most of it away, and then where would we have been?'

William felt the familiar tug of war between the past and present, between his two families. Leah Morgan had given birth to him, then had lost him along with the love of her life in a cruel accident. It must have been terrible for her. Papa wasn't his real father, and never seemed to care about him. But he'd done a selfless thing in saving him from the wreckage, giving Mama the thing she most wanted, most craved: a son.

'I managed to talk to him before he... before it happened. He told me there was an affair.'

Mother turned away to look out of the window, but not before he'd seen the colour drain from her face.

'What did he say?'

'I couldn't hear properly. The wind was too strong. But he said something about you being the victim.' He went to stand at her side, turning to watch her expression.

She plucked a handkerchief from inside her sleeve and mopped at her eyes. 'It's painful to talk about it. But you have a right to know.'

William waited in silence, glancing out of the window at the seagulls wheeling through the air.

She retreated to the chair and sat down wearily. 'It happened just as James was becoming well known. He'd been distracted by a pretty face before, but it was never a threat, because I could help him with the business side of things and look after his interests like no one else could. As far as I was aware, he'd never strayed before, not seriously. This time was different.'

'Why?'

'Because I was pregnant with you. Looking back, I can see I was so overcome with joy that I didn't pay James enough attention. He was caught in a whirl of events, in demand for parties and so on. It was expected that I would stay at home in my condition, so I didn't think too much of it. I only found out when a newspaper reporter revealed the affair.'

William knelt beside her and put his hand over hers. 'That must have been very distressing for you. I don't understand how Father could do that, when you said you were so much in love.'

'We were in love; and that helped us survive it. We both knew it was a meaningless lapse. He begged me to forgive him. Knowing I was having his child made him choose me. You saved us.'

Poor Mother. Now he understood even more her desire to keep him in her life. He was just about to say that there was no need for her to continue the threats to Mama, when she spoke.

'How did Christina react when you told her about your Papa?'

The question caught him off guard. He stood up. 'She doesn't know yet,' he admitted. 'I came straight here.'

'Is everything all right between you?'

She was more sensitive than he thought. Had his agitation given her a clue? 'Not exactly. We had an argument, after she found out I'd lied about who Mama was. Then the message came, and I had to leave for Seaton before we sorted it out.'

'Well, it may be for the best. It's no secret that I had reservations about her. She has a shrewish look; I'm not sure she'd make you happy. The last thing you need is to be held back from your career, when everything is looking so promising. And if you don't respect her enough to tell her the truth...'

'Don't, Mother. I'm upset enough about it without you interfering.'

'Interfering? Really, William! Do you think all my guidance and paying for lessons is interfering?'

'No... of course I don't, I didn't mean that...' Why did he always say the wrong thing? 'I'm sorry, Mother. I'm still in shock from Papa's death. It was awful, seeing him drown like that.'

She nodded. 'I understand. But you need to make up your mind, William. If you don't intend to marry the girl, you need to let her down gently, and the sooner the better.'

He didn't respond. It wasn't the right time to discuss the choice he had to make. 'I'll go upstairs and unpack, if you don't mind me staying for a couple of days. I have a lot of thinking to do.'

'Of course I don't mind. And I promise I won't mention Christina again; you need to make your own mind up. But don't you want to hear about the arrangements for your exhibition?' Her eyes brightened, as they always did when she was planning an event.

'Yes, of course.'

He listened as she told him the curator of the Yorkshire Fine Art and Industrial Institution had agreed to host the exhibition. 'It's quite an honour,' she said with a smile.

'Thank you, Mother. You're being very ambitious. I hope I'm worthy of it.'

'Of course you are. My reputation is at stake as much as yours. That last piece needs finishing, the one with the dancers at the Spa. I'm hoping the flower girl portrait will attract a lot of interest.'

Dare he put forward his idea? 'I was wondering... is it good enough to put to auction? It would be wonderful if we could show a wider audience the plight of the homeless on our streets.'

She smiled. 'You have a social conscience, just like James. It warms my heart. By a coincidence, you might have found a solution to a little problem I have. I already had a portrait booked in an auction, but my artist has been ill and couldn't complete it in time. If I can substitute yours, I won't lose my money.'

How shrewd she was, he thought. But he didn't care how it happened, as long as he had the chance to prick the conscience of the rich and have more people notice his art. 'That's wonderful, thank you.'

'My pleasure. It arrived safely yesterday; I will retrieve it from the Institute and get it sent off to the auctioneer's immediately.'

He kissed her and took his bag upstairs. She seemed genuinely sorry about Papa's death, and the assurances he'd given her should be enough to stop her from making threats to Mama from now on. Shouldn't they?

CHAPTER 38

Tinny sat at the table in the back room with her hands cupped around a glass of water. Her eyes were sore from crying. If Grace hadn't sent for William, they could have at least tried to sort out their problems, even though it seemed hopeless.

Grace. He was bound to see her there; she might even be at his home, helping to watch over Anna Harper. They'd have time to talk, to become close again, in an atmosphere fraught with emotion. She couldn't compete with their shared childhood experiences.

How could he keep so much from her, after everything he'd said about hating the secrets and lies his own family had woven? The betrayal of her trust and her love for him hurt the most. God expected her to forgive, but was He asking too much? It would be hard to believe anything William told her ever again.

Mam came through from the kitchen, wiping her hands on a towel.

'You need to eat, my girl. It's no use pining away and

William finding a heap of clothes on the floor when he comes back. You know how much I hate wasting food.'

'I can't, Mam.' Had he arrived in time? Was his Mama still alive? If not, she'd have to deal with his sorrow as well as everything else when… if… he returned. Either way, it could be some time.

'What if he doesn't come back?'

'Oh lass, don't go thinking like that.' Mam put her arm around her shoulders. 'Of course he'll come back. He loves you, anyone can see that.'

'But we can't compete with his family. They have money and a nice house, and he'll be in his old bedroom with all his childhood memories…' She pulled away. Mam thought it was so straightforward. But then she didn't know everything.

'There's another girl, and I think he loves her.'

'What?' Mam pulled out the chair and sat beside her. 'You never said.'

'She's a friend from home: Grace. They've been writing to each other for ages, possibly since he first came here. Remember that Christmas, when I picked the letter off the floor and William shouted at me? It was from her. She even came here, to the shop, soon after we got engaged, and they had a meeting. I had no idea about any of this at the time.'

Mam opened her mouth, but Tinny held her hand up, needing to finish. 'We argued about it last week, but then he got called home. It's such a mess, Mam.' She twisted her ring round and round, wondering if she would be able to wear it for much longer.

'He's a good lad deep down. Don't worry about things before they happen.'

'I'm not so sure. I don't think I can trust him ever again.'

'After everything he's done for us? Don't his actions speak louder than his words? He's been through a lot, don't forget.'

Her mother had had a soft spot for William from the day he'd come into their lives. But it might all be out of their control, if he decided to stay up north and break his promise to her.

'If I light a candle, will you pray with me?' She took a candle from a drawer in the dresser and lit it from the gas lamp, dripped a pool of wax on to a saucer and balanced the candle in it. Gently, she set it on the table. As she turned off the lamps, the room darkened, and shadows danced on the walls as the flame flickered.

Tinny returned to her seat and with hands clasped together, closed her eyes and sat in silence for a moment, gathering her thoughts.

'Heavenly Father, hear our prayers. Send your healing spirit on William's Mama, and please, Lord, let her recover. Give him peace of mind, that he can confess his wrongdoing and be forgiven.' Not just by God, she thought, but by me too.

'Amen,' said Mam.

She hadn't finished. 'And send him home to me, so we can talk, and better understand each other. We need to find out if we can trust one another again. I promise to be forgiving, but please make William accept that he has to be truthful. In your name this prayer I make. Amen.'

'Amen. That's lovely, Christina.'

She opened her eyes and watched the flame swaying and lengthening, drawing her emotions to its brightest point. 'My prayer will work, won't it Mam? God's always listening, isn't He?'

'Of course He is.' Mam gave a long yawn. 'It's getting late, and we both need our beds. Things always seem worse after a long hard day. Everything will look better in the morning. Keep hoping and praying, my lass, and it will all work out. You're made for each other, you two.' She gave her a kiss, then made her way upstairs.

Tinny sat alone staring at the glow of the candle, continuing to pray, her lips moving silently. Somehow, she didn't think her mother's confidence was well placed. William would be by his Mama's bedside, praying too. Would she be part of those prayers?

There were other reasons for him to stay in Seaton besides his attraction to Grace. If William didn't have the strength to stand up to his Papa, he could be forced to stay there and join the family business. She sighed as she climbed the stairs. The odds weren't good; she'd probably already lost him.

CHAPTER 39

Papa's pleading face came into view, his arms reaching out towards William, pulling him below the surface, dragging him to where the currents swirled and drew them both under. William kicked out for his life, squeezing every last drop of air from his lungs until they were about to burst. It was futile to resist Papa's firm grip, so he closed his eyes and gave in, sinking, drifting down to the sea bed.

His eyes flashed open; he was in his room at Scarborough. It had felt so real, as if he had no choice but to die.

Would he ever be able to paint a seascape again? He'd tried yesterday, but it was unbearable, a reminder of the power of the sea, the wind whipping up the waves in a cruel, murderous storm that swept everything and everyone away in its path.

He consulted his pocket watch. It was no good; lying here wasn't achieving anything. Mother would have already left for her journey to London. He got out of bed, had a quick wash, dressed and went straight to his studio.

The canvas portraying dancers at a society ball stood on an easel, almost finished. It was the final painting for the exhibition. They'd be asking for it soon, and it might take his mind off things if he did it now.

He squeezed a dab of crimson on to his palette and mixed it with a dash of burnt umber to create a cherry red. A gentle touch with the brush in the right places would help to create an impression of fluidity in the silken dress worn by one of the dancers in the picture. The light in the Spa ballroom had been hard to portray, but this subject should appeal to Mother's society friends, a scene of joyful music and dancing that he hoped would evoke warm emotions.

Once he'd cleaned the brush and put it away, he stood back to assess the canvas. Better, but not quite right. He pottered around the studio for a while, tidying away his materials, then decided to go to the Spa for lunch. It might help him decide on the finishing touches to his painting.

The promenade was quieter today, on account of the grey clouds scudding across the sky, bringing a threat of rain. He tipped his face upwards to enjoy the light breeze and the freshness of the air. He'd been spending too much time indoors. Hiding here to avoid facing Tinny was all very well, but it was making him stale.

As he entered the Spa ballroom, the orchestra was tuning up and people were taking their seats at the tables around the edge of the dance floor. He placed his order and settled at a table to enjoy the music. This last painting had been a good exercise in portraying movement; but he could always learn more. He could stay awhile and watch the afternoon dancers, noting the way the ladies' skirts flowed, and the pattern of the light on the burnished floor.

As he finished his lunch, a gentleman passed by the table. 'Would you like my newspaper, sir?' He offered a folded copy.

'Thank you,' said William. He opened it, scanning the pages for any stories of interest. A headline caught his eye:

Record-breaking art auction. He folded the page to a manageable size and read the article.

This week, a painting by a virtually unknown artist broke all records for a portrait of a working-class subject. The Flower Girl, by William Harper, was the subject of frenzied bidding at the Liverpool auction house, in a pre-exhibition publicity tactic which certainly paid off for his sponsor.

How strange it was, seeing his own name in print. Broke all records? He read on.

Mrs Leah Morgan, widow of the celebrated artist James Morgan, has attracted much attention for the risks she takes with young artists, and for her ability to match them with tutors to achieve rapid progress. With this latest addition to her list of protégés, Mrs Morgan has made a wise investment, with a sale price of £70 after costs.

"It's a remarkable painting, far beyond expectations for such a young artist," the delighted buyer said. "It draws you in emotionally, as if you are being personally asked to buy the flower. The quality of the brushwork is quite unique." He asked for anonymity.

William Harper's exhibition at the Yorkshire Fine Art and Industrial Institution runs from the first Thursday in June to the end of the month.

It must be a misprint. Before she left last night, Mother had told him how much it had raised, and it was nowhere near that much. He called the waitress over and paid the bill, then took his coat and strode to the nearest shop to purchase a different newspaper. He sat on a bench in Valley Gardens and found the article. It said the same. This was perplexing. Mother wouldn't take that much commission from him, would she? Perhaps it worked differently for an auction sale.

He'd promised to go and talk to Mr Cooper at the Institution, to check the arrangements for the exhibition. So far, he'd delayed it, reluctant to return to York where he'd have to face Tinny. But it might be a timely opportunity to ask the curator what he could reasonably expect to receive for the picture.

There was no time to waste. He had to get back to Mother's, pack a bag and catch the next train to York.

❧

WILLIAM STOOD in front of the Yorkshire Fine Art and Industrial Institution, gazing in awe at the stone facade with its portico of five arches linking the columns. It was unbelievable, and a little scary, to think his paintings would be on its walls in a matter of two weeks. York was an even bigger opportunity than the Scarborough exhibition. How could he even think Mother wasn't looking after his interests? But he couldn't rest until he had all the facts. He made his way through the arches into the building, asked for the curator and waited.

Mr Cooper emerged, a tall wiry man with glasses and a neat beard. 'Mr Harper, I'm delighted to meet you. It's been a real pleasure planning your exhibition. Do follow me, and I'll show you the space we're using.'

As they were climbing the stairs to the first floor, William asked him about his commission. He hoped it wasn't an impolite question.

The curator didn't seem to take offence. 'I must say, it's good to see a young artist who wants to learn how the business works. Our commission is five percent, and the rest goes to the artist, or in your case Mrs Morgan, since she's managing things for you. She will be taking a fee for her time, naturally, but that's between you and her.' He opened a door and beckoned William to follow him in. 'Here we are.'

William hid his disappointment at not getting the answer to his question and focused instead on the room in front of him. The walls were festooned with hooks in the empty spaces where his paintings would soon be hanging. In one corner there was a set of canvases still on display. 'Are you removing those before it starts?'

The curator shook his head. 'Didn't Mrs Morgan tell you? We've secured a loan of several of your father's works from a local collector. She thought there'd be a lot of interest in how he's passed his skill to you. It's remarkable to see the similarity in your techniques. Art historians love this sort of thing, and you have such an unusual story, being brought up separately and never knowing him.'

William frowned. Mother hadn't mentioned she was revealing this. And she'd always said they should keep their relationship a secret. What had made her change her mind?

Excitement at seeing more of his father's work overtook his misgivings as he made his way over to the paintings and stood in awe, trying to take it all in. One canvas caught his eye, a harbour scene in a storm, with a group of dark rocks at its centre, the waves crashing and spreading over them. He peered at the label. *The Black Middens, Tynemouth.*

James Morgan wouldn't have realised the prescience of choosing as his subject the very place where he would meet his death. The poignancy of it haunted him, yet it was hard to look away. He tried to regain his composure by focusing on an adjacent canvas, a Scarborough scene similar to his own recent portrayal of families enjoying a sunny day on the promenade.

'Forgive me, I forgot to congratulate you on the sale of The Flower Girl.' Mr Cooper gave a slight bow of respect. 'A remarkably successful strategy by Mrs Morgan, putting it to auction. And here you can see why we were so excited by it. Your father had a real talent for portraiture. He came to it relatively late. Such a shame; one can only imagine how he might have progressed if it wasn't for his untimely death.

Here we see the best of the portraits he completed.' He gestured at a collection of four canvases.

William's eyes widened as he recognised the familiar scene at the entrance to the Grand Hotel in one of the pictures. A lady was stepping down daintily from a carriage, wearing a fine oyster silk dress adorned with appliquéd ivory flowers. Her eyes sparkled, and her ruby lips were parted in a smile as if looking directly at the artist.

Mr Cooper stepped closer to the portrait. 'You have impeccable taste, Mr Harper. I think this is James Morgan's finest painting. But with such a muse, how could any artist fail to be inspired?'

William stared at the portrayal of his mother, a young woman obviously in love. She'd said their relationship was special, and this painting proved that. His father must have been besotted with her. He squinted to make out the date. They wouldn't have been able to afford to attend a ball at The Grand at that time, so he'd put her in the picture as if they could. How proud of her he must have been.

The other portraits also featured Mother, pictured in different locations around Scarborough: strolling in the Valley Gardens, standing in St Mary's churchyard looking out to sea, and relaxing at home. Her beauty was beyond doubt. How tragic, when he thought of the loss she had borne later.

One thing wasn't quite right, though, and with Mother away, he couldn't ask her about it. Perhaps it was time to return to Seaton and see how Mama was coping.

CHAPTER 40

The clanging noise burrowed into Tinny's brain, vibrating as if she was standing in the belfry while the hour struck twelve. She meandered between dreaming and waking, resisting the pull into consciousness, burrowing her head under the pillow. Who could be making that much noise in the middle of the night?

The banging continued, insistent and jarring. Not bells. She threw the blankets off and rolled out of bed, putting on her dressing gown and slippers. What was that smell? Oh, Lord, no. The noise stopped as she ran out of the room, stumbling down the stairs, panic rising in her chest. 'Mam?'

At the foot of the stairs, she stopped. An orange glow was visible beyond the glass panel in the door. Was her mother still in there, trying to fight the fire? The noise had stopped. She swallowed a sob and tried to stay calm, gathering up courage for what she had to do. As she opened the door, a whoosh of smoke engulfed her, catching in her throat and making her cough.

'Mam! Where are you?' She dropped to the floor and

crawled into the room. The flames were at the far side; there was no escape that way. Holding her breath, Tinny edged forward, suppressing her panic. She had to get Mam out as fast as possible. The alternative was too distressing to even contemplate.

The acrid smoke filled her nostrils and caught in her throat. She stretched out flat on the floor, trying to find a pocket of air, aware of the roar and crackle of the flames, destroying all their possessions, their livelihood. But none of that mattered right now. She had to get Mam out.

Two pans were next to the table leg. She must have used them to raise the alarm. Blinking in the smoky haze, frantic with fear, at last she spotted an arm stretched out along the floor. She darted forward, lifted her mother by the armpits, and dragged her backwards to the foot of the stairs, before slamming the door shut.

She coughed, and sooty saliva splattered the floor. 'Mam... please, I'm here. Talk to me.' There was no response.

Tinny looked around in desperation. How could they get out? The key to the back door was in the kitchen and she couldn't go back in to get it. She'd never have the strength to force the door open. The only way out was through the window. But even if she could break the glass, she'd never manage to lift her mother. She swallowed a sob.

'Wake up, Mam. We need to get out.' The words choked in her throat, dry and rasping. A knot of panic rose up as she struggled for air.

She leaned over and laid her head on Mam's chest, praying for a sign she was still alive. Why wouldn't she respond?

Tinny lifted her head and pulled herself up to kneel beside Mam, then closed her eyes and started to pray. It was all she could do now. The heat was building up. It wouldn't be long before it broke through. And then they'd be trapped. Was it already too late?

A loud crack rang out from the other side of the door, and a falling beam crashed through the glass panel, scattering shards over them both. Tinny flung herself over Mam.

Then everything went black.

CHAPTER 41

William tried to avert his eyes from the cruel sea as he turned the corner and made his way towards the village green. The house came into view. A pall of gloom hovered over it, the curtains closed in mourning. Perhaps it wasn't a good idea to have come without giving advance notice. Mama might find it confusing or distressing to have him there.

As he entered the hall, the darkness settled around him like a cloak. He stood alone for a moment while his eyes became accustomed to it. The sombre sound of a low note on the piano led him to the drawing room. Mama was sitting on the stool, her head bowed, absentmindedly pressing a single ivory key again and again.

As she turned towards him, her eyes brightened with happiness, transforming her features. 'William! I had no idea you were coming. How wonderful to see you.' She took his hands in hers and leaned in to kiss his forehead.

He felt a surge of relief at how much stronger she looked. 'It was a sudden decision to come, otherwise I would have sent word. I've spoken to Mother, and she regrets the letter. You should be free of her now.'

'Oh, my darling, you don't know how much that news means to me. It's been so hard without your Papa...' She began to cry.

William offered her his handkerchief. 'But something strange has come to my attention. I was hoping you might help me work it out.'

'If I can,' she replied. 'I wasn't in the right frame of mind before, but things are clearer now. Lady Forbes has been such a good friend to me. What have you been doing lately?'

'I've been finishing the paintings for my exhibition. I need to keep earning, at least until we're confident you can inherit Papa's estate.'

Another worry was left unspoken, that he'd be forced to get involved in the shipping business. He said a silent prayer that Lord Forbes would discover all the right plans had been made. But might the absence of a body cause complications? Never mind that; he couldn't let his mind be distracted by things he couldn't control. His priority was to uncover the truth about his father's portraits.

'You must be thirsty after your journey. Do you want some tea?' she asked.

He shook his head. 'Not at the moment, thank you. I was wondering...'

'What?' Her glance was wary.

'Something Papa said when he was out on the pier. About an affair involving Leah Morgan.' It was best not to call her Mother when he was here.

'Please don't... I can't bear to think of him out there, contemplating death.'

It was wrong; he shouldn't have asked. 'I'm sorry, it's too soon, isn't it?'

They sat in silence for a while, William's thoughts

whirring like cogs in a machine. Was there a clue here? It was worth a try.

'Mama, a thought occurred to me yesterday. Has Lord Forbes looked through Papa's personal papers yet? There might be something that might help him make faster progress in sorting out your financial situation.'

'No, not yet. I couldn't face letting anyone touch them.'

That was a blessing. 'Would you allow me to look through his bureau?'

She nodded. 'That will be a help. I'd rather you did it.'

'In that case, I'll make a start straight away.'

William entered the study and lit the gas lamps, turning them up as brightly as he could. It was still too soon to open the curtains; he'd have to manage. The room looked like a shrine to Papa, much like his own bedroom had seemed when he'd stayed in it the night after the tragedy.

The bureau was open, with a few papers resting on the hinged desk together with an inkwell and pen set beside a half-finished letter. William glanced at it, but the first few paragraphs only contained the usual good wishes for the recipient's health. It finished abruptly in mid-sentence. Papa must have sat here, in turmoil over the risk to his business and the potential destruction of his reputation in the community. Did the sudden halt in the sentence mark the moment when he'd left for the pier, planning to end his misery?

William moved the pen and inkwell aside. There were several compartments inside the bureau, holding bits and pieces of stationery and a few business cards, but nothing that looked important. At the right-hand side he spotted a drawer with a tiny golden key. He turned it and pulled, but the drawer wouldn't budge. He prised it open with a letter-opener and tipped the contents on to the top of the desk.

It all seemed to be receipts for various purchases from a

very long time ago. At the bottom of the pile were a few newspaper cuttings. He opened one out. It was a news story about the wreck at Tynemouth, with eyewitness accounts of the storm that had broken up several ships.

William shivered as he read the details of the evening that changed his life. Many more people had perished than he'd realised. He scanned the story, but there was no mention of James Morgan and his family. He set the cutting aside and opened another.

The scandal of the budding artist's affair, he read to himself. An icy tremor ran through his body as he started to read it.

The story of James Morgan's affair with socialite Virginia Lake is the talk of the art world. Opinions are divided on the subject, some saying young artists need more guidance to handle their sudden popularity, so that they won't be tempted by the strange world they find themselves thrust into. Miss Lake's beauty is unde-niable, and many men clamour for her attentions. A young man will naturally be flattered and unable to resist.

Others are setting the blame firmly at Mr Morgan's door, drawing attention to his young wife Leah's first pregnancy and condemning him for his lack of loyalty.

There was a sketch accompanying the article, with James in the middle, flanked on both sides by the two women in his life.

It confirmed what Mother had told him. How hard it must have been for her to bear her husband's betrayal, at a time when she should have been full of joy, preparing for their first-born child. She'd won him back from that woman, but had lost him to the sea so soon afterwards. Just like he'd lost Papa. And she'd carried on his memory, promoting his work and selling his paintings. How devoted she'd been, how courageous, learning the business and making a career for herself.

He re-read the article, then frowned. It must be a simple mistake.

William carefully opened the remaining pieces of news-paper, his fingers trembling as he read more accounts of the storm. They didn't add anything. Then he thought of James Morgan's paintings hanging on the wall in the Institute, waiting to be joined by his own canvases. Father's muse. Of course. The answer had been staring him in the face.

CHAPTER 42

I t couldn't be true, it simply couldn't. But there was no other explanation. How could she do it? All the time they'd spent together, learning about each other... It hurt more than anything he could remember. He started to shake, unable to comprehend it.

It seemed an age before he felt able to face anyone. But he wouldn't get very far in sorting everything out if he stayed here. He put the cuttings in an envelope and hid it in his bag in the bedroom before going downstairs to take tea with Mama. She was trying to be brave, but he could tell she was still fragile. He should stay a while longer. Tinny always said helping others was the best way of forgetting your own problems.

Tinny. Her face appeared in front of him like a ghostly image, her blue eyes searching his face, trying to understand why he'd told her a lie. No, not just one; a whole raft of them. The longer he avoided her, the more afraid he was of returning.

'How long are you staying?' Mama's voice broke into his thoughts.

'I'm not sure. There's something I need to work out, and I'm not sure I can do that here. It's all still too raw, too upsetting. If you don't mind, I think a walk might help. I won't be long.'

He planted a kiss on her cheek and went to get his coat. The clouds had separated, revealing patches of a watery blue sky. He stood at the corner of the green for a moment, pondering which way to go. It was tempting to go into the George and Dragon, but drinking wouldn't make the problems vanish. And he couldn't face walking south, towards the scene of the tragedy. So he turned northward.

As he reached Chambers House, he came to a halt. Should he go and ask Lord Forbes how the settling of the estate was progressing? No, it wasn't polite to arrive unannounced. A handwritten note would be better.

He continued past the house, but found himself turning left at the next corner, then left again, bringing him to the servants' entrance at the rear. Only one person could help him decide what to do.

'William?' Grace looked shocked to see him as she came down the steps towards him.

'I hope I'm not getting you in trouble, turning up like this and asking for you,' he said.

'Five minutes is our limit,' she told him. 'What's happened now?'

'I think I've worked out what's been going on.'

'You've solved it? Leah's going to stop the threats?' Her smile was full of hope and pride.

If only it were all good news. Inside, there was an emptiness. 'I've spoken to her, and yes, she regrets sending the letter; she did it because she was frightened of losing me.'

Grace touched his arm. 'Well done. I knew you could persuade her. Your Mama must be so relieved.'

'It's not quite that simple. While I was in Scarborough, I

discovered that Mother had lied to me about the proceeds of the flower girl painting at auction. It raised much more than she said. Then I went back to York to check the arrangements for my exhibition, and there were a few of Father's paintings on the walls. She's decided to tell my story, and his work will be displayed alongside mine.'

'That's a lovely idea, William. You must be so pleased.'

'No, Grace, it's a disaster. What if the newspapers find out about Mama and Papa taking me from the wreck? They're bound to be curious about why I'm not a Morgan. Anyway, it gets worse. His paintings were of Mother. She was his muse; the curator told me. Honestly, she was beautiful as a young woman. But I wondered about one thing that didn't seem right. She didn't have a wedding ring on in any of the pictures.'

She shrugged. 'Doesn't mean much, does it? Don't you miss out details when you paint someone?'

'No, never.' He thought of the flower girl, with her tattered dress and bitten fingernails.

'But weren't your father's portraits supposed to make the viewer want the woman so much that they had to have the picture? It wouldn't have the same effect if they could see she was married, would it? He would have left the ring off when he painted her. Your letters were full of how Leah was a good business woman. She'd have encouraged him to do the right thing to get a sale, don't you think?'

'Not a bad theory, Grace. But my instinct was right this time.' He reached into his pocket and pulled out the envelope to show her the cutting. 'Look at this. I'll hold it; it's quite brittle. I found it in Papa's desk drawer.'

'An affair? Naughty James,' she said with a faint chuckle as she read the headline. Then her eyes scanned the article. 'At least he went back to Leah.'

He pointed at the drawing. 'That's her.'

She followed his finger. 'She is beautiful, if the newspaper artist's been accurate.'

'No, look properly.'

William saw the truth dawn in her eyes. 'Oh no, William... it can't be. After everything that's happened, are you absolutely sure? It could be a mistake.'

'It's not. The paintings confirm it.' He couldn't keep his voice even.

He felt her arms curl around him, holding him close until he stopped shaking. 'I don't know what to do; it's such a mess. I still haven't been to see Tinny. I've stayed away so long that she's probably given up on me. And now this...' He moved back from her, embarrassed at letting her see his weakness. No, that was Papa's way of thinking. If he couldn't be honest with Grace, there was no hope for him.

'If Christina loves you, she'll wait. This is more important; it's your future. You have to go to talk to Leah, otherwise you'll torture yourself with this. There might be a reasonable explanation. And if there isn't, well, that's a different matter. You need to look after your own interests, William, and stop avoiding confrontation. Dad always says if there's an unpleasant task to be done, it's best to get it out of the way. I'm sure he's right; it's often not as awful as you imagine it will be.'

'How did you learn to be so philosophical, Miss Robinson?' he said with a rueful smile. 'I hate to admit it, but you're right. And I've decided what I'm going to do.'

CHAPTER 43

William walked past the Grand Hotel and crossed over to Mother's house, trying to suppress his overwhelming sadness. Grace had been right; he'd found the answers in the newspaper archives. The exhaustion of several sleepless nights had taken its toll, but it would soon be over.

Dobson was outside, polishing the carriage. Mother had better not be planning to go out soon; he had a lot to say to her. He tightened his grip on the envelope that held the cuttings and stood at the gate for a moment, like Jack surveying the beanstalk, wondering what mood the sleeping giant would be in when he, or in this case she, woke up. William forced himself to open the gate and trudged along the path towards the door. He tried the handle; it opened.

She was coming down the stairs as he entered the hall. 'Oh, hello,' she said. 'This is unexpected.'

'Good afternoon, Mother. How was the London trip?' He held the envelope behind his back as he followed her into the sitting room. At least he hadn't bumped into her when he was in the capital.

'Successful, though the new gallery owner is rather full of his own importance. I'm so sorry I missed the opening of your exhibition, my darling. I have to prioritise, no matter how much I want to support all my artists.'

'You don't have to apologise. I've always said I don't want any preferential treatment. Sales were pretty decent, and there's almost two weeks left.' Could he do this? 'I didn't expect to see Father's paintings there. You should have told me.'

'It didn't seem important, not compared to the news about your Papa. Anyway, I didn't think you'd mind; you've trusted me with the other decisions about your exhibitions and we've done very well, haven't we?'

'Yes, but you've always said you didn't want anyone to know we were related. I'm glad I found out on a personal visit to Mr Cooper, and not at the launch itself.' He focused on Father's self-portrait in the alcove to the left of the fireplace, inwardly asking him for inspiration.

'And how is Mrs Harper?'

Mama, he wanted to scream. She isn't Mrs Harper; she is my Mama, and she is still struggling. Papa may not have been perfect, either as a husband or a father, but he was all she had and now he is gone. Thanks to you. But there was no point in saying any of that.

'I'm sure you can imagine how she is. Much the same as you must have been after the shipwreck.'

'Ah, but it was doubly painful for me; I thought I had lost you too. At least your Mama found out straight away, as I understand.'

William wondered how long they could dance around each other. He could leave now, but it would gnaw away at him forever. Besides, he'd promised Tinny there'd be no more lies.

'I know the truth.'

She flinched ever so slightly, but he spotted it. 'The truth about what?'

'Let's start with the flower girl portrait. You told me it raised fifteen pounds. But the newspaper reports said it brought in seventy, after the auction house costs. That's a rather large difference. Are you cheating me?'

'How could you even think that? You've obviously misunderstood. I was letting you have fifteen pounds of it. That's generous, considering the amount I've paid for your lessons. It's a beautiful painting, and you should be excited that it sold, not standing here accusing me. If we can achieve that sort of money for your work at this stage, think what might be possible in the future. I'm not sure I like your attitude, William.'

'Sarah was right. We should have had a proper agreement.'

She stood up, trying to draw herself to her full height. 'You're a sharp one, no mistake. You must take after me for that. All right, I confess to understating it a little. But don't you see that it's better for you to think you're getting a bigger share of a smaller amount? It's the same thing, but you see it from a different angle. There's no harm done.' He'd seen that false smile when she was negotiating, trying to trick someone into paying far more than they should for a painting. But it was a different matter when she was aiming it at him.

'Oh, I disagree. Because the money that you obtained to start your business wasn't yours, was it? You had no right to it.'

'Of course I did, as James' widow. His possessions passed to me and I was entitled to sell them if I wanted to.'

'But you weren't his widow, were you?'

The silence hung between them like a curtain. As he

fingered the envelope, her expression changed from indignation to curiosity.

'What have you got there?'

'Evidence.' The only way he could get through this was to detach himself from the emotions rumbling deep inside him. He mustn't recall the warm delight he'd felt on the day of their reunion, when he finally knew where he belonged. Focusing on his anger at her duplicity was the only way to get this over and done with.

'You've deceived everyone, haven't you? Playing the grieving widow and mother, a hard-working business-woman who'd succeeded against all the odds, breaking the traditions of the art world. I remember how you said everyone under-estimated you, and you mocked them for it.'

She gave a bitter laugh. 'Everyone knows I'm Leah Morgan, James' widow. How can you say otherwise?'

'There had to be a deeper reason why you wanted me to stay away from Mama and Papa. After Papa died, I found some newspaper cuttings in a drawer. One was from a few months before the shipwreck. A love triangle.' He unfolded the thin piece of paper and showed it to her.

'This drawing here, the lady with the fair colouring, is described as Leah Morgan. The one on the right of Father is a younger version of you. It confirms what I'd seen at the Institute the day before, in Father's portraits of you. His muse, the curator said.'

She took it from him and scanned it, then tossed it on to the table. 'They've got the names the wrong way around. That woman was trying to steal James from me, while I was pregnant with you. She had no shame, and he was no better, running after her.'

'I thought the same thing too at first.' He ran his fingers through his hair. The gall of her, to keep pretending.

'It's a mistake,' she insisted. 'It's hurtful to see it after all this time. Let's just forget about it.'

For a brief instant, William wondered whether that was the best way. But no, he couldn't live like that. 'Oh, I'm sure you'd like to do that, Miss Virginia Lake. Your story is true, but it's the other way around, isn't it?'

She wouldn't look him in the eye. His heart ached at what he had to do, but it was the only way to put a stop to her deceit.

'I've been to London, where I found more articles from the time, revealing the plans you and James were making to run away, even after I was born. That's how you knew about my birthmark; you must have seen me. Did you dare to visit their house? When I think of the disgrace you brought on my mother... My real mother, Leah.'

The words left a bitter taste on his tongue.

'My mother Leah, who also died in the shipwreck. You see, thanks to another cutting in Papa's desk, I traced the name of the ship. That led me to a passenger list in the record office at London, which confirmed that both James and Leah were on board. They were taking me to Tynemouth. James did the right thing in the end, ending your affair and staying with Leah. They both perished in the wreck.'

'I don't have to listen to this. You're deluded.' She started to move away from him, but he stood in front of her and held on to her arm.

'When Mama and Papa lived in Tynemouth, they would have known about the scandal that James brought on his parents through his adulterous behaviour. If I spent time in Seaton, they'd have told me, and I would have put it all together. That's the real reason you wanted me to cut ties with them, isn't it?'

'This is pure fancy.'

Her insistence was astounding. 'Well, your blackmail won't work any longer. Papa kept the cutting all this time. I'm sure he knew I was an orphan.'

He was taken by surprise as she flung herself at him, thumping his chest. He staggered backwards, colliding with a table, but managed to stay upright.

She sprang forward again, but this time he was ready for her, grabbing hold of her wrists.

'Stop it. Now.' This wasn't how he wanted it to end, but her denial only added to the pain. He had to stay strong and finish this, as Grace had told him he must.

She glared at him. 'You wanted a real mother. I offered you that, and more. Why did you have to go prying? You've ruined everything. Being with you brought back so many memories of James. We did have a special relationship.'

'You were nothing but a common mistress with no rights. James may have been tempted, but you led him further into sin. Then I was born, and they stayed together. He didn't want you. But after the shipwreck, you saw an opportunity to impersonate her. It was easy to re-invent a woman who stayed in the shadows.' He let go of her wrists and she slumped back in the chair.

'I did what I had to do to survive. You know what that's like. I thought all three of you had died, and there was no one left to inherit. It was better to learn the art business in London, so I locked up the house and moved down there. News is forgotten sooner or later; but you've seen the article that made everyone think I was Leah. After a few years it was safe to come back. I like the peace and quiet here.'

'Well, your peace is about to come to an end, Miss Lake. Unless you sign an agreement never to contact Mama again, and hand over a substantial settlement in lieu of everything I should have received when my parents died, I will tell the police you've impersonated my real mother and defrauded me of my inheritance. It's a rather more serious offence than giving an orphan a home, I think you'll find.'

'You wouldn't do that. I helped you fulfil your artistic dreams. I can have you struck off the list in every art gallery the length and breadth of the country.'

'For what reason? All they care about is the quality of my work. In fact, you've already recognised the interest my story will generate, and the truth is even more fascinating. I don't think you'll want to attract attention to your crime.'

Every word was agony, even though he knew it needed to be said. How different it could have been. William pulled a document from the envelope, prepared in duplicate by Lord Forbes. 'I've put a figure there for the settlement.'

Her eyes widened as she read it. 'How much? You can't...' Her expression changed as she realised he was serious.

He called Dobson in to witness their two signatures on the documents. The groom made his mark and left them alone.

William gave one copy to Leah and put the other back in the envelope. 'A wise move. We can both put this whole experience behind us now. You have one week to get out of this house and I never want to see you again. I'll expect a cheque and the house keys by next Tuesday.'

He marched out before she could reply, his heart thudding as he strode through the gate and along the street. Once he'd turned the corner, he came to a halt and leaned against the wall, breathless and trembling. It was over. But he was an orphan again.

CHAPTER 44

J ane Robinson looked taken aback to see him. 'William? I didn't expect to see you here. How are you? I'm so sorry about your Papa; it must have been very traumatic.' She stood aside and gestured for him to go in.

'I'm fine, thank you, although a little tired; it's been a busy few days,' he said.

'Grace!' Mrs Robinson called up the stairs. She turned back to him with a warm smile. 'You're in luck; she's home for lunch. I think she's got another half hour before she needs to go back to work.'

William followed her into the living room. It was much the same as the last time he'd seen it, except the rag rug was darker with the soot from the fire and the sofa had even more bare patches. The leather trunk still stood in the corner, waiting for the next set of sailors in need of clothes. Grace's mother gave him a wink and disappeared into the kitchen.

The door opened, and Grace appeared. 'Well, hello,' she said with a smile. 'Is this another quick visit?'

'I'm not sure yet. There are a few decisions I need to make. Shall we sit?'

It felt so good to be close to her. She smelled of rosewater and a fresh summer day.

'I took your advice. I've been to see Leah Morgan.'

How strange it felt, telling the full story of Leah's deception and how he'd handled it, as if it had happened to someone else.

'I can't imagine how much it hurt you to do that, after your joy at finding her. You are wonderful, facing up to it. And I'm glad you listened to me about looking after your own interests.' She reached for his hand and gave it a squeeze. 'I know how much the truth means to you. How awful it must have felt, realising that she'd been so devious for so long.'

'I could hardly believe it. But I was so outraged at what she'd done that it spurred me on. I could have handed her over to the police, but this way was better. I've got what I'm entitled to straight away, instead of relying on the authorities. Anyway, it's probably all worked out for the best. I'm not sure I would have liked the life Virginia Lake had mapped out for me.'

Grace frowned. 'But I thought it was your dream?'

'It was, but I only ever wanted to paint. I wasn't prepared for the business side of it. Most of her clients saw art as a status symbol, trying to outdo each other to have the latest works on their walls. They didn't feel a connection with my paintings. What I'd like to do most are private commissions. You should have seen Sarah's face when I handed over her portrait. That sort of personal reaction means so much more to me than being celebrated in a newspaper.'

'Good for you. I'm so sorry about your real mother though. The number of people you've lost… it just isn't fair. You deserve better than this, William.'

He stood up, ready to go. It was too tempting to stay.

She looked up at him, her expression anxious. 'Have you made a decision about Christina yet?'

The years fell away, and he remembered all the laughter, the teasing and the times when he'd turned to Grace in his misery, wearied by the bullying, or sore from Papa laying into him with the belt. She'd seen the worst of him and still she wanted him for herself. It was obvious from the look of longing in her eyes.

'I haven't seen her yet, but I will when I return to York. But first I'm going to tell Mama I can definitely come to see her any time without fear of reprisals from Leah. She'll be so relieved.'

Grace smiled. 'It's about time your Mama had some good news. And she's the best mother you've had; you can go back to being her son now. I'm glad you came here first, but you need to get along and tell her.'

He felt in his pocket and pulled out the jet pebble. 'You've no idea how many times this has brought me comfort since you gave it to me. But it's time I returned it.' It glinted in the light as he placed it in her outstretched palm.

She closed her fingers around the jet and gave a rueful smile. 'I hope you can make the right decision. About Christina, I mean.'

'I'm sure I will. Thanks to you, I've made my mind up.'

CHAPTER 45

York station was so busy that it took William a while to navigate his way out, but at last he reached the path that skirted the city walls. He'd spent the whole train journey trying to make sense of it, but he still struggled to understand how Leah, or rather Virginia Lake, could have embarked on such a life of deceit. What had she thought when she saw his advertisement? Had she only wanted him because he was all that was left of James, a way for her to hold on to the past? She had obviously loved his father, but it was a forbidden love. How much hurt his real mother must have gone through.

Virginia Lake didn't deserve to inherit Father's house, or the paintings. At least he'd been able to right those wrongs. But what hurt the most was thinking of all the time they had spent together. How could she be so cruel as to let him believe he was her son? Was it merely the prospect of his talent bringing her even more money that had kept them bound together? He would have to stop torturing himself with endless questions, or he'd go mad.

His victory over her might have given him some comfort,

but now he had to resolve his argument with Tinny. It had sounded so simple when Grace had told him what he needed to do. After such a long absence, how would she react when he turned up? With relief, or anger and frustration? It was torture, not knowing.

The streets near the abbey gardens were teeming with visitors. Hopefully Johnny's business would start to improve, now that the weather was getting milder. It was a sorry state of affairs when he hadn't given a thought to his only male friend in York. A visit was definitely in order once he'd seen Tinny.

He turned the corner into Stonegate and made his way to the bakery. Something was different; what was it? A smell. A different street barrow? It wasn't the right time of year for roasted chestnuts. He wrinkled his nose at the odour. Where, which building? He scanned the street then started to run. No, please God, not the shop.

A policeman was standing guard outside. William saw the blackened stones under the window, the charred timber and sooty panes of glass. 'Please… I live here with the owner and her daughter. Are they safe?'

'All I've been told is that two ladies were taken to hospital, sir. Don't know anything about their condition, sorry. I've just been posted here to make sure no one goes in. It happened several days ago, I believe.'

His paintings... His sketches were there too, and Sarah's beloved portrait. He lunged for the door.

'Stop right there, sir. You can't go in, it's not safe.'

'But there are things in there that I need. I have to get them; they're important to me.'

'Not as important as your life, with respect.'

William nodded, a flush coming into his cheeks as he realised he'd put his paintings before the two people who meant so much to him. It was a reaction borne out of shock. He knew where he needed to be.

'Of course,' he said, and darted away, running as fast as he could to the hospital. After everything he'd been through... If he'd been here, it might not have happened. Oh Lord, why? After all the people he'd lost, why this, now?

He ran through the streets in a panic, dodging the crowds. What if he was too late? If he'd missed his chance to say everything he'd planned...

Please let them be there, alive and cared for.

CHAPTER 46

William was so flustered and anxious that he almost collided with a horse and cart as he turned the corner near the hospital. Where was the main entrance? He followed the path, frantically looking left and right, until he found a sign. Inside, the clerk at the desk was busy with a patient. William tapped his foot, counting every agonising second of not knowing.

At last it was his turn and he was given a ward name. He rushed through the corridors and found it, unable to stop himself from grabbing the curtain and sweeping it aside.

Tinny was sitting on a chair, one hand bandaged, watching over her mother in the bed beside her. Please let Sarah be sleeping, not… He couldn't even think it.

'Christina. Oh thank God you've survived. I thought...' In an instant she was in his arms, burying her face against his chest. 'Are you badly hurt?'

She shook her head. 'I'll be fine. But look at Mam.'

Sarah lay semi-prone against the pillow, her eyes closed, a gash across her head and her arms covered in bandages.

'She inhaled a lot of smoke; they're keeping a close watch on her.'

'But she'll be all right. Won't she?'

'They won't say.' She burst into tears. 'I'm sorry. It's just that I've missed you so much.'

He held her close and stroked the side of her face. 'Let it out, my love. You've had a big shock. I'm just so thankful you both survived.'

'It was my fault. I left a candle burning. I'll never forgive myself if…' She let out a wail, raw and wild.

'Hush, don't. Look, she's sleeping soundly. It will take time, that's all. What happened?' He stroked her hair, encouraging her to continue.

It took a while before she could calm herself to answer.

'I was asleep when Mam discovered the fire. I don't understand why the silly thing didn't just come and get me; she must have tried to put it out herself. The first I knew was hearing pans being banged together. It must have been the only way she could think of to raise the alarm.'

'That must have been terrifying. How did you get out?'

'It was awful. The heat and the smoke were unbearable. I have no idea how I found the strength, but I managed to drag her to the foot of the stairs and close the door. Then I realised the key wasn't in the back door. We were trapped.'

He felt her trembling in his arms. 'Take your time,' he urged her.

She nodded, waiting a moment before continuing. 'A ceiling beam collapsed and crashed through the glass in the connecting door, and the smoke came rushing in. I thought we were going to die.' Another sob escaped.

He held her closer. 'It's all right. You're safe now.'

'We wouldn't be if it wasn't for Paul coming to make the dough just in time. He must have seen the smoke. I shouted to him; thank God he heard. It only took him a minute to break down the door and got us both out.'

'You've been lucky. And now I feel dreadful for leaving you for so long. I thought you'd have given up on me by now, that you'd never forgive me for the lies. If I'd been here…'

She lifted her head and kissed him. 'Don't. You weren't to blame. Our argument seems silly now. The last thing I remember before going to bed was saying a prayer for God to send you home to me, and that we could start to rebuild our trust in each other. Then when I was trapped by the fire, I thought I'd never see you again. I'm just glad you're here.'

'So am I, my love. I am truly sorry for all the lies… and for the things I didn't tell you.' He searched in his pocket and pulled out a blue violet that he'd picked from the flower bed outside. He handed it to her.

She took it from him with a smile. 'Good choice: faithfulness.'

'I prefer "I'll always be true". See, I'm learning.'

'I forgive you. But if you ever keep anything from me again…'

'Not a chance. I mean it this time. I've had enough of secrets and lies. They only get you in a tangle and rob you of your peace of mind.'

She squeezed his hand. 'That's what I've been trying to tell you all this time.'

He wanted to stay like this forever, with her cheek against his, warm and soft. A rush of love filled his soul, a longing for her that he'd set aside while he had to cope with everything else. It was flattering to hear Grace tell him how wonderful he was, whatever he did. But with Tinny, he could be himself, flaws and all, and she'd help him to be a better person. They could find their own path together, an equal relationship, giving and taking. With her, he would always know that he belonged.

But there were things to sort out. 'Where have you been sleeping? Not here, surely?'

She shook her head. 'The vicar offered us a room, for as long as we need it. But where will you stay?'

'Don't worry about me. While I was away, I came into some money, so a room at one of the inns will do me fine. I'll tell you everything later. Does Johnny know what's happened?'

'Yes, he's been every day to see Mam. Yesterday she was awake for a while, but she couldn't talk. She's improved a little today though.'

William glanced at Sarah. 'She looks peaceful enough. Hopefully she's on the mend. Has anyone told you how bad the damage is to the building?'

'No, but it's been the last thing on my mind. I've been too worried about Mam.'

'When I got there, I couldn't see the true extent of it. The front is still intact, and the roof seems to be all right, but I couldn't go in. A policeman was standing guard.'

'What about your paintings?'

'They don't matter. Nothing does, except you and Sarah.'

She snuggled closer to him. 'I forgot to ask, how was your Mama?'

'That's another story. You won't believe what's happened.'

CHAPTER 47

TWO MONTHS LATER: JUNE 1881

Tinny yawned as she rolled over in the bed that used to be William's, and smiled at the sight of her mother lying beside her, snoring gently. She eased herself out of bed as quietly as she could, and opened the curtains a little, rejoicing in the blue sky stretching out over the sea. Sunshine for her wedding day, thank the Lord.

The only cloud on the horizon was Grace. Had she been genuine yesterday, when she'd given them her blessing?

After everything they'd been through, she should have more confidence in her fiancé. He'd proved himself faithful in all the things he'd done to help her and Mam after the fire. It must be nerves making her doubt him.

She glanced across to the little lodging house on the opposite side of the green, where William and Johnny were staying, then closed the curtain. She mustn't tempt bad luck on this special day, by seeing the groom before they met at church. Today William would become her husband. Imagine that.

Her heart swelled with love for him. He'd handled that cruel woman Virginia perfectly and ended up with a fortune by their standards. And the first thing he'd done was give the vicar a handsome amount of money to find a clean, warm and safe place for the flower girl to live, and to buy her a set of clothes so she could get a respectable job in a flower shop.

She smiled at the sight of her wedding dress hanging from the picture rail. It was the most beautiful thing she'd ever made, from the full skirt to the dainty flowers she'd embroidered on the front panel as the final touch. It had helped to soothe her worries over Mam's recovery while they were staying at the vicarage. If they'd had the shop to run, she'd never have finished it.

William understood her so well. He could have bought her a fashionable dress, but he'd known she wanted her own unique version. She fingered the beautiful beaded slippers, the one thing she'd let him buy for her. Today she would be a princess. All her dreams were coming true at once; if only Dad had been here to see it.

'What time is it, lovey?' Mam stretched her arms and yawned.

'Half past seven. No need to rush.'

'Nonsense, you need a good breakfast inside you before we get ready. I bet Cook's got it all prepared. She's so organised, that one. We had a nice cup of tea in the kitchen yesterday, and we got on ever so well. Fallen on our feet, we have, being welcomed here. You can take your time deciding about the tea room; I like it here, thank you very much.' She pushed away the covers. 'I'll get a wash while you stand there dreaming.'

Tinny didn't tell her that eating was the last thing she wanted to do. Her stomach was turning somersaults. Tonight she and William would sleep in this room, starting their married life together. It was more than she'd ever dared to hope for.

After a half-hearted attempt to eat, they helped each other into their dresses, and met Anna Harper in the sitting room for a glass of sherry. Tinny hadn't realised there'd been a knock on the door until Ada appeared, followed by a man in a smart suit who was holding a box with a circlet of orange blossom. She took a moment to realise it wasn't the man from the flower shop.

Mam gave a chuckle. 'Well, Johnny, you've scrubbed up well. You're a sight for sore eyes, and no mistake.'

'You look a treat,' Tinny agreed.

'All in honour of you, young lady. I'm right proud to give you away.' He put the box on the table next to her and wiped his eyes with the back of his hand. 'Dear me, you'll have me blubbin' like a baby soon. I can't help it. You're looking lovely, Christina Bennett.'

'Thank you. And soon I'll be Christina Harper. Just imagine.'

'Sooner than you think,' Mam said, nodding at the clock on the mantelpiece. 'Look at the time.'

A draught fluttered around her feet. Johnny must have left the door open. She was just about to ask him to close it, when she heard the latch click. A moment later, Grace appeared, wearing a long dress in a delicate shade of primrose yellow that set off her dark eyes and hair. She'd certainly made an effort.

'Hello, Grace,' she ventured, remembering she should be charitable on her wedding day.

Grace's eyes widened as she looked at them all. 'You look beautiful, Christina. And you're so clever to have sewn a wedding dress. The embroidery… it's exquisite.'

'Thank you. Were you wanting a lift to church in the carriage?'

Grace blushed, then held out a tiny pouch tied with pale blue ribbon. 'I came to give you this.'

Tinny took it from her. 'What is it?'

'A piece of jet. It used to be mine, a touchstone for the times when I was worried. I gave it to William the day he ran away. Please believe me; I didn't realise he was going to leave.'

'I know you didn't; he's told me everything. It's very kind of you, but I've already got my "something borrowed". Anna has lent me her veil.'

Grace glanced at it and nodded. 'It goes so well with your dress. But this isn't a loan. William returned it to me a while ago. It's done its work, so I decided it should be a talisman of joy and security instead. You've made William happy, more than I ever could, so I want you to have it. This can be your "something old". I put a blue ribbon on it, just in case you needed that as well. Please say you'll take it. It came from Whitby originally.'

'In that case, I can't refuse. It was on the day we visited Whitby that I realised I loved William. Thank you, Grace. This means a lot to me.' Tinny opened the pouch and pulled out the pebble. It was cool and smooth to the touch. She'd never seen it before, but she had no reason to doubt Grace's story. Given the trials William had been through, she was glad he'd had an object like this to give him courage.

Grace gave her a warm smile. 'And I'm sorry if I caused you any worry by writing to William. We've been friends since school, and I was distraught when he disappeared. I couldn't sleep for worrying about him. The day he first wrote to me, I cried because I was so happy that he was safe. We did meet in York, it's true, but he told me about your engagement, and he's been nothing but loyal to you in all that time.'

Tinny told Johnny to look out of the window while she

lifted her dress, so that Mam could tie the pouch strings to the lacing on her underskirts. Then she stood still while Mam fixed the circlet to her hair, securing her veil.

She turned towards Grace. 'I wasn't so bothered about the fact that you were writing to each other. I was just disappointed that William kept it a secret.'

Grace nodded. 'I'd have been the same in your position. He doesn't understand girls.' She grinned and gave an unladylike wink.

Tinny's resolve gave way to a giggle. 'How right you are. I'm trying to train him, but it's hard work.' She swivelled round towards Mam. 'Am I done?'

'Oh lass, you are.' She dabbed at her eyes with a handkerchief. 'Me and Anna had best be off to church.'

Tinny held up a hand. 'Just wait a minute.' Now seemed as good a time as any to make a fresh start, knowing she and William were likely to be here on a regular basis. She turned back to Grace. 'I'm not sure how long we'll be staying here for, but I'd like it if you and I could be friends. What do you think?'

Grace brightened. 'I can't think of anything better. We both want the best for William, and he'd be very happy if we could get along. In fact, he asked if I would offer to be your bridesmaid today.' She shifted her weight from one foot to the other and gave a wry smile. 'I told him it was for you to choose. It only proves how little he knows.'

'I'd be honoured if you would,' Tinny told her.

Mam gave a too-obvious cough. 'If we don't get to church, William will think you've changed your mind.'

'Not a chance,' she said. 'Will you just check this veil isn't going to slip, please?'

She stood still while Mam added a few more hair pins.

Anna touched her gently on the shoulder. 'You look

perfect, my dear. Sarah and I will take Grace with us in the carriage and send it back for you two.'

Tinny gave each of them a kiss and stood at the window to watch them leave. She turned to Johnny with a smile. 'Thank you for this. It means a lot. If only Dad…'

'I know, lass. He should be here.' He stepped forward and put his arms around her. 'But I'm sure he's looking down from heaven and smiling at all this. William's a grand lad; he'll look after you, and your Mam too, make no mistake. You've a bright future, just what you deserve.'

She nodded, thinking about everything that had happened in such a short space of time: William witnessing his Papa's death, the fire and the awful discovery about Leah's true identity. Through it all, they'd stuck together as if they were already a proper family. And now they would be.

The carriage soon returned for them. Johnny held out his arm to escort her, with a look so full of love and pride that it made her blush. Ada and Cook were in the hall, handkerchiefs at the ready.

'Good luck, Miss Bennett,' Ada said.

'The wedding breakfast's ready in the dining room for when you get back,' said Cook. 'I hope it's to your liking.'

'Thank you both.' She picked her way down the steps and allowed Johnny to help her into the carriage. How grand she felt, waving to the onlookers as they set off for the church. If she'd been braver, she'd have asked the driver to take it on a circular route around the village first. She suppressed a giggle at the thought.

Alighting from the carriage in the bright sunshine, the wind caught her veil, reminding her of the way her hat had blown off in the street outside Leah's house after they'd told her of their engagement. At least they didn't have to handle her disapproval. She caught hold of the veil and fixed an image of William in her mind, the carefree version of him in their moments of fun. It would be such a thrill, being with him tonight, sharing their love, and in the years ahead.

'Ready?' asked Johnny as they stood behind the vicar waiting for the organ to start. Grace took her position in front of them, ready to do her bridesmaid duties.

Tinny nodded. To anyone else, the rows of empty pews would have been a disappointment, but she didn't need a crowd of onlookers to make it special. The man waiting for her at the altar was all she wanted, together with the love and support Mam, Johnny and Anna would always give her. And Grace too, she thought.

The music began, and she walked down the aisle towards William, bursting with happiness. God had given her a loving, caring man and she would cherish him for the rest of her life.

CHAPTER 48

William exchanged a look of love with his bride as they left the church. They were husband and wife at last, ready to start the next stage of their journey together. Today was a day for celebration, a day to forget the shadows that hovered over him, the memories of those he'd loved and lost.

He held the carriage door open and helped Tinny in, then turned to Sarah. 'Please join us.'

She frowned. 'That's not what's meant to happen. I can walk back with your Mama.'

'Ah, but I have a little surprise for you. Both of you.' He helped her in, and they were waved off by their little group of guests.

The carriage drew up outside the end house on the south-east corner of the green, instead of carrying on to Mama's.

'Why have we stopped here?' asked Tinny.

'Everything will be clear in a moment.' He alighted from the carriage and helped them both down, then produced a key from his pocket and placed it in the lock. 'Follow me.' He could hear whispering from behind as Tinny and Sarah conferred, clearly bemused.

As they walked in, the light from a large bay window on the east wall flooded into the open space, revealing a few tables and chairs, a counter at the back that covered about three quarters of the room's width, and a door in the far corner. He waited for their reaction, trying to keep his face straight.

'William?' Tinny looked around. 'What have you done?' Her cautious tone was the same as when he'd told her he intended to be an independent artist rather than find another sponsor.

'I'm using my inheritance to buy our freedom. This can be an investment, or it can be our home. The choice is yours. And when I say 'our home', I mean the three of us. Sarah, you're as much a part of my family as Tinny is now, and I couldn't bear to take her away from you.'

For once, Sarah had no words. She took out a handkerchief and mopped her eyes.

'You've bought this?' asked Tinny.

'Yes. Let me show you everything first; I'm not expecting you to decide today. Trust me, Mrs Harper.'

Tinny's face was full of wonder. 'Mrs Harper,' she repeated. 'It sounds lovely. I thought I'd never stop being Miss Bennett.'

He beckoned them towards the door at the rear and they followed him up the stairs, past the first landing and up to the second floor. 'Let me show you my new studio,' he said as he pushed open the door.

A long table occupied the centre of the room and a leather armchair was positioned by the bay window in the eastern wall. William smiled as he saw the late morning sun's rays pouring in; the light was as good as in his father's studio at Scarborough. It would be just right. He had already installed two easels, plus a dresser to store his materials.

Sarah walked over to the window. 'The view is simply beautiful. Oh, my goodness, you can see right round the bay. Look at the hills in the distance.'

Tinny went to stand beside her. 'How perfect. I remember you telling me that the sea changes every day, reflecting the colour of the sky. You'll be able to capture it in all seasons.' She turned to him and kissed his cheek. 'As long as you don't stop doing portraits.'

'Don't worry; the commissions I'm getting are a good mix. I'm about to start one for Lady Forbes; she wants a picture of her two spaniels. That will be a challenge,' he said with a chuckle. 'I hope they can sit still for more than thirty seconds.'

He led them back to the first floor so they could explore the bedrooms and bathroom. Sarah was still entranced by the view of the sea from the eastern side.

William surveyed the room. 'If we moved here, this could be our sitting room. Then we'd have the bedroom next door and the other one would be yours, Sarah. But if we want to stay in York, or make our home in another place, I'll just reserve the studio for me to use whenever I visit Mama; I'm sure I can find someone who will rent the rest. They say being a landlord can be fairly profitable. I meant it when I said it was your choice.'

They returned to the ground floor. William leaned against the counter and looked at his wife. 'Are you thinking what I'm thinking? The kitchen's behind there.' He pointed behind him.

Tinny's eyes met his. 'You'd need to knock out a hatch in the wall, to pass food through.'

'That's easy,' he replied. 'It might take a while to find someone who wants to run it, but if I pair it with the accommodation on the next floor, it should be attractive enough. Whoever rents it will have to let me run up and down the stairs when I'm here, unless I can create a separate entrance at the back.'

He gave Tinny a wink, and she started to giggle. 'I had an idea you were plotting something, you rascal.'

'I wouldn't call it plotting. We've both been keeping our eyes open for the right place. You're just disappointed because I found it first.'

He laughed as she put out her tongue at him. Since he'd dealt with Virginia, Tinny had seemed much more carefree. 'I couldn't believe how quickly everything fell into place. You've always told me that when that happens, it's the right thing to do. I'll be able to charge commercial rents; it will be a good investment.'

Tinny skipped across and threw her arms around him. 'Commercial rents, my eye. It's obvious this is far better for a tearoom than anything we've seen so far. Just think of the custom in the summer, with the day trippers. And for the rest of the year, we could offer afternoon teas for local groups, funeral wakes, birthday celebrations... You are giving us first refusal, I trust?'

He looked into her eyes and saw hope and excitement there. 'Of course. These last few months have taught me so much. Now I understand what the most important things in life are. Like being free to choose the path that's right for you, not following other people blindly like I did with Leah... Virginia. You two and Mama mean more to me than anyone in the world.'

He moved back into the middle of the room and raised an eyebrow at Sarah. 'What are you thinking?'

She shrugged. 'Don't expect to get any sense out of me. I'm still overwhelmed that you want me to live with you.

Anyway, I doubt I could add much; our Christina here has it all sorted in her head.'

Tinny smiled. 'You need to take things easy, Mam, but somehow I can't see you putting your feet up completely. This will be so much easier. No more early mornings making bread. We'll be able to choose our opening hours, and I bet plenty of places round here will be keen to supply the produce...'

'It needs a lick of paint,' Sarah observed. 'But it's so much bigger than the old place, and it'll be lovely and bright with the sun shining through those windows. Some nice sheer curtains would stop it getting too hot.'

'You don't need to decide this minute,' said William. 'It's a big step to take, when you've lived in York all your life. I don't mind if you'd rather we stayed there. It's not far to come for visits, and with a studio here, I can still devote time to my art. I could work with two sets of clients.'

'Oh, I'm sure,' she said, glancing at Tinny. 'There's not much to keep us in York, not since the fire. Ever since the engagement, I've been expecting you to take Tinny away, and to think you still want me to be a part of it...' She gave a sniff and her eyes shone with tears. 'You are so thoughtful, but it must have cost you a lot of money. We'll pay rent, naturally.'

'You'll do no such thing,' he told her. 'It's my gift to you for giving me a job and a home. And a wife, for that matter. You're a part of my family now, Sarah, and I love you dearly.'

'It will be great fun to design it,' said Tinny. She gave William a lingering kiss. 'You are wonderful. Thank you.'

He broke away and walked over to the suitcase that lay on the floor by the window, flicking open the catches and pulling out the parts of his telescope. Then he cleaned each one with a soft cloth. It all slotted together perfectly. It didn't take long to assemble the stand and set the telescope on it. As he looked through it, a schooner came into view, rising and falling with the waves. He beckoned Tinny and Sarah over, enjoying their murmurs of appreciation as they took turns to see it.

They were his saviours and his future family, and he owed them everything.

'Here's to a bright future for us all,' he said. 'Now let's go for our wedding breakfast; our guests will be waiting. We can give Mama the good news. She will be thrilled to have a proper family here.'

What a lot of lessons he'd learned since he left here as a boy, frightened and alone. He'd found and lost people along the way, but sometimes the things you were looking for were right under your nose. Belonging wasn't a name on a birth record; it was caring for others and being cared for in return.

Now he could say farewell to his borrowed past. The future was all that mattered.

$\approx$

JOIN MY READER CLUB

As a thank you for buying this book, I'd like to offer you a chance to join my Reader Club. You'll receive free exclusive material, starting with the original chapter from 'A Borrowed Past' which didn't survive the editing process. It's called 'The Lifeboat Rescue' and shows a younger William having an adventure. You'll then receive a monthly news-letter with information about my writing plans including my next book, what I've been reading, snippets of research and much more.

Go to www.subscribepage.com/a7f7t3 to sign up as a member; I'm looking forward to sharing my writing journey with you!

I also blog at https://juliettelawson.com.

May I ask a favour? If you enjoyed this book, please help others to discover it by leaving a review on the page where you bought it. This is my first novel, and you can make a real difference to my visibility. Thank you so much.

AUTHOR'S NOTES

I hope you enjoyed William's story. It was inspired by my research for a parish history book (*Portrait of a Seaside Parish: Holy Trinity Seaton Carew*, as Julie Cordiner), which I wrote as part of a fund raising drive to restore the local church. I discovered some wonderful stories and characters, and felt that this was a community that deserved to be shared more widely.

As this is a novel, the characters are all fictional, and I have taken some liberties with certain aspects to make the story work. I've invented the pier at Seaton Carew, and Chambers House came from my imagination, though there are some rather grand houses on The Cliff which date from around that time.

However, a spooky thing happened while writing the book. I was asked to give a talk on Seaton Carew by the local University of the Third Age (U3A) group, and while preparing my slides, I came across a photo that I hadn't seen before, on a local history Facebook group. It showed a tearoom on the corner of the village green, in the very spot where I'd located Christina's tea room!

The overall feel of the village is taken from historical records, including a diary by my husband's great-grandfather William Scott Lithgo, which provides rich details about the daily life of the villagers, including the lifeboat rescues. His aunt did indeed keep a chest of clothes, cleaned and mended ready for shipwrecked sailors. The villagers used to send wreaths and attend the funerals of sailors who died, often unknown. We have 59 such bodies buried in our churchyard.

The Victorians' preoccupation with social class also came out clearly in my research. The church still has brass card holders on some pews, where the more wealthy members of the congregation paid pew rents to reserve their seats.

York is one of my two favourite cities (Durham is the other) so I enjoyed finding a suitable location for Sarah's shop. I love to walk beside the Ouse and along the top of the city walls, imagining it in days gone by.

I also had two research days on the Yorkshire coast, finding out what William and Tinny would have been able to see while at Whitby harbour and scouting for Leah's house at Scarborough. The staff at the Scarborough Art Gallery were amazingly helpful; the building was a private house at the time of my story, but it was indeed owned by Lady Uppleby. She helpfully added a large dining room a few years before the date on which I set William's exhibition, and as soon as I saw it I knew it was the ideal space for his paintings to be displayed.

Watch out for my next book, which follows Grace's adventures and involves smuggling!

ACKNOWLEDGEMENTS

I have benefited from advice and guidance from many people. Thank you so much to my beta readers: Debbie Young, Tara Greaves, Susanna Bavin, Cath Greene, and Cass Grafton, and the Twitter Ab Fab Writers group members. Your support and encouragement means everything to me.

I will always be grateful to author and creative writing tutor Stephanie Butland for giving me confidence in my writing through a very encouraging manuscript assessment and a fabulous tutored retreat.

The Festival of Writing at York introduced me to many wonderful writers and editors who still inspire me, including Debi Alper, Emma Darwin, Julie Cohen, Shelley Harris, Andrew Wille, and Amanda Berriman.

Inspiring indie authors have also guided me through their generous advice online and in podcasts - chiefly Orna Ross, Joanna Penn, Mark Dawson, David Gaughran, Adam Croft, Paul Teague, Sarah Painter and Dan Blank. My online writer friends have always offered friendship and support - there are too many to list, but I hope they all know how much I appreciate them.

ABOUT THE AUTHOR

Juliette Lawson lives by the sea on the north east coast, at Seaton Carew, one of the early seaside resorts. Her love of family history and local history made historical fiction a natural choice when deciding to write a novel.

Favourite classical authors include Thomas Hardy, Jane Austen and the Brontes, and more recent favourites are Rowan Coleman, Susanna Bavin/Polly Heron, Clare Flynn, Glenda Young, Kate Mosse and Tracy Chevalier.

Juliette Lawson is the pen name of Julie Cordiner, the author of *Portrait of a Seaside Parish: Holy Trinity Seaton Carew* and a series of nonfiction books on school funding and finance. She can mostly be found reading and writing, but she also enjoys walking on the beach, singing in a ladies' choir and her local church choir, knitting, playing with her granddaughters and taking as many holidays as possible!

To follow Juliette on her writing journey, visit https://juliettelawson.com and sign up for her Reader Club news-letter at www.subscribepage.com/a7f7t3 for inside informa-tion about her new releases and writing inspiration. You can also visit her on social media:

facebook.com/juliettelawsonauthor

twitter.com/juliette_author

Printed in Great Britain
by Amazon